– Armada Wars –
Steal from the Devil

R. Curtis Venture

– Copyright –

First published December 2013.
Third edition published May 2016.

ISBN-10: 1505412854
ISBN-13: 978-1505412857

ArmadaWars.com

– By the Author –

Short Stories:

Kudos

Novels:

Steal from the Devil

List of the Dead

The Ravening Deep

This is **vol. one** of Armada Wars.
Reading the books in the correct order
is highly recommended.

– Contents –

– Prologue –
The Fall of Guathelia

Omin pressed his chest into the dirt as hard as he could, flattening his body against the ridge and waiting for his chance to peer safely over the lip of the rubble. He scratched idly and blindly at the Blight marks on his right forearm, trying subconsciously to relieve the constant itching, despite the day's more pressing matters.

High above him a squadron of tactical fighters streaked towards the horizon, headed for Guathelia's capital. Good luck with *that*. He could see the thick black smoke from here, and the bone-shaking sounds of the distant bombardment had stopped hours ago.

Ahead, just over the edge of the rubble that screened him from the street, bursts of gunfire were answered in kind by enemy rounds. The fighting had continued throughout the entire morning. He might never get his chance, unless somebody across the way were actually to win some ground.

A loud *whumph* came from somewhere up ahead, and Omin felt a shudder pass from the ground through his whole body. Then the clattering sound of stones and pieces of debris raining down on what was left of the street: frag grenade.

A pause in the gunfire, and he took the chance to rise from his cover. Just a tiny bit, just for a moment. Then flat again.

"Stay here."

Behind him, also flat on the ground, Halfre raised her dirt-streaked face and looked imploringly at her partner through strands of dusty hair. "Please be careful."

He winked encouragingly, leapt to his feet, and was off in an instant to sprint for the least-damaged building he could see. He reached it in a few seconds, almost tripping over the cracked white stone of the pavement, and pressed his back to what remained of the wall.

The street around him was all but demolished. He saw human limbs protruding from piles of rubble, pale and lifeless, scarlet-flecked maroon marks which he instinctively knew were dried blood. He closed his eyes until he had turned his face away.

The artillery assault on the market town had come in the early morning, when the streets were full of traders setting up their stalls. None of them had stood a chance against the bombardment.

Quick as a flash, Omin peered around the corner of the ruined building. Nobody was in the adjoining side street, but he saw what he was looking for. He quickly dashed halfway down and dropped to the ground next to the fallen bodies. Three Imperial shock troopers, all that remained of a Mobile Air and Ground Assault fire team, taken out by *Them*. Nobody had yet had the chance to recover the bodies. Or the equipment.

He grabbed at an assault rifle first, yanking it from the gloved hands of its late owner. He held it inexpertly, one hand under the barrel, the other on the stock. He found the hand guard and the pistol grip, and touched the trigger.

"Unauthorised user," the rifle bellowed.

Caught by surprise, he dropped the gun. He had not expected that, and in the relatively quiet refuge of the side street the curt voice had sounded dangerously loud. He glanced up and down the way, afraid of the attention he might have inadvertently attracted.

Nothing.

He pushed the rifle away, and stayed low as he moved to the next soldier. He saw the woman was lying across a shotgun, her face thankfully pressed against the ground.

"Sorry." He pulled the weapon from beneath her. She rolled onto her side as the shotgun tugged her clothing, and he saw her face was flattened where it had been pressed against the stone flags; mottled purple-brown where blood had pooled within the sallow flesh and already started to degrade. Her upper lip had been squashed beneath her nose to reveal a row of neat teeth, and a stiff arm lifted a yellowed, rigid hand from the ground as her body tilted. The grasping fingers reached for more life.

"So sorry."

He tested the weapon, with the same result. "Worlds damn you," he growled under his breath. This was not what he had intended when he risked his life — and Halfre's — coming back to find a weapon.

A pistol next, taken from a thigh holster. *Unauthorised User*. He did not waste his time checking the other weapons the corpses possessed.

He pulled open a pouch on the armour of the nearest trooper and found it contained a grenade.

It was perhaps not very practical, but it was better than nothing. He took it, then searched further to find just one more.

Two grenades. Hardly the arsenal he had anticipated.

Taking his spoils he ran back to Halfre, as quickly as he could while trying to stay down low. He found her still in the same spot, and dropped to the ground beside her.

"Did you find one?" She asked.

"Plenty," he said. "But they won't work. I think only the owner can fire them."

"What are we going to do?"

"Same plan as before, only we will have to be much more careful. I found these." He held up the grenades.

"One each?"

"Um, I guess so. Do you know what to do?"

"Omin! I *have* seen the holofilms."

"Sorry, it's just I never really imagined you fighting in a battle."

"Neither did I. Pop the cap, press the button, cook it off for a couple of seconds, then throw."

"Did you really just say 'cook it off'?"

She smiled coyly, and he passed her one of the grenades along with an approving smile. Handling it delicately, as if it might explode at any moment, she placed it carefully in her pocket.

"There's still fighting going on in the streets here," he said. "We may need to find another route. Especially if we're not going to be properly armed."

As if to make his point for him, something tore sharply through the air nearby and collided with one of the few buildings still standing. Not more than a hundred metres away from them, chunks of white stone and dark grey mortar were blasted outward. The entire side of the building tore away, collapsing in pieces across the street, and a wall of dust billowed in all directions.

"Quick," he said. "Come on!"

He grabbed her hand and hauled her to her feet, then sprinted downhill, curving to follow the perimeter of the town. He was so very glad that this side of the market district was verged by a man made embankment; had they been fighters they would have been disadvantaged on the low ground, but as things were they at least had some cover. They would be very unlucky to be caught by stray bullets.

Behind them, the marketplace and its attendant buildings were pulverised systematically by mortar fire. For a time, the echoing gunshots closest to them stopped.

They circled the southern edge of the town, stopping to hug the dirt whenever the fighting came too close. Omin found himself wondering how long the battle might go on for; it had been hours already. Surely either side could just vaporise the whole area? Probably best to not think about that.

"This is it, isn't it?"

He stopped and looked to where Halfre was pointing, over the crest of the incline, and saw that she had spotted the familiar twin statues. Headless and scorched they might well be, but they did indeed mark out the entrance to the Bright Way.

"It can't be far now," he said.

They scrabbled up the banked rubble, which had slid down from the embattled town, but just as they reached even ground both dropped flat immediately.

In the wide space of the Bright Way, a couple of blocks away from them, several MAGA fire teams were retreating. Three groups were stepping carefully backwards, firing into side streets as they converged on each other. Another group popped smoke, a couple of canisters creating a white screen across the road to cover the retreat. The soldiers finally came together and took up defensive positions. They hunkered down behind stone planters and street furniture, their combat armour skinprinting to mimic the surroundings and obscure the outlines of their bodies.

After a moment something began to move in the smoke. Omin could see a shadow, the vapour being disturbed and displaced, but the overall shape seemed fluid, difficult to discern. He could barely tell if it was deep inside the cloud, or emerging from it. His eyes told him it was both, but his brain disagreed. Try as he might he could not fill the perceptual gap, and it hurt him to attempt it.

It was one of *Them*.

Three short, tightly controlled bursts of fire from one of the MAGA troops, and the shifting shapeless presence melted silently back into the wall of smoke.

The world seemed to pause and inhale.

From Omin's vantage point, beyond the end of the Bright Way, the attack came without warning. Figures darted from the side streets, dozens of them, leaping recklessly into the Bright Way and fanning out across the wide avenue. They were human, Omin was sure — he could clearly see as much from where he was. Some wore civilian clothing, some overalls, others still what looked like flight suits. Some were armed with guns, some metal bars, others carried lumps of stone;

anything they could use to shoot, batter, or pelt.

And he was sure they were all smiling.

The horde descended on the MAGA troops with frightening speed. Many fell as they crossed the intervening space, gouts of red bursting from their bodies as they took hits from the soldiers' weapons. Others jumped over the bodies, paying them no regard, and fearlessly kept running, those with guns of their own firing back at the troops haphazardly.

Omin saw a middle-aged woman in a yellow dress bring a metal bar down on a soldier's arm, shattering the bone. The man cried out in pain as his arm snapped and half of it swung uselessly downwards, still holding his rifle. Yellow Dress kicked him in the chest, sending him sprawling backwards, and without a moment's hesitation she began to club him to death with a horrible vigour.

Not far from Yellow Dress was a young man with cropped hair and a tattered navy blue jacket. His face was already streaked with what looked like dried blood. Blue Jacket dropped to the ground as his nearest companion reeled backwards with blood bursting from her chest. He ignored her as she crumpled in a dead heap, continued coming forward with a strange animal gallop, one hand and both feet propelling him towards the shooter. In his free hand he held a pistol. He raised it as the trooper reloaded, fired three times, and killed her outright.

As proficient as they were, the MAGA troopers did not stand much of a chance against the tide of violence. Within moments, the sound of gunshots had stopped.

Omin sank back down beneath the level of the street, carefully and quietly, desperate to attract no attention. He saw Halfre was lying on her back, facing away from the battle. Tears had sliced through the grime on her face, and she clutched her grenade in both hands.

He placed a hand over hers, and she looked at him. "Not yet." He mouthed it silently, and she nodded slowly.

He risked a very cautious peek back into the Bright Way. The motley gang of attackers were mostly standing where they were, swaying slightly. A few of them dragged three of the soldiers across the ground, and Omin realised — when he saw one struggle feebly — that they were still alive. Then, silently and without discussion, the horde turned as one and disappeared into the nearest side street, taking their captives with them. The dead were left where they had fallen.

"Is it safe?" Halfre asked.

"I don't know," he said. "Stay down for now."

They waited for a few long minutes. The slowly drifting curtain of smoke, which had obscured the far end of the Bright Way, eventually cleared. The sounds of fighting had all but ceased, and Omin guessed that those ill-fated troopers had been among the last Imperial forces in the town.

They had to escape.

"It's as safe now as it's ever going to be. Let's go."

He took her hand, and they clambered up the embankment to street level. Wasting no time whatsoever, Omin half dragged Halfre across the junction and into the shade on the east side of the Bright Way, as close as possible to the building line. Without a word they picked their way quickly across the broken masonry and smashed paving stones, moving with refreshed urgency towards the town centre.

As they approached the scene of the slaughter, Omin could feel Halfre hanging back. He pulled her on, just as unwilling to linger at the graveyard as she was to enter it.

Together they peered cautiously into the junction where the inexplicably murderous mob had disappeared, and saw that it was clear. They ran across the intersection and continued on.

"I didn't recognise them," Halfre said.

"What?"

"Those people who killed the soldiers; I didn't recognise any of them."

"Why would you?"

"They were just ordinary people, weren't they? But not from this town. I know the faces of almost everybody who lives here."

"It's a market town. There are always strangers."

"Did they look like traders and shoppers to you?"

Omin gave no answer.

"Thought not."

Up ahead, the road widened and Omin could see what remained of the circular walls of the formerly domed commerce hall. They were coming to the end of the Bright Way.

"It's this right," Halfre said.

They entered the side street, and ran as quietly as they could for the next three blocks. The street entered a wide plaza, enclosed on three sides by ruined buildings, open on the far side to an orderly array of roads. The space was filled with the town's communal vehicle fleet, many of them smoking wrecks.

"Let's find one that still works."

"Okay."

They walked into the abandoned communal transit hub, picking a route through the stands and the ranks of motionless transports, struggling to see any that had escaped the bombardment unscathed. Here and there were craters in the ground, those vehicles which had been nearby now twisted scraps of metal and plasteel, pushed outwards by explosive impacts. Omin tried to ignore the bodies.

His heart leapt into his mouth when he heard the voice.

"Hold it."

He looked to his right, and in a corner between two battered wagons saw there was a trooper sitting upright on the ground, rifle aimed at them.

"Identify yourselves."

"I'm Omin, this is Halfre."

"Who are you with?"

"Uh... nobody. Ourselves."

"You're not Them."

It was a statement rather than a question, and the trooper lowered his rifle. Omin saw that he was leaning heavily against one of the wagons, and had been in the process of applying a field dressing to his side.

Halfre went forward to help him.

"Rifleman Delanka, Second Platoon. All that's left of it most likely. I got separated from my squad; scouting ahead when the enemy got the drop on them. Didn't even get a chance to help them."

"We saw people killing soldiers," said Omin. "They looked like regular people. They killed a lot of them but they took three away."

Delanka groaned, and Omin found it difficult to

tell if it was because of what he had said, or because Halfre had tightened the bandage.

"I don't know why, or how, but it looks like They are using civilians as ground troops."

"Who are They?" Omin asked. "We don't have a clue what's happened."

"I have no idea," Delanka said, "and I'm not sure anyone does. They hit the system hard. Must have taken down everything we had up there before we even knew about it ground-side. That fireball that hit the atmosphere just before dawn? That was the *Vehement* de-orbiting."

Halfre gasped.

"Oh it gets worse. I guess you could see the attack on the capital from here?"

"We saw," said Omin. They could hardly have missed it even if they had tried.

"Yeah, they knew what they were doing all right. One well-executed orbital strike, and the planet was theirs. Everything they've done since then has just been mopping up."

"Is anyone coming to help us?"

"Gate's not responding, so there's no way to tell. My guess is They took it out first to stop us sending a distress call."

"What's going to happen to us?" Halfre asked.

"Hard to say. They have the upper hand right now. Only 104th Battalion were on the surface when the attack began, and most of our assets were still on the *Vehement*. I won't lie; it's a bad situation."

"I saw fighters earlier, headed north." Omin said.

"Air support would have come from Camp Camillion. My guess is the 104th have plotted up there and established an FOB."

Halfre looked confused. "A what?"

"Forward Operating Base," Delanka said. "They'll lead the counter-attack from there. Assuming there's anyone left, that is."

"We were going to find a vehicle and head south," Omin said. "Come with us. We'll go there instead, to the base."

"Are you insane? The moment you set off in one of those things you'll have every enemy soldier in the town on you. Not to mention their ranged weapons."

"What else are we supposed to do?"

"Pick a direction and start walking. Running is better."

"We'll never make it on our own."

"I'm not going to be much good to you, reckon I'll just slow you down."

"Aren't you even going to—"

Omin dropped to the ground, the sentence hanging in the air. He pressed a finger to his lips and both Delanka and Halfre fell silent immediately.

Yellow Dress was standing at the entrance to the plaza, the way he and Halfre had come in.

On hands and knees, Omin edged around the nose of one of the wagons until he could see her. She was now shuffling into the plaza, at right angles to their hiding place, and he figured that if she began to turn, he would have more than enough time to duck out of sight.

Yellow Dress still carried the metal bar, shiny in the midday sun except for the far end, which glistened darkly. Thanks to the massacre in the Bright Way, he knew why. Her brown hair was matted and untidy, her dress was torn, and she now limped with each step. She must have picked up an injury during the fight. Even at that distance, Omin could see her cocking her head this way and that, like a predatory bird listening out for the tell-tale scrabbling of insect life. Once, she might have been a teacher, a doctor, or a musician. But not any more; now she was a monster.

And she was *humming*.

He could hear it clearly across the wide expanse of the plaza, even with the intervening vehicles. A slow, wistful melody, utterly alien yet strangely homely at the same time. He had never heard anything like it.

As if to warn off any appreciation, Yellow Dress began to bash transports as she walked, hitting their side panels with the metal bar.

BANG!

Her lurching steps were punctuated by the jarring sound, and the occasional pattering cascade of safety glass.

BANG!

Seemingly oblivious to her limp, she stalked stiffly up and down the rows of vehicles, her head still moving this way and that in sharp feral jerks.

BANG!

Without warning, a young girl burst from a hiding place behind a wagon close to Yellow Dress. She ran towards Omin and the others, and he ducked back to cover instinctively.

Yellow Dress released an unholy shriek as she began to give chase.

"Get back," said Delanka, shuffling towards Omin and exchanging places with him.

The girl ran by, crying as she went, and Omin's eyes briefly met hers. He could see that she was terrified.

Yellow Dress lumbered into view, the bloodied

bar held aloft, passed them by, and then stopped. She began to turn.

A sharp *crack* split the air, horribly loud in the space between the wagons, and Yellow Dress fell backwards, her punctured skull hitting the ground with a wet crunch. The single shot echoed around the plaza.

Halfre was up in an instant, and ran after the girl. Omin was too slow to stop her, and she disappeared quickly amongst the rows. He heard her soft calls fading as she went.

"Halfre! *Shit*."

"Don't let her get too far," Delanka said. "We need to stay together."

"Thought you were leaving us to it?" Omin snapped.

Delanka looked at the metal bar, still held fast in the dead woman's tight grip. Tufts of human hair were stuck to the bloody coating. "I've reconsidered."

He winced as he rose to his feet, slinging his rifle over his shoulder and pressing his palm flat against the dressing. A bright red stain was already spreading through the bandages. "Go and find her, quickly."

Omin ran, following the path he had seen Halfre take. He could no longer hear her, and started to panic. Reaching the end of the row, he called out as loudly as he dared.

"Over here," he heard her say.

He found her next to an upturned vehicle with smashed windows. Inside, he could see the young girl sitting on the roof, her legs drawn up to her body and her arms clutching her knees.

"Come on, it's okay," Halfre was saying. The girl shook her head.

Omin dropped to the ground once more, and smiled through the empty side window. "We're going to leave the town," he said. "You should come with us. It's not safe here."

"Nowhere is safe," the girl said. She could not have been older than twelve.

"You're safer with us than on your own," Halfre said.

Omin nodded. "We're with a soldier."

The girl came out of the vehicle with her arms held out, and Halfre scooped her up.

"Delanka changed his mind," Omin told her. "He's coming with us."

"Where is he?"

"He was behind me."

Halfre's eyes widened, and she hissed at him. "Omin!"

He followed her gaze, and his blood ran cold. Standing in the nearest entrance to the plaza, with a sickly grin smeared across his bloodied face, Blue Jacket and a half dozen others stood watching them.

"Go!" Omin yelled.

Blue Jacket and the others watched as Halfre ran from them, still carrying the girl. They remained where they were, but turned their attention back to Omin.

He pulled the grenade from his pocket, popped the cap, and pressed the red button: one, two.

He threw it high overhead so that it came straight down amongst them. As it fell, Blue Jacket screamed and broke into a run. A moment later, the others did the same.

It was a moment too late.

The grenade exploded, blasting fire and metal shrapnel into the surrounding vehicles, walls, and people. Shredded bodies were thrown through the air, slamming into unyielding plasteel and tumbling raggedly to the ground. But still Blue Jacket kept coming.

Omin had already turned to run the moment the grenade left his hand. He sprinted as fast as he could, weaving left and right whenever he got the chance. When he heard the blast he chanced a quick look back, saw the plume of smoke rising and a thin veil of powdery haze spreading outwards.

Blue Jacket apparently did not intend to waste time bobbing left and right. He jumped onto the flat bed of a wagon and appeared to scour the plaza for signs of movement.

Omin was out of breath by the time he reached the far side of the plaza, near the end of the wall and close to the junction of the outbound roads. His lungs burned, and he had a sharp pain in his side. He wanted to be sick.

Someone roared on his right, and he turned to see Blue Jacket leap clumsily from a vehicle, down to the open ground between them. He scrabbled across the paving stones and raised his pistol towards Omin.

The crack of a single shot once more filled the plaza, and Blue Jacket's face disappeared. The body flopped forward under its own momentum, hitting the ground heavily.

"Fuck you, Buddy."

Delanka rolled the body with his boot and pulled the pistol from its hand. He checked the civilian handgun over. "Here." He offered it to Omin. "It's not user-encoded. You can fire this one."

Omin took the gun. "Halfre..."

"We're here."

Halfre and the girl emerged from behind a low wall. Omin ran to them and threw his arms around both.

"We need to shove off right now," said Delanka. "We just made enough noise to bring Them here from the capital."

"The FOB then?" Omin said.

"The FOB. Let's just hope it's still there."

With Delanka covering their rear they left the smouldering ruins behind, and set off on the road to Camillion.

— 01 —

Hammer

Singularity is never an easy state. Mind, body, machine; all become one. In the twisted and churning throat of a wormhole, there is a moment in which thoughts become environment. Matter touches the mind, and flesh is extruded out into space it was never supposed to occupy. Small mercy then that the transitional jump experience lasts a mere instant, indelible and enduring as it might be in memory.

Those who travel the gulf between the stars usually have one thing in common: they will gladly endure a single paradoxical instant of shattered unity, if not exactly acquire the taste. An infinitely unpleasant fraction of a second is a small price to pay for the opportunity to stride across eternity.

With a groan of relief, *ICS Hammer* emerged into normal space. The wormhole waited obligingly for the battleship to drift clear of its aperture before evaporating silently into the void, shut down remotely from the other side. Fragments of hull plating travelled gracelessly with *Hammer* as she listed, tumbling alongside the great ship. They were prisoners of the momentum they had shared with her before being wrenched from her side by the tidal forces of the unbound wormhole. She let them go. A seasoned veteran, she was accustomed to the ravages of interstellar transit.

She awoke. Formation lights blinked on and portholes regained their gentle glow. Her primary engines thundered into life as the main reactor emerged from hibernation, and her entire superstructure shuddered in ecstatic response. Hundreds of sensor palettes across her outer hull continued the private chatter that the wormhole had interrupted so abruptly. *Hammer* was becoming aware of her surroundings, sounding them out. She reached out and felt the shape of what was around her.

There was not much to feel. Millions of kilometres away, a pale yellow star burned tirelessly, futilely showering its three barren planets with warmth. With no receiving gate to deliver the ship safely and precisely to a sterile area, *Hammer* had arrived outside the star system intentionally, far from any objects that might have dealt her a fatal blow. She reached out yet further, probing the interior of the star system, and diligently looked for a clear space near her destination. Another jump, vastly shorter and accordingly more accurate, would take her there only once her crew were satisfied that nothing ahead might endanger her arrival.

On the command deck of the *Hammer,* Captain Aker Santani watched how the chattering chaos gave way to reason only with the greatest reluctance.

Her command crew shouted to each other in clipped sentences; rapid bursts of raw information, free from the complications of grammar and conveying only pertinent facts or urgent demands, timed perfectly to fit between the blaring honks of system alarms. White emergency lighting cast the entire compartment in a crisp, vivid light, revealing each minute detail of everything it touched. Acrid smoke drifted low across the pale deck plating, thick and brown, curling around ankles and undulating as it fled the unseen electrical fire that had loosed it.

"Report!"

Santani called out in no particular direction, knowing full well that somebody would have the presence of mind to register the question and pass an orderly and comprehensive response.

She had made over fourteen thousand jumps prior to this one, and she was frankly starting to get tired of the hysterical responses some officers exhibited when a few small pieces of the great ship fell off in transit, or when parts exploded without warning. Even the more seasoned officers seemed to be unnerved on this occasion. Santani had realised some time ago that her command staff were often so surprised, that on the whole it was better to throw a question wide open rather than query an individual who might not answer. Command, she had found after many long years, brought some funny little lessons with it.

It was the COMOP officer who answered. Communications and Operations. Well, he ought to know after all.

"Pulsar locks confirmed, resolving local stellar locks... arrival confirmed at target system."

"Status?"

"No hostiles detected, Captain. We have fires contained on four decks. Two hull breaches: one isolated, one causing problems on deck four. Off-ship comms are down."

Well well. Detailed yet concise. Give the man a small medal.

"What kind of problems? On deck four?"

He swept two fingers across a holo display: invoke diagrammatic. "The emergency hatches in this section won't close; fire took out a relay junction, so the breach was able to evacuate the air." A pulsating red icon: touch to read. "Oh no... two missing, possibly spaced."

"Damn it all to the Deep!"

Santani was never one to accept the loss of crew members easily. Now she was faced with the very real prospect that before their mission had even begun, two of her people had suffered one of the loneliest and most grisly deaths imaginable: blown out into space by the very air that was supposed to keep them alive.

"Active sensors?"

"Not picking up anything that looks like it might be a person," the COMOP officer replied, "but then there's always the possibility they didn't leave the ship that way."

Santani grimaced as she realised his meaning. Presumably an explosion had been the cause of the breach. Had they been in the immediate vicinity at the time, then there was a good chance her missing crew members had left the ship in pieces. As good as the sensor resolution was on *Hammer*, it would take forever to check every potential object. Nevertheless, she hoped guiltily that they had suffered this quicker death.

"Get me a headcount at the earliest," Santani said.

"Ma'am," he said, and turned back to his station.

"We'll hold position for repairs." Again, she addressed the entire command deck. "I want a full report within the hour, and get *him* up here. I'd like to speak to him before he goes gallivanting off to Herros."

With a wave of her hand she dismissed her own holo from before her, and then arose from her chair. Moving with purpose, Santani walked briskly from her central position to the rear bulkhead of the command deck, opening the hatch which allowed immediate access to the wardroom. She stopped briefly to look back at the men and women who hurriedly worked to stabilise the injured *Hammer*.

Young. That was her overall impression. Young in years, and young in service. The old days had slipped away. She could not be sure quite when it had happened, but it was evident in that so few of her crew from the old days had managed to remain with her. A transfer here, a retirement there. The occasional death, on duty or otherwise. Bit by bit, that was how it must have sneaked up on her. Gradually, over her many years, she had been dealt a worse hand than that which she was accustomed to playing.

And now she was not only playing schoolmistress to these graduates, but also ferrying a Shard of the Empress.

What was he, mid-thirties? Seemed about right. Not exactly fresh from the academy then, but to an old hand like her even the very best examples of the next generation would only ever be pimple-faced usurpers.

They don't know how good they have it these days, she thought. Not a clue.

From what she had seen of his files — and that

was admittedly not much, such were the requisite security levels for most of them — he was your typical operative of the Throne. Brusque, taciturn, and sometimes ruthlessly effective. She had widened her search to the logs made by other captains who had carried him from place to place, and found they had all said much the same thing: does not play well with others.

If he thinks he's dragging me into the hornets' nest without knowing why, she smouldered, *he's got another think coming.*

Even the look of him annoyed her. He was just so… *ordinary.* Not at all what one would rightly expect when instructed to receive the living embodiment of Her Majesty's will. His figure was nondescript, reasonably athletic but not in any sense muscular, and his face was plain. His dark hair was rather unimaginatively cropped short, and his eyes tended to the dull brown side of what could have been a captivating copper.

She snorted involuntarily, and her brain made the decision to end this line of thought. It did not become her to disparage the man before he had even shown his capabilities. She turned her thoughts back to the mission at hand, and the capabilities of her relatively inexperienced crew.

Fleet Command were right to trust that new recruits would receive exemplary training on her ship, but even so she would give anything to have her old command team back. *Her* team, from back in the day. When the war against the Viskr had been all that mattered, and the despicable term 'backfill reinforcement' had not yet suffered its ugly birth in some planet-side bureaucrat's comfortable office.

Had she been seriously injured at the Siege of

Laeara, for example, she believed that any one of her command team would have stepped up to the mark without a second thought. She would have trusted her ship, her crew, her own life, to any one of them.

But now... well it was less than impressive to see officers who lost their cool after a rough jump. Granted this had been a particularly nasty one; the great distance from the Kosling system to Herros, with no gate at this end to bind their emergence, had made that all but inevitable. However the ship was rated to withstand much worse; none of the damage she had sustained today had been critical, and it remained to be seen whether there actually were any casualties. From the pandemonium that had swept the command deck after the ship dropped out of the wormhole, anybody would have thought the worlds were ending.

Try fighting in a battle when there's actually a world at stake, Santani thought.

All those years ago, at Laeara, Admiral Betombe had split his battle fleet to defend several priority targets. It had been a real, honest-to-goodness struggle, and the cost of failure would have been measured in millions of lives, not in bulkheads and reactor coils. Back then people had known how to stand firm and get the job done.

The old team. Oh there were a few still serving with her, but it was not the same and never would be again.

Although she was confident there were none serving on the *Hammer* who were not competent to be there, she was also acutely aware that a good majority of her crew had never met with fire. Their mettle had not been tested. She had little faith in war games or even live-fire drills; for Santani, actual combat performance was the only metric by which a battleship could be judged properly. War was simply a theoretical concept for many of this crew; too many.

And from what little she knew of the purpose of this trip, the jump from theory to practice might well be imminent.

◦ ◦ ◦

Wind swept across the dry and tortured rock where nothing ever grew, changing direction quickly and without warning, tirelessly vindictive as it plucked and tore at everything it touched. It carried a fine dust with it, abrasive yet cloying, gradually eroding any surface it contacted, merely burning and stinging to the naked skin yet still capable of reducing great boulders to powder, transforming them after its own kind.

Always the high plateau, close to the cliff edge. Always the same place, the same conditions. Every visit he made to this place was essentially identical.

He pulled his hood forward and down as far as he could, shielding his face from the incessant pain of the dust storm. Bracing his body against the winds, he leaned first one way and then the other, managing to remain upright as the force of the gale shifted direction randomly. It was simple enough, once one learned to anticipate the wind. And he had been here many times before.

He was early. The Emptiness had not yet manifested. As far as the eye could see, there was only the lifeless crust of the plateau; a desolate wasteland of rock, strewn carelessly with boulders, persecuted relentlessly by the powerful exhalation of this nameless planet's vicious climate system. There were no animals and no plants; not even hardy lichens would colonise this place. It was entirely dead. What could be seen of the sky through the morass of the dust was an ugly brown, blotched with sickly orange where light struggled feebly to penetrate layer upon layer of cloying, odious cloud.

This was not a place that welcomed living things.

Then there was the sound. He was certain it had not been there when he arrived, but he struggled to remember precisely when it had begun. It was at such a high pitch, and descending so slowly, that for all he knew it might have started either seconds or minutes ago. Regardless, it was now well within the limits of his perception, and he remembered precisely what this incongruous signal heralded.

He turned to face the edge of the cliffs, where the horizon touched the gangrenous sky so unwillingly. The sound dropped lower, lower still, descending in pitch until it reached a sonorous rumble that seemed to dissolve into the general chaos of the wind and dust, lending its own strength to theirs. The ground itself trembled.

With an ear-splitting crack, the air tore open some ten metres away, halfway between him and the cliff edge. Blackness boiled out into the world, a vertical spill that towered over him, reflecting nothing. Wispy tendrils lashed and curled at the fringes, the main body tapering to nothing at top and base, wider in the middle, a rip in the world into which light could enter, but never leave.

The pain was immeasurable, and everywhere at once. There was nothing that could be done to abate it, as he had found on so many previous visits, and so he simply clenched whatever he could and stood defiant.

The winds were howling now, as if angered by the intrusion of the void upon the eternal dance they performed. Ever-shifting gales began to fall into order, whipping around the plateau, becoming cyclonic. Pebbles and smaller rocks now skittered and clattered over each other as the force of the raging air bullied them across the indifferent ground.

Yet around the deep blackness was absolute calm. Stretching out from it, and almost reaching him, was a region in which no wind blew. It was only in this protected area where the dust drifted lazily back to the ground, and the tiny pebbles were as still as the boulders. It was a tempting thing indeed; to retreat from the violence of the dust and the air by taking a few simple steps forward.

But he would not. Even as the gales became an arid hurricane, now picking up rocks that tumbled haphazardly through the air, he remained rooted to the spot. Forces that should have torn him to pieces hurled stones spitefully at his body. The familiar sound of bones being snapped and crushed was somehow audible to him over the din, but he remained impossibly intact, impossibly immovable. It was as if his body were being broken from beneath him, from around him... but his *presence* remained exactly where he wanted it.

He had only one response this time, for that great dark empty rent in reality, the bane that tested him each and every time.

"Why don't you go and fuck yourself?" He snarled it, angry and frustrated.

As it so often was in these situations, his death was violent and painful.

The waking world pulled him back.

Elm Caden awoke from his violent demise in the same moment that *Hammer* chose to emerge from the wormhole. He wondered whether the turbulent exit had influenced the end of the dream. Probably not; it usually ended that way. The fatal barrage of rocks, and the visceral assault of the interstellar jump, had simply coincided.

He had seen enough of the galaxy to know that coincidences were sometimes just coincidences. Play out enough events in a big enough space, and you get repeating patterns. It simply happens.

Caden dressed himself under the glare of the emergency lighting, serenaded by the repetitive sounding of incident alarms. He was not concerned with either; he had known before they jumped that the exit would be a bumpy one. He had already run the numbers, and knew the ship could take it. The crew would manage. Besides, barring some unforeseen technical catastrophe, there was little he could contribute towards damage control that they would not be able to achieve themselves. Better to stay out of the way for now.

He scooped up his personal link and clipped it to his collar, pressed once and held. "Throam," he instructed. Release. The link chirruped agreeably, and a private channel opened.

"Oh, you're alive," said a gruff voice. "I'm so glad. It was such a rough trip, I was afraid you'd die of fright."

"Very good," Caden said. "I am — as you point out — quite alive. I anticipate Santani will be summoning me at any moment. Check our kit, and have Eilentes run pre-flight. If the situation is passive, I'll meet you on the hangar deck."

"The fun never ends with you." Throam sounded amused.

"On the hangar deck," Caden said.

"Did you call me a dick?"

"No, I said deck. Hangar *deck*."

"Are you sure?"

"Yes."

"Just checking," Throam said.

"Dick."

Caden smiled thinly to himself as he closed the private channel quietly.

"No, you're the dick, you dick."

Throam's voice was broadcast in the clear over the ship's comm system. Despite himself, Caden laughed out loud.

— 02 —

Captain's Prerogative

"This ship, *my* ship, has taken a severe beating," Santani said. "I may have lost two crew members. I won't know for sure until the damaged sections are fully secured."

Caden stood at ease before the captain's desk. He scrutinised her as she spoke, without indicating he was doing so. Old habits die hard.

Aker Santani was leaning forward, resting one elbow on the edge of the desk, her right hand propping up her chin. With her other hand she casually held a small holo, suspending it above the desk just off to her left, as if by giving time to Caden she were deferring some important reading. Wearing a pair of half-moon spectacles, presumably some ancient but fortuitously prescribed heirloom, she tipped her nose downward slightly so that she could glare at him over the tops of the lenses.

All non-verbal signals indicative of a dressing-down, he surmised. Irritated, impatient, uncertain precisely what latitude she has for interference in this operation. Wanting to apply a stamp of authority, but not willing to fight for it. Not yet, anyway.

Apologies, Captain, but I am a Shard. Typically hierarchical interactive psychology will not work on me. I stand on ceremony for one alone, and She is not here.

"We knew it would be a difficult jump before we left Kosling," he said. "I know Fleet worked up the numbers. They got them right too; I checked."

"I didn't bring you in here to show off, Caden" she said. "I'm unhappy about the whole situation. Very unhappy. This ship and the people on it are my responsibility. We've only just arrived— no, we're still *outside* the system, and I've already taken damage, possibly casualties."

"We are all of us in a dangerous occupation," he said. "I don't appreciate being made responsible for it."

"That's true," Santani said. "But you are the one who was ordered to come here. I don't see why my crew should have to share the risk with you."

"You know as well as I do, Captain, that a transport vessel wouldn't survive transit to Herros. No destination gate means no wormhole stabilisation. Nor would it have been a suitable vessel for the mission parameters. I required a heavy battleship."

"And how lucky we were to be stationed at Kosling when you decided to leave."

"It wasn't luck. You are stationed there so that you may be of use to the Empire."

"At your beck and call, you mean."

"This bickering is pointless. You've been given your orders, I expect you to follow them and to show the decorum associated with your rank. *She* expects it."

"Rank? Ha!" Santani laughed out loud. "What would a Shard know about having rank?"

"I may be outside the system; that doesn't mean I don't understand it."

"I rather think it does."

"Then you are mistaken, Captain. Hugely mistaken."

Santani's link chirruped, and she clicked it at once. "Go ahead."

It was her first officer who spoke. "We found them Captain, trapped in a damaged section. Jump casualties are now officially zero."

"Thank you, Mister Klade."

Santani clicked her link again, and the channel closed. She returned her attention to Caden, her glare now softening to what looked like mere irritation. The interruption and the welcome news it brought seemed to have broken the tension.

"We can at least be thankful that your crew members are unharmed," Caden said.

"Yes, I'm sure you're very relieved. I still have damage to contend with. You should know that even if nothing else is to go wrong, I want assurances that this mission of yours is worth it."

Worth it? He had not expected *that*.

"As you know Captain, the missions allocated to Shard operatives come directly from Her Most Radiant Majesty."

"That doesn't answer my question at all."

Caden was again taken aback. "The Empress herself commands it. Therefore assume that it *is* worth it."

"I don't like it. Nor do I like assumptions."

"She is not concerned with whether or not we like it. She tells us to go, so we go. She tells us to do, so we do. It is the privilege of the Throne."

"Privilege won't keep my people safe."

"Given the right circumstances, nothing will,"

Caden said. He did not like the way this conversation was going.

"In fact, in this case, I'd say privilege is going to get my people killed. We don't even know what we're being sent into."

"We're here exactly because we don't know, and that's all I can and will tell you. I suggest, with the greatest respect to you, Captain, that you have some faith in the Throne."

"Faith in the Throne," she said. He thought he heard a note of derision in her voice. "You can file that with 'privilege'."

There was a quiet pause as each regarded the other. Caden now sensed that the captain was not trying to be obstructive, nor was she trying to assert her own brand of authority. No, it was something else entirely. Despite the cynical approach, this was a commander who needed to be reassured. Blameless really; she had not been briefed. One could hardly expect her to ferry a Shard operative across the galaxy blindly, on a heavy battleship, without developing any misgivings.

Be patient.

"She fully expects us to return, Captain."

"How do you figure that?"

"She wouldn't have sent such a resource as a Shard operative if she expected never to see us again. Although I say it myself, we are a rare breed and an important resource."

"That comes across as fairly arrogant, Caden," she said, "but I have to agree you are probably correct. And that's not such a bad thing."

"I'm sure you have other reservations, and I would imagine you want to minimise any possible risks. So I'll simplify matters. If *Hammer* can open a wormhole for us, I'll enter the system only with

Throam and Eilentes."

"Are you sure that's wise?"

"If preliminary scans had turned up a hostile force at or near Herros, I'm certain you would have mentioned it by now."

"Correct, the system interior certainly appears to be passive from here. But even so, bear in mind that at this distance our sensors are telling us what the landscape looked like about seven hours ago. There is a risk of ambush."

"Minimal I would say; whatever happened here happened days ago. I think it's better all around if we act as a vanguard: the risk to *Hammer* is reduced, we're less visible to sensors if there is a hostile force present, and if the worst comes to the worst, you'll have time to receive our telemetry before you retreat."

"And you get to operate without uninitiated observers?"

"That too."

She considered this carefully. "You wanted *Hammer* to bring you here, yet you're leaving us at the periphery while you go in alone?"

"You just agreed that if there were a significant enemy presence at Herros, we'd probably have picked it up," he said. "If it turns out that the situation is hostile, and it's more than we can handle, we will re-evaluate."

"Very well. It's your choice. Make your preparations, and notify me if you require support. *Hammer* can always jump to Herros after you have made an initial assessment."

"Thank you, Captain."

"There is just one more thing, Caden."

"Go on...?"

"Please advise Mister Throam to exercise some

discretion when using the comm system."

Told off by the captain. Caden could not help but smirk slightly.

"That applies to you as well."

◦ ◦ ◦

Rendir Throam glanced up from his work as Caden strode purposefully toward him and the shuttle. He returned his attention straight back to the arms and equipment laid out before him on the hangar deck, knowing full well that the Shard would want to leave as soon as was possible.

"How are we fixed?"

"Nearly there," Throam said. "Final checks for my part. Think Euryce had some kind of problem in the cockpit."

"I'll check with her," Caden said. "I think the good Captain Santani is worried we're going to get her crew killed."

"Aren't they always?"

"Just so you know, she also said not to be a dick with the comm system."

"Did she really? You know I will get you back for that, right?"

"I know you'll try."

"I won't just try; you're doomed. That's three I owe you now. Watch your back."

"You're actually counting, aren't you?" Caden said over his shoulder as he disappeared up the access ramp into the rear compartment of the shuttle.

"You'd better believe I'm counting." The counterpart muttered it, lifting an empty supply crate clear of his working area.

On the deck plating, Throam had carefully arranged everything that they would need when they arrived at Herros. Everything they would need, and then some. He had run enough missions with Caden to know what they were likely to want immediate access to in the most probable scenarios.

First and foremost were three sets of body armour of a light flexible sort, which each of them would wear over their base layer regardless of whatever else they carried. Throam, Caden, and Eilentes; they would all have this protection as a bare minimum. Plasteel fibres woven into panels that covered the chest, abdomen, shoulders, sides and back, with additional shaped plates to protect the neck and femoral arteries.

Next to these he had placed the outer armour that he and Caden would almost certainly don before they arrived. He had already checked each piece for cracks, ensured no seals had perished or separated from the armour itself, and run the diagnostic routine built in to each suit. He had tested the skinprinting function, and smiled with satisfaction when the outer layers shifted quickly — from their default white and grey digital urban camouflage — to mimic the darker hatchings of the deck plates. Finally, he had also checked the webbing, mag-tags, and straps that they would need to carry the rest of their equipment: all in order.

Eilentes had her own set of armour stowed in one of the cabins on the shuttle, and he knew she had checked this herself. Unnecessarily so, since that set had only just been issued, but it was always gratifying to see someone exercising a good habit.

Two large plastic crates with chunky handles came next, each of them bearing the red and blue emblem of Life and Rescue. Essential in any situation. One crate was simply a duplicate of the other: field medical kits, ropes, basic rescue equipment, metallic blankets, and a body bag. Time and time again, previous experience had demonstrated the value of carrying redundant supplies.

A similar pair of crates held the basics that would be needed to keep the three of them alive should they become stranded. Water, ration packs, solid fuel blocks, power cells, air scrubbers, a beacon, more metallic blankets, and a collapsible survival tent. All of them in date, with intact seals. Excellent.

A final duo of crates, these with thick walls and adorned with the blue and white symbol that represented Tech and Systems. Each was filled with a flexible foam lining, impregnated with a protective wire mesh that acted as a Faraday cage. Entombed within, resting snugly in their sculpted recesses, were spare communication links, holographic storage, and an interface tool.

The final arrangement was his favourite, and the one which had occupied most of his time; weapons, beautiful weapons.

At the back lay three long plasteel cases, none of which he had checked. Eilentes had warned that she had done it herself, and he knew better than to interfere once she had closed the lids. Her long range rifles, she had once said, were her own trustworthy arsenal. No hands would ever touch them but for her own.

Everything else, on the other hand, was entirely in his purview. Caden had no reservations about picking up a weapon that his counterpart had stripped, cleaned, and loaded; as far as the Shard was concerned, it was the same as doing it himself. This suited Throam well, for he loved the job. It had become almost a ritual.

Two times Moachim M46 short-barrelled assault rifles: check.

Two times Moachim P16 rapid fire pistols: check.

One times Lancillon Industries 10/W compact mini-gun: check.

One times BromCon Type II shotgun: check.

Eight zadaqtan throwing blades: check.

His own dagger, with ankle sheath: check.

Ten frag grenades: check.

Six density grenades: check.

Four packs gel explosive: check.

Big grin: check.

Nothing had ever satisfied Throam quite so much as ensuring that a huge pile of unborn devastation was ready to be played with. It certainly beat the prospect of carrying it all, even if the majority of it would be split between him and Caden.

Throam wiped sweat from his thick brow with his forearm, then ran his hand over his scalp. A fine spray of moisture flicked off his black hair as each short bristle sprang back to its natural place. He was by no means tired, but the task of sorting the equipment and moving it all around had not been inconsiderable. It was fortunate then that neither was he; at nearly two metres tall, and giving the honest appearance of being just as wide, he was only just starting to get warmed up. That warmth was the real problem; a natural consequence of being built like a tank. He was beginning to regret starting the day with a chest session. But it was worth it, to finally have everything in its proper place.

Starting with the stackable crates, he began to lift the kit into the waiting shuttle.

° ° °

Euryce Eilentes moved gracefully from console to console, swiping and pressing the interactive holos which gave her access to the shuttle's flight systems. She was not happy.

An hour beforehand, when she had come to the hangar deck to run pre-flight checks on the small craft, she had found several critical problems with the flight control module. Re-installing the shuttle's operating system from the backup core had been simple enough, but she had then needed to go through each of the primary systems in turn, inputting her customisations as best as she could remember them. That would teach her to forget to create a preferences file. Noted for next time.

The shuttle was effectively theirs, requisitioned from Fleet Command a few days beforehand for the purposes of Shard operations. Eilentes had flown it only once before, when she had transferred it from Fort Kosling to the hangar deck of the *Hammer*. Perhaps it had been somewhat premature of her to spend so much time customising the various systems while she waited for the rendezvous with the battleship.

But there were better things to worry about. This was her first Shard op, and she had never before worked with Caden. It was not in the remit of the pilot to get involved in the Shard-counterpart dynamic, so she could avoid accidentally causing ructions between him and Throam easily. But that same factor might well prolong her status as a third wheel. Even though she had previously run missions with Throam, many times in fact, as far as this specific trio went she was still going to be the unknown quantity. The outsider. The newbie.

If you want to be truly needed, you have to shine.

Mama's words were as true to her now as they ever had been. She had first been given this advice when she reached her final year at the Commerce Authority Piloting School on Kementhast Prime. Later, when she retrained at the Imperial Flight Academy, her mother had repeated the suggestion.

And how Eilentes had shone.

It's just nerves, she told herself. I can do this, and I can do it well. I'll just treat it as a practical exam, like at the academy.

"Are we good to go?"

Eilentes looked back from the cockpit and saw that Caden was standing in the main compartment, leaning against the edge of the intervening bulkhead. He waited patiently for her answer, a faintly amused expression on his otherwise neutral face.

"A few minutes more," she said. "I had a bit of a problem earlier."

"Nothing serious?"

Definitely do *not* give the impression of incompetence. "Oh no, not at all. Just a setback. We're flight-capable."

Caden smiled at her, and she found herself wondering if the tales of his cold and aloof manner had been exaggerated. Anything passed around the fleet that could reasonably be called a 'tale' was usually precisely that.

"What exactly are we here for?" She asked.

"That can wait until we're away from the *Hammer,*" Caden said. "I'd rather not run the risk of being overheard."

"There's nobody else on the hangar deck," she said.

"Doesn't mean we can't be heard."

She felt instantly foolish. The Shard had been sent to the far end of space by the Empress herself, on a mission so secretive that not even the ship's captain had been briefed. Of course he was going to play it safe.

She would need to be more mindful in future that she was no longer simply piloting ships. Now she was a part of something bigger and more important. Secrets would need to be kept, and interests protected. Not least of which was the interest they all shared in staying alive. Careless words could cost lives, if not their own then perhaps those of others.

"I can wait," she said. She smiled back at him.

"Are either of you lazy assholes going to help me with all this shit? Half of it's yours anyway."

Eilentes looked past Caden and saw Throam stumbling into the cabin, a plastic crate tucked under each arm. She knew that expression. He was feigning difficulty; the crates might as well have been empty for all the trouble they were really giving him.

"Sorry. I'd love to help, but I'm busy." She slapped and pawed at the cockpit holos in a patently meaningless way.

"I just don't want to," said Caden. "But I can see you're doing a grand job."

"I'm supposed to keep you alive." Throam dropped the crates almost onto Caden's feet. "So I can still pummel you, as long as I don't go too far."

"Your problem though is you always go too far," said Caden.

Eilentes smiled secretly to herself. Yes, that was certainly one of his problems. The Shard was a good judge of character. She supposed it went with the territory.

"Better come help me then."

Caden shoved aside the crates Throam had dumped so unceremoniously, and followed him back down the ramp. Eilentes heard his retort even from the cockpit.

"I've never liked you, you know that don't you?"

Neither of them had got it right. She hauled the crates into the correct position and latched them down securely. The last thing she needed when the shuttle left the artificial gravity of *Hammer* behind was a bunch of kit floating through to the cockpit.

I was wrong, she thought. This isn't going to be like an exam at all. It's going to be just like living in halls. Always tidying up after stupid boys.

– 03 –
A Free Man

Urx. An ugly name for an ugly planet. Maber Castigon had hated every second of the years he had spent on this primitive, miserable, noxious world. But then, he was supposed to have hated it. That was the general idea.

"Look directly at the sensor," said the guard.

Castigon stared directly ahead, his face a blank mask. A single light blinked on the front of the camera, and that was that. Exit image recorded.

"Go to the next room."

Evidently satisfied, the guard gave Castigon his single instruction then paid him no more attention. He gestured at a holo, pushing the exit image into Castigon's file and marking it to be appended to Imperial records during the next databurst.

I'd love to snap your neck, Castigon thought. Ten Solar years I spent on this absolute hole of a planet; you could at least acknowledge me.

One good twist. He imagined the noise that would make.

"Go to the next room," the guard said. "Go now."

Castigon realised he had remained seated and staring for several long moments since the guard first told him to move. He had been so busy thinking about the sensation of the man's briefly painful death, and the expression that would be on his face as he realised the finality of what had just happened to him.

He went to the next room.

"This way please." A distant voice beckoned him the moment he passed through the doorway.

Castigon walked across the concrete floor and glanced around at the stark, white walls. No windows, no décor, no features. Just the one steel desk in the centre of the room, and a man standing behind it with one hand resting on a plasteel container. The room seemed immense for just one desk.

"You will no longer be referred to as 409-966, Citizen," said the man. "You are now once more Maber Castigon, a free man of the Empire."

"I never stopped being Maber Castigon," he said.

"Quite." The man took the lid off the container. "I believe you will find everything in order."

Castigon peered over the rim, and recognised the possessions he had brought with him to Urx. All except one item, which he picked up and turned quizzically.

"A transport chit," the man said. "You'll be taken from Urx to Imiron, free of charge. There is a probation office at the starport, and you are required to visit. Once validated there the chit can be exchanged for one more trip to any planet of class two or lower. After that, you're on your own."

"Imperial routes only?"

"But of course. Nobody else will accept that chit."

Castigon sighed to himself. They were so predictable.

"A reminder that the Empire knows where I

am," he said. "Just like this enormous room is supposed to remind me that I am a small and insignificant thing, being sent back out into a great and mighty society."

"I just work here, Mister Castigon."

Castigon began to remove his effects from the container; first, neatly folded clothes. "You know if I were the disturbed sort, the ones you people seem to want to put in here as often as possible, that kind of thing might actually make me more likely to come back."

He lifted a pair of shoes from one side of the container. At least whoever had packed it had put the dirty soles on the bottom, with the clothing on top. Someone more vindictive might have done it the other way around.

"I mean, I'm sure it works with rational people," he said. "Reminding them they did a bad thing, they needed to be punished, and they'll be watched. I would imagine most people take the hint."

A personal link. Not charged.

"But there are so many people in here with real issues. I can't imagine that serving out a sentence feels like much of an achievement to a crazy when they get told they're going to be subjected to surveillance for evermore."

A holo. Not charged.

"Not to mention that telling someone they're small is a pretty bad idea, if their crimes were a product of their own sense of insignificance. You know, if they think that murdering a few dozen people will make their name live forever, and so on."

A short dagger in a black sheath. The sort carried by counterparts.

"The really damaged ones." He met the other man's gaze directly.

He turned the sheath over twice, and felt the handle of the dagger.

"If I were one of that sort, this whole experience might just be too much."

He drew the dagger, inspected the blade carefully. Light glanced off the polished metal, perfect reflections revealing the quality of the blade and the obsessive care lavished on it by its keeper.

"I could decide it's too hard to even go back out into the world," he said. "Or I might think that I'll eventually end up back here anyway, and decide to speed things along."

He pointed the blade at the man behind the desk.

"I might decide to do something that would extend my stay."

The man looked down at the blade, then brought his eyes back up slowly to meet Castigon'-s. Those impassive, fathomless pools.

"As I mentioned, Mister Castigon," he said, "I just work here."

○ ○ ○

As was his custom on the last day of the local week, Proconsul Maggine worked late into the night. The slightly sweet sea air was so warm that he had left the balcony doors open, allowing a balmy current to meander through his office. No need to turn on the environmental systems; the temperature was just right. With his quarters in the House of Governance facing out onto the coastal cliffs, the gentle breeze carried the scent of the ocean rather than the cloying odours of Lophrit's capital. He was quite content to breathe in the night air.

He swiped across the next unopened item in the stack of tasks displayed by his holo. Another petition from a Raised citizen, yet again relaying the inane objections of an Ordinary. How tiresome. It was entirely obvious to him that the more prestigious elements of Lophrit society had not quite grasped their roles, despite the planet being settled half a century ago. Still they continued to bring trivia to his desk. Still they failed to screen the problems and desires of their less fortunate peers, issues which they were quite capable of diverting at their own level. He would have to discuss the matter with the more prolific offenders, and ensure that they understood properly how society was supposed to function. This one in particular could deal with the Ordinary himself, and Maggine tapped out a reply to that effect quickly. The petty issues of Ordinary citizens were just not interesting. The fact that they only had such mediocre things to complain about was exactly why they were considered... well... ordinary.

A splintering crack sounded off in the far distance, and almost immediately the sharp noise was followed by the rumble of air crashing and rolling high over head. Maggine registered the sound, but barely moved. He loved a good thunderstorm, especially the great violent shows that Lophrit could muster in her humid atmosphere. If he were able to finish his remaining tasks quickly, he could sit out on the covered balcony and quite safely watch the glorious display in its cataclysmic entirety.

He flicked to the next item, and found it more interesting. A request to establish a permanent gate relationship with a Gomlic trading post, on a world just across the border? Intriguing. His predecessor had always rejected such ideas, but gate security was more refined these days. The Gomlic world was less than three thousand light years away, upstream on the Sagittarius arm. He requested a comprehensive cost-benefit report from the sender, and closed the item. The stack of tasks plopped down once again, one step closer to completion.

Another crack, another rumble. The thunderous sound seemed to wash across the building, shaking the window panes ever so slightly. He hoped Lophrit would indeed put on the spectacular performance that the thunder promised.

A legal matter was next, and he quickly came to his conclusion. He was experienced with the civil claims system and wasted no time in making a decision. He sent the item across to the courthouse for their records.

Another great sound of bones snapping in the sky, another rumble of displaced air.

Maggine opened the last item in his work queue with a sigh of relief, and began to read. Of course, it would be a particularly grief-ridden petition. Just as he was beginning to think that his working week was coming to an end, naturally that was the best possible time for a four-way dispute between inter-married families to reach his desk. He began to read the circumstances, and found himself aghast that these people could even live their lives in such a—

The noise was so sharp and loud that he thought for a moment it had deafened him. Until the pressure wave came, he was sure his eardrums had been blown in. But then the thunder followed, battering the roof, and the walls shuddered. Furnishings in the office swayed from side to side, an antique pen jumped from its holder and rolled off the edge of the desk. He felt the jarring collision through his legs, sensed somehow that air had been pushed straight down on top of the building. A further sound, without doubt an explosion, rampaged violently on the heels of the thunder.

At that moment the alarms began to sound.

Maggine ran to the balcony and looked up into the night. Neither of Lophrit's moons had yet risen above the horizon, and the stars were bright in the cloudless sky. And yet something was slightly amiss.

It took a few seconds before he realised that stars were going out. Not randomly, not one at a time, but in patches; irregular shapes, growing slowly and blotting out the firmament. His ears picked up a low, throaty rumbling across the water. The sound of engines.

It was then he understood it had not been thunder he heard; these sounds were the shock waves caused by atmospheric splash-downs. Now panicked, he dashed along the balcony, hand trailing along the balustrade as he made his way around the outside of the building. Everywhere he looked he could see the dark patches blotting out the night sky, gradually growing bigger. A new sound then started, repetitive and angry, quick snapping sounds followed immediately by equally short thuds. He rounded the next corner of the balcony, coming to the city-facing front of the building, and skidded to a halt.

There, over the roofs and towers of his beloved city, the orange beads of tracers streamed one after another into the night sky, straight lines criss-crossing each other as dozens of batteries tracked their targets. Anti-drop defences, activated before he had even been informed of any problem. The orbital platforms must have fallen already.

He saw small explosions high in the inky darkness, where the streams of tracers ended so abruptly. Brief ripples of light illuminated artificial contours, edges, protrusions. White streaks answered the defensive barrage, fringed with orange, bolting from the sky and slamming straight through buildings. Gauss guns. Gauss guns firing on an Imperial city! Nothing of the kind had happened in almost a generation.

Trembling, knuckles whitening as he gripped the balustrade, he looked out toward the city centre. The great triple tower of the communications building was gone. Simply gone. He guessed that its fall had been the source of that first explosion he had heard.

If the orbital defences had been overcome before the surface had even been warned, and the comms towers were now destroyed, that meant that in all probability no distress call had yet been sent. Maggine already knew there were no ships visiting Lophrit that were capable of opening their own wormholes.

He ran back to the office and pawed at his holo. For a moment his hands shook so much he could not find the right menus. He willed his fingers to co-operate, swiped and tapped, and eventually located the emergency interface.

Security code? Oh by all the many worlds. He vaguely remembered setting a password years ago, and guessed at what he might have used. Success! The menu folded outwards, and he was prodding at the pane marked 'Incursion Protocol' before it had even formed fully on the holographic display.

"Insufficient Network Access," the holo replied. "Check Gate Connection".

"You cannot be serious," Maggine snapped. He jabbed sharply at an active area to run a diagnostic on the system's jump gate.

"Gate absent," said the holo.

◦ ◦ ◦

Castigon stepped from shadow to light, and brought his hand up instantly to shield his eyes against the glare. As much as it pained him to admit it, those years spent in Urx's infamous Correctional Compound One had robbed him of the memory of so many experiences. In this particular instance, it seemed his eyes had forgotten exactly how they should handle daylight.

When he had first arrived, he remembered, everything inside the facility had seemed dim and gloomy. Try as he might, he could not recall the exact time when he stopped noticing. He must have been in there so long that his brain had compensated, without him even perceiving a difference. The daylight now was blinding to him.

A rumbling came from behind him as the gates closed, further confirming his freedom.

He narrowed his eyes against the painfully bright sun, and started to trudge up the empty road towards the city. In his hand, he carried the chit that had been placed in with his personal property. He turned it over and over in his fingers.

They would grant him passage between star systems, at considerable expense, but they could not quite reach to a lift into town. And they wondered why people these days had no time for the government.

Oh, and only passage to planets of class two or below. So no chance of taking in the sights of Damastion then, or finding his way on Kementhast Prime. He would not be allowed to land on High Cerin, and a visit to the Meccrace system was out of the question. Nor would he be permitted access to Earth.

Well, not legitimate access.

He came to a natural bend in the road, where it curved away to follow the contours of the land, and turned back for a moment to take a last look at Correctional Compound One.

Sunk into the ground itself, in a vast basin of naked rock, it gave the unappealing impression of being a discarded lozenge. Of the three stories that were above ground, only the top one had windows; the privilege of daylight was reserved for staff. It was below ground level where the inmates languished. Out of sight, out of mind.

What had surprised him about the subterranean prison was that even through the rock and concrete and thick metal doors, the smell still pervaded every nook and cranny. The distinctive and tangy odour of Urx, a scent not unlike the combination of manure and old fish, somehow permeated every level of the ostensibly sealed facility. It clung to everything, and he loathed it. Worse still, for some elusive reason the smell defied habituation; one simply never got used to it. Every day spent on Urx was another day living with that rank stench. Day in, day out, for ten Solars, he had felt like he wanted to retch.

And the Blight! Oh by the worlds, the damnable Blight was everywhere.

Urx was a contaminated planet, one of many Imperial colonies which had come to be thoroughly infested long before anyone realised that interstellar travel could spread microbes so very far and wide. Granted very few humans had ever had a severe reaction to the Blight, but when it got a foothold in even a minor cut or scratch... *hellish*.

Other species were not so lucky, but mankind seemed to have a natural resistance to the curious little symbiotic complex of virus, bacteria, and fungus. It was just unfortunate that the composite organism was still capable of causing such misery when it infected open wounds: itching, scratching, pus, dead skin, more scratching, secondary infection, prolonged healing time, and most likely permanent scarring. Castigon now carried several Blight marks, and he recalled the torture of each infection with an abiding bitterness.

Funny that he should have been tormented by such relatively trivial matters, when the violence and malice of his fellow inmates should have been of primary concern. But then Castigon was hardly an angel himself.

He was not foolish enough to think that his survival had been relatively easy, but he would admit that he had learned a thing or two during his stay. One had to, stuck underground and surrounded by people who, without the shadow of a doubt, thoroughly deserved to be there.

One thing had interested him above all else. It was a subject he had researched carefully and guardedly in small pieces, learning over many months, gleaning information from various different sources without putting himself at risk.

He had discovered there was a thing they called the Backwaters: a clandestine mixture of back channels, systemic security failings, and corrupt officials. About which — he was reasonably sure — the Empire knew absolutely nothing. What was surprising to him was not that it was so well developed and successful, but that even he had never heard of it before.

He had learned that the Backwaters were routinely used by criminals, smugglers, and society's least desirable elements in general. At a price, the Backwaters could get you access to anywhere, or to anyone.

When he first learned of it, when he realised that even the intelligence analysts at Eyes and Ears were probably in the dark about it, he had been concerned. It could only have been the counterpart training that made him worry. After a few more years, he had quite stopped caring. All that mattered now was how he could use the information for his own ends.

Class two or below. Ha! He snorted, flicked the chit into the dirt by the side of the road, and started walking again. He would see about *that*. He would gladly accept the free ride to Imiron, but after that he knew exactly where he was going and it certainly was not class two or below. The crass mind games, played so commonly in the name of civilisation, no longer mattered to him. No; now there was only one thing on his mind.

It was time to settle some old scores.

– 04 –
Quiet as the Grave

The shuttle bucked hard as it dropped out into normal space, and Eilentes felt the familiar sensation of having every nerve in her body stretched away to infinity. As the stars outside became almost static points, and the flood of opalescent light faded from the cockpit canopy, the almost unbearable sensation quickly trickled away.

"Jump complete," she said. "We're on approach to Herros."

"Thank you *Hammer,*" Caden said.

The wormhole projected by the waiting battleship stayed open behind them, but quickly closed down to a much narrower diameter. Close enough to avoid the problem of signal degradation, *Hammer* would now send and receive telemetry through the wormhole, thereby staying in real-time contact with the shuttle and her crew.

"Nothing worth mentioning in range," said Throam, "and the station is silent."

"Station?"

"Gemen Station," said Caden, "is the reason we're here. Two days ago it went dark; no databursts, no scheduled transmissions, nothing. Total blackout."

"What in the worlds are they doing all the way

out here?"

Caden turned away from his holo to look directly at Eilentes. "Medical research."

"Yeah right."

"Well that's the official line," he said, turning back to his holo. "Take it or leave it."

"Do you believe it?"

"Of course not; it's complete rubbish."

"I'm showing green lights for all stealth plating," Throam said. "It won't hide us, but it will make us look much less like a shuttle. Think we can risk an active sweep?"

"Do it," Caden said.

Throam tapped in commands, and the shuttle's sensors started to probe more urgently into the space surrounding Herros.

"Our mission is fairly straightforward," said Caden. "Secure Gemen Station, establish cause of blackout, neutralise any hostile forces, recover assets."

"Nothing orbital," said Throam. "Starting a sweep of the surface."

"If you have assets worth stealing, you don't put them out in the middle of nowhere without any form of defence," Eilentes said.

"They didn't. There's supposed to be a task force stationed here," said Caden. "I'm not entirely happy with how conspicuous their absence is."

"I'm with you on that."

Throam's holo flashed up a blinking green icon: no contact. "We're clear as far as sensors are concerned. Nothing on the surface that we shouldn't be expecting to find."

"So no defence force, but also nothing hostile in the system as far as we can see, and nothing out of the ordinary on the planet?"

"That's about it, yes".

"You sure there isn't a Viskr battalion waiting down there?" Caden said. "If this turns into another Fort Tochi cluster-fuck, I'm going to stab you again."

"Reasonably sure, yeah: there are no transmissions, no large energy signatures, and the only metallic structure big enough to give a reading this far out is the station. You stab like a child by the way."

"Curious."

"He stabbed you?" Eilentes had a note of genuine concern in her voice.

"Ha, yeah. A bit," said Throam.

She stared at him for a few seconds, unsure whether the two men were testing her credulity. Next one of them would probably ask her to go for a long weight. On the other hand she already knew that Throam was damaged goods, and so far Caden did not seem quite as robotic as she had been led to believe he would.

"Eilentes, I think it would be best if you keep the boat ticking over while we check out the station, just in case we need to make a quick exit," Caden said.

She found herself disappointed. It was the military equivalent of 'you wait in the car'. Well okay, she thought. I suppose it beats getting shot in the face on my first trip out. My moment will come.

"We're coming up on our insertion window," she said.

Herros now loomed in the forward canopy, a great ball of muddy green which seemed to roll slowly without ever changing position. It hung in the middle of their view, gradually growing larger, the thick unbroken atmosphere crawling sluggishly across the surface in a futile race against its own indifference.

"Time to show us what you can do then. Take us down."

Caden and Throam moved easily into the rear compartment, almost weightless in high orbit of the planet, and dressed themselves for combat. Protective plates, outer armour, webbing. Each of them holstered a pistol to the left of the abdomen, then clipped an assault rifle to the mag-tags on their back plates. The magnetic patches built into the armour accepted the weapons with a satisfying *shunk*, grabbing at the black metal and pulling it greedily into place. Secure, but easily accessed. The mag-tags would grip each gun jealously unless the weapon reported that an authorised user had taken hold of it.

While Throam stocked pouches with tubes of explosive gel and clipped grenades to his webbing, Caden strapped a longer pouch to his front armour plate: the set of eight zadaqtan, glossy throwing blades which could penetrate even a human bone. In close quarters combat, particularly in an environment where projectiles or energy discharges posed a hazard, the distinctive blades could easily ensure he was the last man standing. At least, they did so the way he used them.

"Check me?" Throam said.

Caden checked each of the seals on Throam's armour carefully and methodically, and tugged at his webbing. "Down," he said.

Throam stooped, and Caden finished his checks around the shoulders and neck. The helmet seal would have to wait until Throam had returned the favour. "Squared away. Now do me."

"Maybe after I check your armour."

Eilentes smiled to herself as she nudged the shuttle into its descent trajectory. Throam was still essentially the same then; confidently incorrigible with his close friends. From experience, she knew that for him to speak to Caden in that way must mean there was significant trust between them.

She wondered if since last they met Throam had managed to become a more sociable animal. She hoped so; last time around he had unwittingly made a real mess of their chances together. She shared the blame. Letting him walk away without knowing how she really felt? That was not a decision she had enjoyed making, despite him being blissfully unaware of it.

The shuttle trembled, its outer hull buffeted by the gradually thickening atmosphere.

"Hold on back there," she said, "we may experience some turbulence."

○ ○ ○

"A word, Captain, if I may?"

Santani looked up from the repair summary that scrolled across her holo. Klade stood patiently in front of her, deferentially positioned just off to one side.

"You may."

"I've just been informed of something unusual, and given the nature of our deployment I thought you'd want to know."

"Go on,"

"As you know, sensor palettes shut themselves down during wormhole transit, along with a number of other sensitive systems. They power up automatically when the ship hits normal space."

"I'm familiar with the process," she said.

"In the same moment that sensor functions resumed when we arrived here, they recorded a large gravitational spike."

"How large?"

"'Vast' would perhaps be more accurate."

"The echo effect perhaps?"

"No, it was considerably bigger than us, even if you account for any distortion caused by the wormhole."

"But scans of the surrounding space were negative when we got here."

"Yes Ma'am, they were and they still are. The sensor logs show that the gravity spike vanished as we emerged."

"So what you're saying is, something left the system when it detected our incoming wormhole?"

"That is one of the possible explanations, Captain."

"Something with an immense mass profile?"

"Apparently so."

She grimaced. "I'm not sure I like that idea."

"Well, it's also possible that it was a power surge in a sensor palette. We did take a beating."

"I'd very much like to know which it was, Commander."

"Of course. I've already downloaded the sensor logs for analysis, and taken an imprint of the system software to be scrutinised by Tech and Systems. It'll all be sent back in the next databurst."

"Keep me apprised," said Santani. "If the readings were accurate, Fleet Command will want to know about it. Something huge prowling about out here; that's going to have them worried."

"Yes Ma'am."

"And I'd like to be ready in case it comes back." She leaned towards him and lowered her voice.

"The last thing anyone on the command deck needs to see is me shitting myself."

○ ○ ○

Resting on the landing pad of Gemen Station, the shuttle was poised gracefully, as if ready for flight at a moment's notice. Eilentes remained in the cockpit, scanning dutifully for any signs of opposition and ensuring the engines remained on standby.

Caden and Throam emerged from the rear of the shuttle, rifles raised, sweeping the landscape around the landing pad as they stepped off the ramp. As soon as they were clear, the ramp folded up neatly into the shuttle.

They made their way across the pad, still sweeping the area, advancing cautiously on a secondary entrance to the station which allowed access to the landing area. They arrived at a wide trapezoidal doorway, sealed by huge metal doors, and Throam stood off while Caden popped the cover protecting the entry controls.

"We've got power," he said. "That's reassuring."

He tapped the largest button, the one that would normally operate the doors. The imposing portal remained stubbornly inert. The edges of the button illuminated, now fringed with red light.

"Lock-down," he said.

Throam shifted his weight between his feet and scanned the horizon, waiting while Caden used a holo to bring up codes for the station systems. The mission pack he had been given prior to joining Throam and Eilentes at Fort Kosling was, for a change, very comprehensive.

"Got it," he said, and tapped a series of numbers into the keypad.

The glow at the edges of the main button changed to green, and he jabbed it once before stepping back to raise his rifle. An opening mechanism rumbled behind thick walls, the two overlapping doors separated, and escaping gases blew dust outward. The short length of corridor beyond the opening began to glow as wall-mounted light panels came to life.

"Euryce, you copy?" Said Throam.

"Lima Charlie," she said. "Go ahead."

"We're about to enter the station. Sensors couldn't get anything back, so chances are you're going to lose us when these doors close."

"Acknowledged. I'll leave a light on for you."

They stepped inside, and Caden easily found the controls that corresponded with those on the exterior. The doors closed behind them, sliding into place and sinking into their locking grooves with a resounding *thud*. Whoever had designed this facility had certainly known how to protect an entrance.

A brief flicker of light bounced around the chamber as internal sensors swept the entryway. The two men were registered, and a holo appeared on the wall: Air Exchange Procedure, Please Stand By.

Moments later, the atmosphere of Herros had been pumped out of the room and replaced with processed station air. Caden's armour confirmed it was breathable, and he gladly broke the seal on his helmet visor.

"One door down," he said.

"There could be anything outside this airlock."

"I suspect we've missed the action, otherwise I wouldn't have had Eilentes bring the shuttle in so close. And she'd be with us."

"You sure about that?"

"Whatever happened here, it's resulted in an entire task force going MIA. Whoever did it is probably long gone. We'd have seen something by now if they were still around."

Throam looked unconvinced. "Unless they're all behind this door."

"They'd have sentries at the very least, whether that means guards on the outer doors or vessels in orbit. You don't knock out a fleet to get to your prize, then completely ignore everything else while you play with it."

"I guess there's only one way to find out," said Throam. He angled himself towards the inner door and hefted his rifle.

"Actually, there are two."

Caden swiped his fingers across the holo that had appeared in the airlock moments before. He invoked a security interface, used another code from the mission pack, and brought up the station logs.

"Okay," he said, a little disappointed. "Security holos have been wiped, transit logs, communication logs... everything."

"So we'll be doing it my way then." Throam was still facing the inner hatch, holding his stance patiently.

"I suppose that will make a change."

○ ○ ○

Eilentes monitored the holos vigilantly while she waited in the shuttle cockpit, listening out for the occasional bursts of audio that somehow managed to escape the station's shielding.

"One door... anything... lock" — the words came in fits and starts, punctuated by crisp bursts of static — "entire battle... something... prize."

She was far from concerned. Even in those meagre fragments, she could hear that the tone of their speech was conversational with no hint of alarm. Whatever they were saying it was most likely an assessment of what they had found or expected to find. She knew that very soon, as they ventured deeper into the station, the fragments of audio would stop.

She keyed the controls for ship-to-ship comms. "Ground party to *Hammer*, come in."

"Go ahead ground party," came the reply.

"We're on the surface; no opposition. Your path is clear. Feel free to drop in any time."

"Acknowledged, ground party. We are inbound to a distant orbital. *Hammer* out."

She watched a holo as passive sensors picked up the intense energy burst of a flaring wormhole, and the heavy battleship registered immediately. *Hammer* had dropped into the system interior, a safe distance from Herros but close enough to lend assistance should the need arise.

Now she could relax. The battleship's many sensor palettes were far more sensitive than those on the shuttle; if anything hostile turned up uninvited, *Hammer* would be training her guns on it before Eilentes was even prompted for a reaction. She stretched as best she could in the contoured pilot's seat, ran her fingers through her hair, and thought of Rendir Throam.

Ten Solars it had been, more or less, since they went their separate ways. They had spent almost a year together on the *Embolden* by the time Throam's long-awaited notice had come, when he was finally released from his battalion to fill a freshly vacated counterpart role. He had seemed almost indifferent to the end of their relationship, and for a while she had told herself he had waited so very long to become a counterpart that he could hardly have thought about anything else at the time.

More fool me, she thought.

There had been precious little contact after he left. She realised she was not alone in that — worlds knew he was hardly the most sociable person she had ever met — but it still cut deep, even though all his old squad mates on the *Embolden* had complained about exactly the same thing. He's like this with everyone, they had assured her.

But that was just it: she had hoped *she* would mean more than that to Throam. Being a part of 'everyone' was exactly the same as being just anyone. And even though she knew it wasn't true, a part of her associated being 'just anyone' with being no-one at all.

The worst part though had been the moment they were reunited, just a few days ago. He had spoken to her as if she were nothing more than an old drinking buddy.

"How the fuck are *you*?"

Yes there had been a hug, one of those amazing hugs she had always looked forward to at the end of a hard duty shift on the *Embolden*, but that was basically it.

She had truly loved him by the end.

In some ways it was perhaps a blessing that he had been approved for pairing with Caden. She and Throam had been drifting apart in the final couple of months; her completely infatuated, and him seeming to not really notice that their casual relationship was changing into something else. The man could be so dense sometimes. If it had not been for the sex, she would probably have ended it to spare herself some pain. The sex had almost been worth it on its own.

Before she retrained for the Navy, Eilentes had piloted commercial ships. There had never been many people she was in regular contact with, and none who could be relied upon for a long term commitment, so like most people in that career she had sought physical comfort when and where the chance presented itself. Not that such opportunities were frequent; she would hardly say she had slept around.

Rendir Throam was the first soldier she had bedded. He was better than everyone who had gone before, men and women alike. Well, *woman*. There had only been one, so maybe it was not a proper comparison. Eilentes had given it a fair try, and although she did not really see what all the fuss was about there was always the possibility she had just bunked up with the wrong girl.

No woman would ever come close to Throam though, that much she could say for certain. Even though she was reasonably tall herself, his chin had only just started where her head left off. He would lift her with one hand and toss her on the bunk, sometimes growling playfully while she had fits of giggles. His skin was always burning hot, and the medi-training cycles favoured by his MAGA unit meant he usually had more testosterone than his body knew what to do with. She had never objected to him sticking those needles in his buttocks when he stayed in her quarters.

So yes, the sex had *almost* been worth it. Almost, but not quite. It was fair to say that Eilentes had grown very attached to Throam, and she had wanted much more from the relationship. But whatever she did, whatever she said, it never seemed to sink into his big, daft head. It was as if he had reached a point where he had what he wanted, and then stopped thinking about what else he might have had. What else *they* might have had.

And then there was Caden. She had been warned that Shards could appear aloof and disinterested, but even so his attempts to get to know her over the past few days had been anaemic at best. He and Throam, on the other hand, had what looked like an easy and well-practised partnership going on. It was entirely possible Rendir was getting it from the Shard these days. It would not have surprised her one bit; judging by the size he had put on in the past decade he was definitely still on the gear, and that had always made him so horny he would try to knock boots with anyone too slow to escape.

Paranoid much, Euryce? Maybe it's simpler than that, she thought glumly. Maybe he really *did* get over me that quickly.

Even though she had told herself years ago — in no uncertain terms — that she was done with being upset, she had to wipe away a tear.

○ ○ ○

"Quiet as the grave," Throam muttered. "I don't like it."

"It's not just you. Something is very wrong here."

For several minutes now, the two of them had stalked cautiously through empty white corridors, passing deserted laboratories and work spaces. Everywhere they went was the same: minimal power, pale blue emergency lighting, holos on standby, tools and personal effects laid aside as if their owners had just walked away for a moment.

"Why is it not all torn up?"

"I have no idea." Caden said. "I have no idea, and I don't like that at all."

The deeper they got into the station, the less comfortable Throam became. He saw no bodies, and no signs that weapons had been fired. There was no damage whatsoever, in fact, and nothing that would indicate a struggle had taken place or a siege had been mounted. Not even a single barricade. He had anticipated so many scenarios, and this had not been one of them.

"Where are we now?"

Caden checked his holo. "Auxiliary research level. Everything interesting looks like it should be down below."

"Control room?"

"Right in the middle of the level beneath us."

"What are you thinking?"

"I'm thinking we secure this level first, since it's part of our exit route. Then we make a beeline for control and use internal security to check out as much of this place as possible. While we're there, see if there are any backup security holos."

Throam nodded. "Works for me."

They resumed, working their way stealthily and systematically through the corridors and labs, offices and meeting rooms. Throughout the entire level, everything was the same. Other than the lack of people, there was no sign that anything was particularly amiss.

Throam was unnerved by the silence. Give him the clamour of a battlefield, and he would be perfectly happy: he knew where he was with gunfire and explosions. But this, this was almost forbidding. Something about the quiet and the stillness and the absence of any life... it screamed out at him that they should not be there, they ought to leave immediately. Whatever had happened to the people living and working here, it could easily come for them next. He felt a knot tightening in his stomach; it was a foreign sensation to him. He had charged across burning earth before, directly into enemy ranks. He had leapt across chasms and 'chuted straight through storm systems. He could not remember the last time he had been this nervous; but then the threat had always been visible before. Clear danger he could deal with. It was usually just an opportunity for him to make something much less threatening.

After what seemed like an age, Caden stopped in his tracks. Throam realised they had come full circle. Satisfied that the whole level was clear, they returned to an elevator station they had come across earlier. Throam prised the doors open, and in the dimly lit shaft they could see an emergency access ladder was built into the wall. He reached out to grab a rung.

"Don't trust the lift?" Caden said.

"If there's anyone down there, the noise would give them a heads up."

"You're starting to think like me."

"I agree, I've been around you far too long."

"Not quite what I meant."

Throam climbed down into the murky shadows, followed by Caden, and before long they found themselves on the level below. It looked essentially the same as the one they had just left; all sloping white walls, pale blue emergency lighting, and grilled flooring.

Caden consulted his holo. "This way."

Minutes later they were in the main control room, a large circular chamber containing two concentric rings of work stations and holos. The walls were given over largely to glass panels; from virtually any angle, they allowed a direct view out into the adjacent corridors. In the centre of the room was a large, round console, designed to allow several users to work together.

Caden moved to the central station. "I'll hook in."

Throam waited patiently while Caden worked at the console, moving around the room quietly and visually scanning each window in turn. Despite the lack of any presence so far at Gemen Station, he did not intend to allow anyone to get the drop on them.

"I'm bringing up the cameras."

Holos around the room began to display the feeds from cameras all over the station. They showed yet more corridors, tech bays, labs, offices, storage spaces; all of them devoid of life. Not one chair was overturned or glass partition cracked.

"This is starting to weird me out," said Throam.

"Stay frosty, these cameras don't cover every corner of the station."

"If someone jumps out at me, I *am* going to shoot first."

"Good." Caden tapped a corner of the console holo, and the display flipped from the camera feed to a security interface.

"It's the same here," he said eventually. "Logs have been wiped clean, security holos are also gone. There's nothing of any use. All we have is the live camera feed."

"What about project files?" Throam asked. "Can you see what they were working on here?"

"I don't have access," Caden said. "That's outside the mission profile."

"*You* don't have access?" Throam could hardly believe it. He was accustomed to the Shard having authority to act at will, being capable of going anywhere, seeing all manner of information, and knowing everything that mattered.

"Apparently not."

"Then how are you supposed to know what assets to recover?"

"I expect it'll be obvious. We'll need to search the rest of the station."

"We pretty much need to do that anyway. Last time I checked, personnel took priority over 'assets'."

"Here, this looks like it might qualify."

Throam looked at the holo Caden pointed to, and saw an immense room which appeared to be a storage area. From end to end, it held row after row of plasteel containers, each twice Throam's height. On the side of each container he saw an emblem he did not recognise: three concentric five-pointed stars, sharing a common centre, each one smaller than the one it sat upon. The middle star was inverted, so that the points of each fell into the interstices of the one behind it.

"Gear adrift," Throam said.

Caden pushed his personal holo into the camera feed display, intersecting them. With his finger he flicked at the text labelling the camera location. The legend slid across from one holo to the other, and snapped into place automatically on the map his own displayed.

"Let's go and see what we've got."

– 05 –
Gear Adrift

Castigon had been a free man for just over a day when he arrived on Maidre Shalleon. Just setting foot on the class one planet, a minor crime in itself for someone of his particular status, felt so very good. If only the probation services could see him now, they would have fits. They would be particularly annoyed by his current activity; relaxing in the warm sunshine on one of the plazas which were dotted around the outside of the main transit hub, he sipped an ice-cold drink casually and watched the world go by.

So many people coming and going. Hurrying and bustling this way and that, striding across the plaza as they went scurrying about their lives. Important meetings, connections to make. Racing to the appointment, to the starport, to get back home. Oh such urgent scurryings.

He sneered at the utter pointlessness of it all. These people knew nothing of the galaxy. Maidre Shalleon was one of the pampered worlds, coddled by the central administration and indulged in every way imaginable. Truly, this planet deserved its class one status.

Looking across the small sea of chairs and tables arranged in arcs outside the café, he amused himself by imagining stories for the people he saw. The young couple who had never seen each other naked. The older lone woman waiting for someone, anyone, to talk to her. The group of laughing girls who had no idea that there was a madman watching them. They could all die tomorrow and the universe would not notice.

He saw a man across the plaza, walking out of the cool shade of the tunnel that led away to the transit hub. The man looked around as if lost, then walked straight towards the café. As he approached, he seemed to take pains not to look at Castigon. Yet despite the many empty chairs he sat at the table next to him.

"The weather here is outstanding, as was promised." Castigon leaned slightly into the gap between their tables. "I must bring my mother next time."

"If you do," said the man, "see that you take her to the city museum."

"I hear the landplant exhibition is virtually complete."

"The relics of colonisation have indeed been lovingly restored."

Confirmation. This was the person he had arranged to meet.

"And if I wanted to visit the famous game preserves of Maidre Shalleon?"

"Ah," said the man, "then you would of course need to prepare yourself for the hunt."

"Quite as I expected. And where might a man such as myself prepare for that activity?"

The man leaned towards him. "As it so happens, I may well be able to assist you."

○ ○ ○

Dozens of empty containers. Hundreds even.

Every one of them unlocked, some with their lids and hatches not even closed properly, just resting against the seals. Each container had a metal shell inside, with a hard foam lining shaped to accommodate specific parts. Whatever they had once held was now missing.

"Cleaned out," said Caden.

"These had warheads in them," said Throam. "I'm sure of it."

For a long moment, they looked at each other in silence.

"Well," Caden said, "I guess now we know what sort of 'medical research' was being conducted on Herros."

"That's just great. Let's build a shit-tonne of weapons on a virtually defenceless planet at the ass end of nowhere. Then when they get snatched up by who-fucking-ever, we'll just send in a couple of chumps to sort it all out."

"All right, don't lose your head. We've dealt with worse."

Caden started to walk along the rows of containers, looking for anything that stood out. A slight difference between them, objects left behind, even a smear of dirt. At this point, with the security logs wiped and the staff missing, he would gladly take any clue he could find.

Behind him, he could hear Throam muttering to himself, throwing out the occasional curse and thumping the sides of the metal containers. He was quite happy to leave the angry counterpart where he was; a few minutes alone was normally all the time Throam needed to calm down and become useful again.

He reached the end of the first row. Nothing.

Rounding the container at the end of the row,

he turned back on himself, now between the first and second rows. He could still hear Throam's blazing monologue.

Again, nothing.

He continued with his search, walking up and down the rows, scrutinising every surface and panel to no avail. In the distance, Throam had quietened down considerably; partly due to the distance, but mostly due to running out of uniquely colourful curses. Caden was now approaching the final containers rapidly, and the hope of finding that vital piece of evidence was fading with every step.

Failed before you even started.

He stopped immediately.

"Did you say something?"

There was a pause, and then Throam shouted back. "No, why?"

"No reason."

He took another step, then stopped again—

—leaned against the nearest container as the room began to swim, the periphery of his vision becoming a thin yellow ring which danced and wriggled, *Pathetic,* the floor and walls ahead stretching away into a bright white tunnel that was somehow fallen into darkness, blackness, night, bent over slightly to suppress the wave of nausea rushing suddenly upon him, *Give up now and save yourself the embarrassment* free hand waving in the air, trying to find something solid to anchor on to, the floor heaving beneath his feet, and there on the rolling floor right under his face was a pair of black boots, with black trousers above them, *You can't even stand* trousers that were right in front of his head, combat style, where is that humming coming from, but where is that humming even coming from, and the legs leading up from each shoe to join in the middle, raising his head, legs leading his gaze up and up to where the trousers must end, where the body must begin, *You should never have come here,* but no, there's no body above those legs, they just melt into the inky dark of the tunnel vision and become another part of the nausea, the blackness, a sensation of falling —

"Are you okay?"

Throam's voice came from behind him, and the room snapped back into place. Eyes watering, Caden coughed and realised he was almost bent double by the side of a container, still leaning on it for support.

"Yeah, I just... felt a bit odd."

"Odd how?"

"Queasy. Jump sickness. I'm fine, really; it's passed."

"You don't look fine to me."

Caden stood upright and composed himself. "Seriously, it's nothing."

"You know just because I don't say anything doesn't mean I don't notice," Throam said quietly. "It would really help if you'd clue me in."

"I'm fine, that's all you need to know."

"You're not though, are you?"

"Drop it," Caden said, "that's an order."

After a long pause, Throam's expression shifted from concern to annoyance, then melted to resignation. He knew better than to press the matter.

"You good to move on?" He asked.

"Yes, there's nothing here. Nothing we can assess without forensics, anyway."

"Next section then?"

"Next section."

"'That's an order'," Throam mimicked. "Sometimes it's really hard for me not to punch you."

The counterpart turned and walked away, towards the same cargo doors which had allowed them access to the storage area.

Caden paused for a second, looked around slowly, and followed after him. The episode was already fading fast, his body and mind forgetting the strangely disconnected feeling of it all. He had just one question on his mind.

Why now?

◦ ◦ ◦

On lush grass, dappled with spots of dancing gold light, Elm played with his starships beneath the great old oak. Shipped in from Earth at tremendous expense, the massive gnarled tree had been a mere twig of a sapling when its roots first touched the soil of another planet. Long, long before the boy was born. Damastion money was old money.

"Damastion is always most beautiful in the spring, dear," said Mother. "I simply could not imagine living anywhere else."

"Oh my, but there really *is* nowhere else," said the ornately coiffured lady sat beside her.

They laughed together, and Mother fanned herself lazily. As mild as the weather was, the warm morning had drawn from the ground and vegetation a moisture which now lay thick in the still air. The humidity could be oppressive, if one allowed it. The lady twirled her parasol absently.

"I have it on good authority," said Mother, "that the proconsul himself will be leading the proceedings next week."

Hoisting her skirts slightly, she adjusted her position in the garden swing, turning to face her companion so she could more easily appreciate the response. The lady was accommodating, and marvelled obsequiously at the honour that was to be bestowed upon the family Caden.

"Oh, how wonderful," said the lady. "You simply *must* have the entire ceremony recorded."

"Recorded, dear?"

"How many people can say the Imperial Proconsul has waved them off to work?"

"Well you know my dear, they now say the war might be all over by the end of the month."

"You don't say?"

"Can you imagine?" Mother said, folding her fan and tapping it against her empty palm. "At the tribute ceremony the proconsul will honour those fighting out of Damastion, and my Modim might never even have to join the campaign."

"It still counts, of course," said the lady.

"Oh, but of course!"

They both laughed.

Two destroyers soared through space, spattered with the golden light of multiple explosions. They collided with a disappointing clack. As accurately as they were decorated, Elm was tiring of these painted ships. He wanted more intricate toys, like the ones he had seen through shop windows in the bustling city of Galloi. Wooden toys were for children, and he was already nine Solars old. Old enough to wash and dress himself.

"Mother, can I play with Brehim?"

"'May I', dear. 'May I' play with Brehim." Mother corrected.

"May I?"

"Brehim isn't here, dear."

Mother and the lady continued their conversation, which with Elm's prompting now turned towards the educational prowess of the ornate lady's youngest son. Just two Solars older than Elm, and Brehim already had an electronic toy battleship, one which even fired little orange missiles.

Elm was so very bored with the wooden toys.

He clambered to his feet and rubbed his legs where the pale imprint of grass blades marred his skin. Mother always made him wear shorts and a mock naval tunic when she was entertaining company of status.

Dropping the wooden ships on the grass, he wandered out from the shade of the great old oak, and into the bright sunlight which washed through the grounds of the estate.

Father would be somewhere nearby. It amused Father greatly to covertly observe the pretensions of Mother's social encounters. It was a secret to nobody on the Caden estate, other than his own wife. Father liked to don the hat he wore when hunting flightless birds on the estuary, and he would hide in the gardens with a pair of antique field glasses. Father called this naturalism. Elm did not know the word, but Father said that it was best to catch Mother in her natural habitat. He had once said she was a predator.

Perhaps Father would agree that the wooden toys had stopped being suitable. He knew what it was to enjoy himself.

Elm tottered across the lawn in the direction of the nearest shrubbery, and disappeared amongst the curling branches and wide, rubbery leaves.

Inside the giant native bush, the air was cool and damp. Fist-sized beetles hopped from branch to branch, buzzing in annoyance at the intrusion into their quiet domain. Elm reached out inquisitively to touch the purple, oil-sheen carapace of the one nearest to him. The furry beetle reared on its four hind legs, unfolded a set of opalescent wings from beneath its exquisite shell, and with a thick, leathery buzzing sound it launched itself into the air.

He watched it circle and weave as it gradually created distance between them amongst the twisted loops of the branches. On any day, beetles were better than wooden toys.

The distraction ended when the fleeing insect was no longer in sight. He began to work his way deeper into the shrubbery, his small frame navigating the lattice of branches with ease. It did not occur to him that an adult would find such passage much more troublesome than he. The air was very still now, icy cold.

Elm was almost at the centre of the sprawling mass of limbs and leaves before he decided that Father was almost certainly not hiding there. Having made the effort to arrive, he sat cross-legged in the dirt for a few minutes, quietly appreciating the secret heart of the place. He played with twigs and pieces of dead leaf, extracting entertainment from the detritus as only a child can. The hidden world was totally silent, and after several minutes had passed he began to feel how alone he was.

He was not a sheltered child, by any means. He had been to Low Cerin with Mother and Father only months before. He had witnessed with innocent eyes the widespread poverty of that under-privileged planet, the street people staring back at him blankly as Mother virtually dragged him past. Their eyes had looked through him, as if those people had somehow become stuck behind an impenetrable wall and long since accepted that they would never return to the world. They made him feel guilty just for being loved.

No, he was not sheltered. But never before had he experienced for himself the deep pang of true isolation. There had always been someone there with him, save for when he slept. Even then, Mother and Father were only separated from him by a wall. But here, amongst the spiralling loops of the rubbery-leafed shrub, there was only the silence and the cold. Even the beetles had fled from him.

The feeling twisted into a tight, hard coil, grew long spines that sought out and pierced any emotion that might threaten to dispel it. It gnawed at his heart and clawed at his mind. It watched him through unblinking eyes that peered from every dark corner of inky shadow beneath the bushes. It saw. It knew his name. It rasped formless words. It mocked him.

By the time Elm found the way back out to the lawn, and ran on wobbly legs back towards the great old oak, vast and pendulous mountains of cloud had started to block out the sun.

The warmth of that day had vanished.

◦ ◦ ◦

"Who in the many worlds is this?" Throam said.

They entered the lab cautiously, sweeping each side of the fatal funnel that the relatively narrow doorway formed, covering each other as they cleared the room visually of any potential threats. Any other than the one they could already see.

She stood motionless, thin arms by her sides, hands resting lightly against her thighs. Her gaze was locked on the featureless wall before her, lank brown hair partly covering her face, lips moving ever so slightly in silent recitation.

"Turn around," Caden said.

The woman did not move, or indeed show any sign that she had heard.

"Turn around, now!"

No response.

Caden began to approach her, slowly, and in the corner of his eye he saw Throam move out to the side. If she attacked suddenly, the counterpart would need a clear shot.

The woman remained rooted to the spot, mouthing wordlessly at the wall, her lips barely moving.

Caden mag-tagged his rifle to his back plate and drew his pistol. Holding it in his right hand, pointed straight at the woman's head, he reached out with his left hand and prodded her shoulder. The one nearest to him, so that if she whirled around he could push her away and create space between them.

No response.

"You've still got it," Throam said.

"Hey." Caden ignored the counterpart's jibe. "Snap out of it."

He pushed the woman's shoulder again, harder this time, and she tilted forward slightly before returning to the same position. Again, there was no response.

Caden backed off. "Catatonic?"

"Sure seems that way. Who do you think she is?"

"No idea," said Caden. "But I don't think she's meant to be here."

"What makes you say that?"

"Because everyone is gone. If she's staff, why is she here alone when the others are missing?"

"If she's *not* staff, why is she here alone?"

Caden glared at Throam, then turned his attention back to the woman. He took her by the elbow, gently but firmly, and pulled her towards him. As if remembering the movement, she took a single faltering step. Her eyes remained fixed, her lips continued to move feebly, but she stepped forward all the same.

"So we can walk," he said. "Well *that* certainly makes things easier."

He moved her gradually towards the doorway.

"Stay behind. If she makes a move, drop her."

"You're the boss," Throam said.

– 06 –
The Blank Woman

Fort Kosling was truly vast, and dwarfed the eleven-hundred metre *Hammer*. Next to the massive bulk of the Imperial fortress the heavy battleship was a mere splinter. She had slunk quietly into one of the many apertures which dotted the equatorial prominence, before being directed to a docking pier. The internal space in which *Hammer* arrived had been immense, a giant geometric cavern criss-crossed with guide beams. Dozens of starships rested there, decorating every pier.

As they docked, Santani had announced on the ship's comm that no crew member was to leave the ship. Caden, Throam, and Eilentes however had been allowed to disembark. It came as no surprise to any of them to see four men waiting at the end of the umbilicus, all dressed in dark grey with purple piping: the public uniform of Eyes and Ears. The men had waited for Throam, Caden, and then Eilentes to clear the umbilicus, then one had nodded in curt acknowledgement before they entered the narrow passage in single file, heading towards the passenger lock of the *Hammer*.

"I wonder what that was all about?" Eilentes said.

"Probably just rumour control," said Throam. "They'll want to check what the ship's holos have stored about Herros before they let anybody leave."

"Paranoid much?"

"It's normal for them."

"It's not like we landed in the middle of the Rodori Grand Bazaar," she said. "This is a military installation."

"Yes, the very *best* place to be if you want to lose control of a rumour."

Caden looked around and saw that the umbilicus had brought them to a fairly standard arrival lounge, the kind which was supposed to offer some measure of recuperation if a long wait were likely. Nobody had come to meet them, suggesting a wait was indeed in the cards.

"Welcome to Fort Kosling." A recorded voice sounded over the comm system. "This facility is a controlled environment. Please wait while we assess contamination threats. For your own safety, follow all directives given to you by our debarkation staff after leaving the arrival lounge."

"Warming," said Throam. "I feel welcome."

"Might as well get comfortable," Caden said. "We may be here for a while."

As he sat down his link chirruped.

He clicked the link. "Caden."

"Shard Caden," came the reply. "This is Intelligence Operator Occre Brant. I believe you're responsible for the package that just arrived?"

"We haven't found the person responsible yet," Caden said pointedly.

"Controversial," said Brant. "Well, it's certainly one of the larger packages I've received lately. By the time you're out of quarantine I should have her name."

"Where will I find you?"

"Arrivals know who you are. There's only one place you can go from the lounge; when you check in they'll send you my way. You won't need to report to anyone else."

"What's your involvement exactly?"

"I'm liaising between Eyes and Ears, and Fleet Command. I can't get into it right now, but as you probably gather there are common interests in this situation."

"Yes, I imagine there are."

"Ha. I'll see you in a couple of hours."

"I'm very much looking forward to it," said Caden, and closed the channel.

"Occre Brant? I'm sure I know that name." Throam said.

"Never heard of the man," said Caden. "I expect he'll be the usual cagey interrogator."

"He sounded very cheerful for an interrogator."

"True. I'm not expecting miracles though."

"When have you ever?"

Caden smiled slightly. Throam was right; he was typically quite pragmatic in his expectations of people and organisations alike. Once Caden had a good view of the rules that governed a personality or a role or a committee, he was usually able to get an accurate feel for how each would react to certain circumstances. Prediction was one of his most useful skills.

"How long do you think?"

Caden looked across at Eilentes, who had sat down on one of the plain sofas so thoughtfully provided by Arrivals. She had crossed her legs and was now toying with her raven hair as she waited for his reply.

"Probably a few hours," he said. "The air system will be monitoring what we're exhaling. I'd guess we'll need to provide blood and saliva as well, if they want to make a proper job of it."

Right on cue, a panel opened in the far wall and out slid a sampling station. The recorded voice delivered a new message.

"Biological samples are required for threat screening. Please provide the samples, following the instructions on the holo."

"I've never had to go through checks this thorough before," said Throam. "Usually it's swab and go at the desk."

"You've never come back from Gemen Station before."

"You think its something to do with whatever they were up to out there?"

"I'm certain of it. It makes sense; there's a chance we've been exposed to something, and somebody who knows what that is doesn't want to take any risks."

Throam and Eilentes provided their samples, each using swabs to collect saliva and lancets to draw tiny amounts of blood. As they bagged and labelled their samples, Caden waited in silence for his turn, his mind working constantly. There was an oddness about this mission he had been sent on.

The Empire maintains a secret facility.

They build and test weapons there.

Someone attacks it, and steals the fruits of their labour.

The Empress sends me to find out why.

We find an oddball woman and nothing else.

On our return, Eyes and Ears are expecting us.

We're tested for a contagion.

Those are the facts.

Sometimes it helped him to get the main points together in a neat list, but this was not one of those occasions. Something was missing from the puzzle, and it was not a trivial piece. Many questions formed in his mind. The only thing of which he could be relatively certain was that Shard involvement had been inevitable: neither E&E nor Fleet Command would want to sully themselves by dealing directly with whatever dirty little catastrophe they had brewed on Herros.

But then it could always be worse: it might be that he was now involved because they suspected an inside job. Occre Brant was going to have to explain one or two things.

◦ ◦ ◦

Santani was staring at Klade when he looked up from the system overview. Holding her compact holo in one hand, resting the other hand on her hip, and just staring.

He flashed her a brief smile and raised his eyebrows; in response she flicked her eyes briefly towards the wardroom. Then she walked nonchalantly across the deck and disappeared through the hatch. He gave it a moment before he followed her, tapping away at his holo, scheduling repairs to the minor systems they had not deemed a priority after the damaging jump to Herros.

He looked casually around the command deck, saw nobody was paying any particular attention, and went after her. Finding the wardroom empty he walked across it towards the hatch that led to the captain's own office. He stepped through, and remained silent until the hatch had closed fully behind him.

"Captain?"

"The data the sensors collected when we jumped to Herros... you did transmit it before we returned?"

"Yes, it went in the first databurst after we dropped at this gate."

"Good."

"Is something wrong?" He knew even before he asked. The captain's face was the same as it always was when she was troubled.

"It's too early to tell, but I do know one thing. I've never been comfortable with the idea of Eyes and Ears crawling all over my ship."

"They had me scrub every sensor reading we've taken since we first left Kosling," he said. "They also checked through navigation and transmission logs."

"So they'll know that you've passed the sensor readings to Tech and Systems?"

"I presume so, yes."

"I understand they've also been to sickbay?"

"Swarmed through it. Every part of it scanned; no idea what for."

"It's where *she* was."

"Whoever she is, they're certainly going to some lengths for her."

"They are at that."

Klade waited while Santani drummed her fingers pensively on the edge of her desk. He was accustomed to her reflecting for minutes at a time; although he had only served with her for five Solars, his term as the ship's first officer had been long enough for him to learn her habits and moods. He sensed that a bold decision was being made.

"Okay, we let them carry on until they're finished. I've never had my ship grounded before by

Eyes and Ears, and I'd like to see how these matters generally pan out when they get their way."

"But... that's not all?"

"Not in the least bit, no. The moment we're free to communicate off-ship, you get on to Tech and Systems and see what they've made of those sensor readings. Don't lose a second — you can bet your ass that they'll also be getting a visit from our inquisitive little friends."

"As you wish, Captain. I'll see to it myself."

○ ○ ○

"Apologies for being late, after you've already spent the past three hours in quarantine."

Occre Brant smiled apologetically and gestured for Caden to sit down. The Shard had been waiting alone in the spacious office, scrutinising the various paintings Brant had chosen to display.

"Half of my job seems to be spent waiting for something or other," he said, matter-of-fact.

"Yes," Brant said. "Well, you'll be pleased to hear that all of your tests came back negative. For all three of you."

"I don't suppose you're going to tell me what we were tested for?"

"Nope. Sorry."

Caden sighed under his breath, and sat down in the chair that Brant had indicated earlier. He took a long look at the man opposite.

Brant was about the same age as Caden, perhaps slightly older. His black hair was cut short, emphasising a strong brow and solid jaw. He had a stocky build, and an air of physical confidence which Caden suspected was backed up by capability. His clothing was neat, clean on, and not decorated beyond the identification of his rank. Other than that he was essentially unreadable. Caden had not encountered anyone who gave out so few signals in a long, long time.

Except for one thing: his facial expressions were entirely genuine. Caden had seen enough liars and fakers to know when a smile was true.

"I'm actually late because I've had a little difficulty getting an ident for your survivor," Brant continued. "She wasn't on the staff roster for Gemen Station, although of course that's exactly what we were expecting."

"We?"

"You and I." Brant smiled. "Well I certainly wasn't expecting her to be Gemen staff; from your records I think you've also seen enough to know it couldn't ever be that simple."

Caden nodded in agreement, noting with interest that Brant had looked up his service records and wanted him to know it.

"I'm guessing there was no local DNA match either?"

"You're not wrong. No match on the records held at Kosling. We've got a DNA query running now on all the civilised worlds, expedited of course. I expect a result within the next hour."

"That soon. Why 'survivor'?"

"Excuse me?"

"You called her a survivor. Why is that?"

"Simply because she's obviously been through some kind of trauma."

"No other reason?"

"None."

"Where is she now?"

"Medical, getting the most thorough examination of her life. The doctors down there are not going to leave anything to chance."

So there it was; Brant had not expected them to

return with a survivor, and so accordingly he had not been prepared for it. Medical were checking her out in detail because they had no idea who she was, or what she carried with her.

I'm not the only one with questions then, Caden thought.

"Anyway," Brant said. "To business. Eyes and Ears have a forensics team at Gemen Station now, along with a computer interrogation unit. Fleet are naturally beside themselves at having lost an entire task force, and they're sweeping the system with a fine-toothed comb. *Fearless, Resolute,* and *Keeper* are out there right now."

"They won't find anything, will they?"

"I doubt it. Whoever hit Herros did a very good job of it. No alarms raised, nothing left behind. Except for your strange lady of course."

"Of course."

"So, Shard Caden. Tell me what you found there."

Caden related the details of the expedition to Brant, describing how they had found the station intact but abandoned, how the security systems had been wiped and the research databases locked down. He recalled the storage room full of empty containers, finding the woman standing alone in a laboratory, getting her to the shuttle with Throam and strapping her safely into a flight seat before returning to complete their search. The labs devoid of life, the holos empty of data, the storage spaces stripped of contents. He left nothing out, save for his hallucination in the storage room... if that was what it was.

Brant listened intently, his eyes never leaving Caden's face. At length, when the Shard had completed his account, he nodded slowly.

"Well, this is disturbing," he said. "It sounds like a very surgical strike. I'm not sure which is more worrying; the theft of the weapons or the abduction of every soul stationed on Herros."

"How many people?"

"Should have been sixty-eight when we lost contact. That's comparing the last roster they filed with our newest transit logs, so it could be slightly inaccurate."

Caden grimaced. Sixty-eight people, all of them vital resources. But more than that, they were also wives and husbands, parents and children, friends, carers, and lovers. Brant was looking at him; saying nothing, doubtless expecting nothing. Caden knew just by the expression on his face that they both understood the loss in exactly the same way. It did not need saying.

"The weapons they were developing," he said. "What were they?"

"For the most part, they were chemical in nature."

"Is that it?"

"That's all I am authorised to tell you."

"You do realise that I carry the authority of the Empress?"

"As does Eyes and Ears, and by extension as do I."

Caden raised his eyebrows, genuinely surprised. Most of the time a mention of the Empress, or even the mere suggestion of Her expectations, was enough to guarantee cooperation. But now twice in the same day, the comments had been brushed off as meaningless. Like Santani, Brant did not appear to be impressed. Perhaps out here, near the border with the Perseus arm of the galaxy, the idea of Imperial rule was taken less seriously than it was in the core systems.

Well maybe by *you*, he thought.

Brant seemed to sense his feelings. "Look, I'd like to share more with you, really. But there are limits — severe limits — placed on what I can divulge about this."

"I insist."

"Insist away, I still can't tell you."

"So let me get this straight," Caden said, "I have been sent to Herros to investigate why it went dark, because the Empress would really quite like to know. Meanwhile there is another organisation also working directly for the Empress, with a fairly good idea about what's been going on, an idea it just won't share."

Brant looked amused. "No, you're not reading the situation correctly at all."

"So explain it to me," said Caden.

"The Empress knows full well what was going on at Herros, as we have been operating under Her instructions. She hasn't shared it with you because you don't need to know. You aren't instructed to solve the mystery of what the Empire was doing there; you're instructed to solve the mystery of where the weapons and people went, who has them, and why."

"You don't think the nature of those weapons might have a bearing on things?"

"Not really, no."

"You really are difficult, aren't you?"

"I'm just stating the facts."

"You remind me of me, only much less so."

Brant laughed, and gestured at Caden. "Sit on this."

"Not while I'm on duty," said Caden, not missing a beat. "Look, is there anything you can tell me that would help me do what I was sent to do?"

"Yes, there is." Brant's face became serious.

"I'm all ears," said Caden.

"This is not the first blackout."

"You mean other stations have gone dark?"

"Stations, colonies, and also ships."

"So what happened with the others?"

"No idea. Gemen Station was the only one classed as a high priority."

"Tell me you'll be following up on the others?"

"Not personally, and my superiors feel that's a routine task for the Navy patrols to see to. Communication failures happen all the time; there's nothing to indicate that this sudden spate is anything other than a statistical fluke."

"You're kidding, right?"

"I didn't say I agreed with it. I'm just telling you what I've been told."

Caden was silent. Multiple blackouts were not a good sign. As Brant had suggested, it could have been a simple coincidence of technological failures. Incidents did occur together sometimes, without any actual connection between them, hence the word 'coincidence'. But although he had his own views on coincidences, something did not feel right; at least one confirmed attack on an Imperial facility, and who knew how many others had occurred. More worryingly, who knew how many were occurring right at that very moment.

"I would strongly urge you to reconsider. Feed it back up your chain of command: those blackouts need to be investigated."

"Oh I already have," said Brant, "but it's falling on deaf ears, if you'll pardon the pun."

"Try harder."

"There's no point. Eyes and Ears is very much a

top-down organisation. If it makes you feel any better, chances are my superiors have a very good reason for whatever it is they're thinking."

"It doesn't make me feel better."

"I didn't really think it would, if I'm honest. Believe me when I say that I sympathise."

The doors to the office opened, and a woman walked confidently into the room. She was tall, almost as tall as Caden, and slender. Thick red hair cascaded over her shoulders, framing an angular face with pale, almost perfect skin. She wore the same uniform as Brant, and despite her severe expression Caden had to admit that it certainly looked better on her. Bright green eyes speared him for a brief moment as she strode defiantly across the room and thrust a holo at Brant.

"We have her," she said. "The Blank Woman."

Brant took the holo with a curt nod and turned back to Caden. "This is Intelligence Operator Peras Tirrano, my colleague."

"Colleague, friend, some would say natural complement."

Caden sensed an immediate change in the air, to which Tirrano seemed oblivious. All of a sudden, while she had been talking, Brant's open manner and friendly expression had disappeared entirely. Caden took in her movements, the subtleties of angle and poise, the briskness of her motion and the ferocity in her voice and eyes. Efficient, but impatient. Calculating, relentless, and almost certainly vindictive.

"Not those who know me well," said Brant.

"You can be cruel, my love," said Tirrano.

"The Blank Woman?" Caden intervened carefully. Brant looked at the Shard as he drew Tirrano's attention, and Caden saw clearly the appreciation in his eyes.

"That's what they're calling her in medical," said Tirrano. "The woman from Herros. You know; because she's blank."

"I'm not sure I understand what you mean."

"You didn't notice? She's vacated the premises. Very little evidence of thought or personality going on in there. I thought you people were supposed to be keen observers."

"She's called Amarist Naeb." Brant read from the holo that Tirrano had delivered. "She was part of a geological survey team that went into the Deep a couple of years ago."

Tirrano interjected with what she had already learned. "The survey was part of the search for colonisation candidates along the fringes of Imperial space. Her team followed up on a probe that pinged exotic minerals; it was a planet not far into the Deep Shadows. It's never been flagged for colonisation, but they carried on with their survey nonetheless. Been there ever since."

"So what was she doing on a deserted research base?" Caden said. "Something is very wrong with this picture."

"Charlie-Charlie Sixty-Twelve-Five Echo." Brant read aloud the colonisation catalogue number from Tirrano's holo. "I have a horrible feeling I've seen that before."

He swiped his own desk-mounted holo and brought up the Eyes and Ears intelligence report database, tapping and prodding until he found what he was looking for.

"It's on the list," he said quietly. "No databursts or other contact for a few months."

"How has this not been investigated?"

"Flagged as lowest priority," Brant said. "Looking at this entry, it seems it's actually not that unusual for them. After they arrived quite a lot of raw data was sent back, followed by scientific papers which were only of interest to very specific groups. Since then there's been a significant drop-off, with family messages and service requests arriving every few weeks, plus the occasional new finding."

"So it wouldn't look particularly odd then?"

"No, not at all."

"What does it matter? It's a geo-survey team on a barren planet nobody wants," Tirrano said.

"It matters because they're all on their own out there," said Caden.

"Yes, where they chose to put themselves."

"Also, it matters because whatever happened out there was probably a prelude to Gemen Station. Herros is right on the fringes of the Deep Shadows, a couple of good jumps away from the Viskr border. So is the location you just described."

Tirrano snorted. "We don't even know if this Naeb woman was taken from there, or if she left on her own."

"I think we can all take a good guess at that," said Brant.

"The fact is, it's currently the only lead," said Caden. "I'll head there and get eyes on the place. Then we'll know for certain."

"Not yet," said Brant.

"Why not?"

"Because we've not found out what she knows."

○ ○ ○

"There you are."

Throam looked up at Eilentes and seemed to

take a second to recognise her. She knew that expression; he had been lost in thought. It was not like him to think about things too deeply or for too long, but when he did it was to the exclusion of all else.

"Hey," he said. "Where have you been?"

"Where have *I* been? Where have *you* been? I've been looking all over for you."

"I was right here the whole time."

Throam smiled, and she knew immediately that even if he had been somewhere else, he would now stick to his story.

"I went to check out the facilities," she said. "You know they have a sharp-shooting range here that's a klick long? A klick!"

"Impressive."

"Impressive is the word. This place is huge."

"Did you shoot?"

"No, the loaners they have down on the range aren't worth squat. I left all my kit on the shuttle, just like you did. We'll have to recover it from *Hammer* before she leaves."

"We'll have time."

"So." Eilentes sat down on the seat next to his. "What have you been doing?"

"Nothing much. Just came here for a bit of quiet."

He waved casually at the panoramic window of the observation lounge, shielded glass that curved across most of the outer wall. She followed his gesture and saw the local star field, the distant planet crawling lazily across the darkness, the great ships moving at port speed between the fortress and the Kosling system's gate. She had to admit, as awe-inspiring as she found the scale of it all, it was certainly a relaxing view.

"I actually meant generally, in your life. I've not seen you since Brankfall. That was ten Solars ago, right? Ten Solars!"

"Same old shit," he said. "Running around the galaxy, trying to stop people blowing Caden's head off. It's a full time job. You?"

"Same old shit. Just different places."

"You any closer to a command?"

"Not been my priority for a long time. Did you ever listen to a word I said?"

"Yes of course, you said you wanted to command a battleship."

"I never said any such thing! You *know* how long it took me to get my emancipation card approved."

He smirked, and she realised that once again she had fallen for it. She slapped his arm. "Wind-up merchant."

Throam laughed and pretended to recoil from the blow. She crossed her arms and leaned away from him, giving him the same disapproving look Mama used to give Papa whenever he brought some new piece of junk to the dinner table.

He beamed back at her until she melted.

"You were mulling over something when I came in," she said at last. "Want to share?"

"It's nothing really. Just something is up with Caden."

" I *thought* you were watching him when you came back from Gemen Station. What happened?"

"I'm not really sure. He's changing, but I can't exactly say how. He won't talk about it."

"How do you mean, 'changing'?"

"Used to be he'd zone out sometimes, just once in a while. But now it's different. It's like he has some kind of anxiety attack. But I've never seen him panic about anything."

"Hasn't he been checked out?"

"Oh yeah, all the time. We both get the full works before every mission; it's regulations. But they never find anything wrong."

"Shouldn't you tell somebody? If he won't talk to you about it I mean."

"Like who? The Empress? He technically doesn't have a commanding officer."

"Ah yes, I see your problem."

"Maybe I'm just worrying too much. If it was serious, I'm sure he'd say."

"Wouldn't make sense to put you both at risk."

"No, and he certainly knows it."

Throam went quiet again, staring at the floor. She knew she would lose him to his own thoughts if she did not give him something else to talk about.

"Are you and Caden...?"

He stared at her dumbly, not understanding what she was trying to ask him. Clearly he had not changed that much then.

"Are you two an item?"

He looked like he did not know whether to laugh or shout. "Worlds no! Only one of us would survive *that*."

She thanked the universe mentally, and grinned at him as if she had just been joking. "What's he like? I mean they have a bit of a reputation, the Shards. People in the fleet say they're unemotional and not worth trusting."

"Unemotional?" Throam smiled again. "I wouldn't say so. I guess Fleet usually only see him when he's on a mission, and it's not his job to be emotional."

"Because that's surplus to requirements, right?"

"Exactly. As for not being trustworthy, well that's a right load of shit. There's nobody I'd trust more with my life."

"Not even me?"

"Definitely not you, with your crazy-ass flying. You'll be the one who finally kills me."

She slapped him on the arm again.

– 07 –
Fresh Meat

Castigon vented a stream of curses into the night sky of Fengrir as he scratched his right leg furiously. Of all the times for him to pick up a small cut, it had to have been just as he arrived on one of the contaminated worlds. Perhaps the inflammation would teach him to be more careful in future.

He had nicked his skin on a sharp metal edge while unbundling himself from a most undignified hiding place. Arriving on the planet as a stowaway, he had had little choice but to choose stealth over comfort — being caught by immigration control was not really an option by this point.

Hours had now passed, and an infection had well and truly taken hold. The scratching did not really help, truth be told, and he had tried to avoid it for as long as he could before being driven to relieve the infuriating agony. Yes, there was definitely Blight in that tiny wound. His dear old friend, back for another game of 'guess the scar radius'. The sensation was dry and electrical, as if a live circuit were flexing and sparking and burrowing just under the surface of the skin.

But he had learned his lessons well on Urx, and even in his frenzied clawing he took pains to avoid tearing the actual cut itself. He tried to rake his nails only across the healthy skin surrounding it, digging in as if he could press the sensations out of his flesh by coming in from the side.

Whoever had said it was not worth vaccinating humans against the Blight had clearly never had this experience, he decided. He made a mental note to find out precisely who he would need to talk to about that. He could be *very* persuasive.

He was only half joking with himself, but even so that would have to come much, much later. Right now, he had some important business to attend to. Thanks to the Backwaters he was surprisingly far ahead of schedule. He had believed — as he languished in his cell back on Urx, in those early days of incarceration — that his mission of re-education would take him years.

And yet here he was, just days after his release, walking on the very same soil that his first target now trod.

○ ○ ○

"This is seriously boring."

"We aren't here to enjoy ourselves, I'm afraid."

Ider Firenz already found her younger counterpart irritating. She could not for the life of her see how this man could possibly have risen to the rank of company captain, much less imagine what he must have done to earn his position next to her.

"I really don't see why we're needed here anyway."

He was perhaps right — on a purely practical level of course — but Firenz knew well that it was better to have a Shard on hand when the need arose, rather than be without and suffer the consequences. And if she had to be there, then so too did he. She started to open her mouth, to tutor him on the topic of due diligence, but immediately changed her mind.

She had no intention of recommending to keep him on when they were done on Fengrir. Why waste effort on him? The Empress would just have to try again, and may the light of a thousand suns shine down upon Her most radiantly fat behind.

"I'm going to stretch my legs," he said. "Will you be okay?"

"I survived Ottomas," she said. "I think I will survive the ambassador."

"Ottomas Endures," the counterpart said. He got to his feet.

"Until the Last Breath," she replied. At least he could get *that* right.

Appatine strolled quietly away, heading clockwise around the perimeter of the square. She assumed — no, hoped — that he would continue to watch the people in the crowd as he went.

The Lem Bataan visitor had been talking for almost an hour now, with the translation from his link routed through an audio system kept permanently in the public space. She was glad for the translation; the piping and fluting voices of the Lembas usually gave her a headache after just a few minutes, and hours of it would surely have finished her off. The amplified translation was just enough to ensure she could not hear the ambassador's natural voice.

As far as she could tell the Lemba had not said anything worth hearing yet. His circuitous speech did not command her attention, for she was true to her role and watched carefully for danger, but she was fairly certain that as yet his purpose on Fengrir had not even been spoken of.

Even with a cursory glance, she could see that

none of the people gathered here were cause for any real concern. Not even the Coalition had bothered to turn up to this particular event, and they were usually so determined to cause disruption. If you could call it that: informing the citizenry they ought to feel unhappy about the things that made them unhappy was — in her view — a complete waste of time.

Politics, she thought, is the only true constant.

"It is vitally important that nothing upsets the delivery of the ambassador's message." The Empress's Chamberlain had looked down his nose at Firenz with visible distaste, as if the distance between their holos were not great enough for his liking. "Vitally important, you see? She expects you will do your duty, Shard Firenz. Oh yes, She does indeed expect that."

She scanned the crowd yet again.

Vitally important? Ha! The Lemba was still warbling out his meandering friendship greeting, in the customary way of his people. The Lem Bataan Confederation considered every citizen to be part of a huge family, and it was clear the ambassador was applying that traditional view here. He presumably had not noticed that most of the people listening had not been there when he started. They were stopping to see what was being said, then moving on to deal with the day's business.

Imperial citizens are not like your people, she thought. Good luck with the speech though.

Perhaps Appatine's laconic appraisal of the day was entirely justified. At least the man said what he thought; many in his position would not have the stones for that, knowing as he did that they were being evaluated constantly. Maybe she *would* wait until the end of this pointless mission before deciding whether to write off his chances of becoming a counterpart. Worlds knew, candidates with a big enough set of balls were hard to come by these days.

° ° °

Castigon had been very, very careful. It would not do for Ider Firenz to see him just yet. He was certain that his was a face she would remember until the day she died.

The counterpart was a different matter. He had never seen the lad before, and judging by his apparent age that was to be expected. While Castigon was being tried prior to his detention at Correctional Compound One, this knuckle-dragger would have been scratching his big ape head on the back row of some provincial classroom. He certainly didn't look the type to make a point of following the civilian news feeds.

Probably best not to be seen though, he thought to himself. Dear Ider might have shown him my files.

It was doubtful, seeing as the lad was plainly a probationer, but Castigon was not in the mood for taking risks. Not any more, not the reformed and rehabilitated Maber Castigon. He had had a long, long time to think about what went wrong at Ottomas.

Rehabilitated! Oh he made himself laugh sometimes.

He stepped silently back into the sharp-edged shadows beneath the square's peristyle, and made for the exit nearest to the House of Governance.

It was not far between them; proconsuls of the Empire were fans of speaking in general, more so of being heard. The public square was often one of the first things to be built in a colonial town. Castigon walked past the grounds once, turned the corner of the next street along, and stopped to think.

It was the standard layout, with a large set of double gates set into a high plasteel wall. The gardens in front of the receiving hall had a wide spinney of flowering trees right in the centre, surrounded by a small wall of its own. Festive, to be sure, but also a defence against vehicles driven at the building by suicidal attackers. Not that *he* planned anything quite so melodramatic.

If he had not minded the risk of being identified, he would be able to waltz right in there and take a look around. He would have needed to come up with some ruse, yes, but that was not a problem. The security systems however might be his undoing. It would possibly be sufficient to rely instead on the utter lack of imagination behind the Empire's policy on civic architecture.

Anyway, it was not like there was any chance he would be able to plant anything in the building before evening came. The doors and windows would be sealed at sundown, and the entire building swept for weapons and devices. It would not be opened again until the guests began to arrive for the reception, and even then access would be policed thoroughly.

Ah well, he thought. I'll wing it, just like on Ottomas. I hope this one doesn't go balls-up as well.

○ ○ ○

Mostrum Appatine, as it turned out, scrubbed up very well indeed. Firenz could not help but glance sideways as they made their way up the steps to the receiving hall, and found herself warming to the idea of having him as her counterpart.

No, that would not do at all. She was here to do a job, not to slobber over fresh meat. A close shave and a dress uniform did not make someone suitably capable, in any case.

The doors were wide open, and soft music floated out into the warm night. Lem Bataan music, if she was not mistaken. Accompanying it was the deceptively delicate scent of *tchok*, a Lemba delicacy. She hated *tchok* with a passion.

As they passed through the entrance, Firenz cast her eye casually over the duty guards. Local civic security, and judging by their bearing not one of them had military service. Still, at least each of them carried a Moachim P16 rapid fire pistol — someone evidently believed they should have reliable side-arms. She hoped they had received adequate training.

"You're here, here at last. Welcome. Please come this way, quickly as you like!"

One of the proconsul's staff was bustling towards them, bowing halfway to the floor before seeming to recall that Firenz and Appatine were not honoured guests. He aborted the attempt and half-waved, half-flicked his hands towards a panelled door on the far side of the reception hall.

"Come on," Firenz said to Appatine.

They took up their positions near the door, nonchalant, as if they were simply guests of lower rank. The moment the ambassador entered the public area, responsibility for his personal security would pass from his staff to Firenz and Appatine. Low key was the order of business; few proconsuls enjoyed having body armour and sub-machine guns in amongst the guests at their functions.

"You remember the layout?" She asked.

Appatine nodded. "Every corner, every stair."

"Good. If anything happens, we'll need to get them out by whatever route is safe."

Someone was coughing in a manner that was altogether too regular, and Firenz realised the music had stopped. She turned back to face out into the hall, and saw that the other guests were standing silent, drinks and canapés in hand.

The same man who had beckoned them in was now standing in the centre of the room.

"Ladies and Gentlemen," he said. "The Honourable Chellis Bel-Osanda, Proconsul of Fengrir, Governess of all the lands and titles therein."

A smattering of light applause built up as the proconsul descended the curving staircase. Firenz guessed that most of the attendees must have no idea about proper etiquette.

The door behind them clicked, and opened wide.

"His Excellency Ohl Ain, Ambassador of the Lem Bataan Confederation. His Attaché, Doctor Irim Su."

Again there was the patter of inappropriate applause. Firenz sighed to herself, although she had to admit that she had stood through far more than her fair share of ceremonies such as this. On Fengrir, even the cream of society probably did not get out very much.

Proconsul Bel-Osanda showered the ambassador with munificent greetings, both he and the attaché looked properly ingratiated, and moments later the music had started again.

Then came the dreaded mingling. Firenz added mingling to the top of the list of things she despised about this mission. If anything were to go wrong it would be now, while her clear line of sight to the Lembas was so frequently disrupted.

As if to reward her prescience, the universe chose that moment for the lights to go out. There were a few gasps, one or two glasses were dropped, then came giggles as the guests composed themselves. Firenz tapped Appatine twice on the arm: eyes open.

"Apologies, Ladies and Gentlemen. We will have the power fixed momentarily. Everything will return to normal in just a few minutes."

But the gunshots disagreed.

Flashes of light came from the entrance lobby, quick bursts of automatic fire. Firenz saw the civic guards illuminated from behind, like puppets in spasms as their strings were jerked harshly by an insane performer. People were already screaming, a table went over with a crash, and the room became a whirlwind of moving bodies.

Firenz shouted to Appatine over the din. "Protect the ambassador!"

○ ○ ○

After so many years, Castigon was back in his element at last. He dropped the guards on the door with ease; they had not been paying proper attention. Big mistake.

Walking calmly, he strode through the entrance and straight into the heart of the chaos in the reception hall. People were running, yelling, tripping; they did not matter. To him, they were simply moving cover.

A civic guard ran down the staircase, corkscrewing around the outside of the hall, P16 raised in front of him and sweeping from side to side as he struggled to identify the threat. Castigon pushed a woman aside to shoot the guard twice in the chest, and the man tumbled down the final few steps. More screams, more panic. Should have kept the high ground, Castigon thought, stayed safe behind the marble. Should have identified your target *before* advancing, you fool.

He saw a rectangle of blue light on the far side of the room: a doorway, with emergency lighting beyond. Dark figures were being bundled through — it would almost certainly be the honoured guests.

He shoulder-barged his way past a male, sending the gasping functionary sprawling on the floor. He began to run at the doorway, raising his pistol, and fired repeatedly. Bullets bit deep into the heavy wood of the closing door, until finally the gun clicked empty.

He got to it just in time, wedging his boot into the gap. With both hands pressed against the door he could not possibly reload, but what good would the weapon do him anyway if he could not reach his target?

Whoever was behind the door was strong, but not strong enough. With a final shove Castigon forced the door open, pushing his opponent backwards. A pistol skittered across the floor of the corridor, and he could not tell if it was his or the other's. All he knew was that his hands were now empty.

Appatine was filling the gap between them within half a second, and Castigon ducked just before a clenched fist entered the space where his face had been.

The lad seemed much, much bigger up close and personal. And he had been *fast*. Castigon though was hardly an amateur himself.

He brought his hands up to guard his face and neck, bobbed to the side as Appatine threw another heavy punch. This time the counterpart was ready for a dodge, and changed his angle as Castigon moved away. The knuckles missed, but Appatine's forearm slammed painfully hard against the side of Castigon's head. His ear began to throb immediately.

The left fist was already coming in from below, and Castigon shifted his centre of mass deftly over his right foot, blading his body sideways to present a narrower target. He grabbed the back of Appatine's unguarded neck, and brought his knee up hard as he pulled down with his hands.

Even as Appatine's nose exploded over Castigon's knee, his arm — so nearly a weapon — became trapped between both of Castigon's.

The counterpart went down, and Castigon pulled his opponent's wrist back against the shoulder joint, pushed all of his weight against the forearm through his left knee, and wrenched. Disappointingly, Appatine's scream drowned out the double *pop* of the breaking bones. Ah well.

Castigon kept his weight on, and drew a black push dagger from the sheath around his ankle. Without hesitation he drove it firmly into the counterpart's back, levering it forwards as the blade sank in. There was another popping sound, and Appatine lay still.

Castigon did not delay in leaping to his feet and trotting down the corridor, hugging the wall as he went. He scooped up the dropped pistol and checked the clip: what do you know, full. It must have belonged to the young counterpart after all.

The corridor took a hard right, and then another, and both corners slowed him down. He hardly fancied being shot through simple carelessness. Then another door. He took a run-up, barged it open; his momentum carried him into the room, and he allowed himself to slide across the floor.

No contact. The bay windows were open, and thin white nets were pushed to the side. The delicate scent of night-blooming flowers was in the air. A sickly glow illuminated the room, light from the local sun bouncing off a fat, rusty orb of a moon that looked as though it had struggled to heave itself above the horizon.

He edged out onto the veranda. On the lawn, headed for an armoured diplomatic vehicle, he saw the ambassador and his attaché. They were surrounded by civic guards, and the Shard was bringing up the rear. He levelled the pistol and fired over their heads.

"Go! *GO!*"

He could hear Firenz shouting across the gardens, could see her as plain as day in the bright orange light reflected off Fengrir's bloated moon.

As the guards continued their retreat, shepherding the Lem Bataan away, Firenz held her ground. She took up a defensive stance, kneeling, blading her body and aiming her side-arm at Castigon.

Ah Ider, you always were predictable.

"Close enough," she barked. "Identify."

Castigon smiled, not that she would be able to see it at that distance, and held his arms out to the side. He continued to move towards her with slow and measured steps.

"Stay where you are. Who are you?"

Castigon stayed silent.

"Toss the piece."

"Get real, Ider." He moved closer still. So close that he was able to see the recognition register on her face: a beautiful moment.

"You! *Murderer!* Butcher of Ottomas!"

"If you say so."

"You won't get to him," she said, levelling her sights with his eyes.

"Him who?"

"Ambassador Ain."

"I don't even know who that is."

"You're not here for him?"

"No, I'm here for you."

He was faster than she was, as he always had been. While her bullet sailed on towards the veranda windows, destined only to burrow into remarkably expensive wood panelling, his punched a hole through her head. He watched her collapse backwards, her back hitting the ground with a hollow thumping sound, and he felt nothing for her.

So she *did* remember my face until the day she died. Huh.

– 08 –
Fill the Silence

Behind the mirrored glass of the observation room, Caden stood in silence with Brant and watched intently. He had the feeling that Tirrano, standing tall and imperious over the seated Blank Woman, was now in her element.

"Why were you at Gemen Station?" Tirrano asked. "What was your objective?"

Amarist Naeb did not even appear to register that anyone was talking. Seated in a metal chair, still hooked up to a bag of saline solution, she fidgeted and mouthed silent words as Tirrano asked her questions. Naeb's eyes darted around and occasionally she smiled faintly, her head bobbing as if in agreement with some question asked from far away.

Eternal and harmony and everywhere and infusion
serendipity and sensation and luminance...
...and calling and celebration and agony
unfamiliar words screamed from all sides
quiet screaming

"Where are the personnel?"

Still Naeb did not respond, but continued her

quiet reverie. Tirrano looked back at the dividing window and shrugged at Brant. From the way she moved, and from her facial expression, Caden could see that she was done with the easy questions.

"Who are you working for? Tell me now."

Naeb made a sound that might have been part of a laugh.

"If you don't start to co-operate, and answer my questions, I'm going to have to resort to other means."

waves of faces, white spiral waves
clamour...
Belonging
only flashes
the horrible beauty of it all

Tirrano moved behind Naeb and held her head in both hands. She bent it back and to the side, forcing Naeb to look up at her. "Who has the weapons?"

Naeb gaped blankly at Tirrano for a few seconds, then continued her wordless whisper, her eyes leaving Tirrano's face and drifting off to gaze at something beyond the walls.

the song, forever the song, oh by the worlds
by all the many worlds
don't ever let it stop
don't let it stop
don't
don't!

"Answer me!" Tirrano shouted, raising her hand high. She slapped Naeb across the face, hard, leaving a white imprint which turned red quickly. Naeb's head snapped to one side with the force of the blow, then lolled indifferently. A trickle of bright blood oozed from one nostril. Tirrano raised her hand again.

the song, our song
fading
no oh no please don't stop please

"I said, answer me!"

"That's enough!"

Tirrano looked up at the Shard in the doorway, at Brant standing behind him just outside the room. She glared, and Caden read the expression. The interfering Shard, sent to stick his nose in where it was neither wanted nor needed.

"I think we can safely say that you're not getting anywhere," he said.

"Not yet. I'm just getting started."

"No, you're done. Leave her alone. She's a patient first, a suspect second. You already said it yourself; she's blank. Slapping her about is not going to get us anywhere."

Tirrano turned to look at Naeb, then back to Caden. She looked past him, appealing to Brant. The operator shook his head slightly.

Her eyes burned with resentment. "You don't know what you're doing."

"I usually find it's best to understand what I'm doing *before* I leap in," he said. "I want you to leave."

She opened her mouth as if to reply, then saw

Brant's face and said nothing. Without a further word, she left the room.

"Get the Doc back in here," Caden said to Brant.

Brant left, headed for the adjoining medbay, and Caden stared at Naeb. She stared back, her lips now motionless. Her eyes fixed on him, no longer darting around. She smiled, a wide, loose, gaping smile. The smile of an idiot.

"Fill the silence," she said.

"What?"

She smiled back. And then her eyes flicked off to one side, following something invisible. The wordless recitation began again, and she was away once more in her own world.

"Amarist, tell me what you mean," he said. But she was gone.

Brant returned with the corpsman who had overseen Naeb's examination. The woman was clearly nervous, Caden noted. Like Naeb, she did not seem to know where to look. He imagined she was probably ill at ease, coming in to a room where a patient of hers had clearly just been interrogated.

"Doctor," he said, "can you tell me about her condition?"

"Well, as I said before she's physically not in bad shape," the corpsman said. "Under-nourished, but nothing too serious. Her immune system has taken a battering recently, but she cleared screening — no infections. I think her mental state should be the primary concern at this point."

"You're telling me. Has she been lucid at all while you've been with her?"

"Not once. No, she's been like this the whole time."

"The whole time. Any idea why?"

"It's most likely some form of post-traumatic stress. I have to confess that's not my area, but she'll be seen by a specialist soon."

"What would you say if I told you she just spoke to me?"

"I'd be very sceptical. The way she is right now, if she *did* say something, I'd caution that it was probably gibberish."

"I want you to check her for everything you can think of."

"Of course. Am I looking for anything in particular?"

"No, just anything... not right."

"Oh, I see. I think. As you wish."

Caden turned his attention to Brant. "Post-traumatic stress. I think I had best get to that planet as quickly as possible."

"I agree," said Brant.

"Please keep Tirrano away from her."

"That I can do," he said. "But who's going to keep her away from me?"

○ ○ ○

"Oh, you are having a laugh," said Santani.

"I'm afraid not Captain," said Caden. "I need a ship, and we got on so famously earlier that I couldn't think of anyone else I'd rather travel with."

Even on the small holo display, Caden could see that Santani was hopping mad and she was making no effort to hide it. He decided to push her a bit further.

"Also, our shuttle is still in your hangar and I really can't be bothered to come and move it."

Santani declined to rise to the bait. "The coordinates you sent me, they're in the Deep Shadows. Practically within spitting distance of Riishi. If any of the Viskr defence forces look out the window while they're taking a dump, they'll be able to see us."

"You exaggerate, Captain. It's nearly three thousand light years away from the homeworld. Anyway, we won't be going alone."

"Elaborate."

"Gladly. I had a word with Admiral Pensh, and he's agreed to also send *Stiletto*, *Sai*, and *Dagger*."

"That's reassuring."

"Yes, well I'm not oblivious to the fact that the Deep is largely unexplored. Or the fact that this bit of it borders Viskr territory."

"I'm very glad you noticed."

"I am known for the keenness of my observations."

"Except when it comes to spotting that you're not wanted."

"Everybody has their blind spot."

Santani sighed. She looked to the side and muttered something, and Caden realised that Klade must be in the compartment with her. Him, or some other trusted officer.

"We're still effecting repairs from your last ride out with us," she said. "We'll be combat-ready in six hours."

"The other ships will be here by then," Caden said. "I'll have a mission briefing ready for you when they arrive."

"I can't wait."

Santani closed the channel, and her image disappeared instantly from the holo. Caden leaned back in his chair and looked across the desk.

"I think she likes you." Brant said.

"I thought you worked in intelligence?"

Brant smiled to himself. Present throughout, sitting in silence, he had been able to see Santani through the translucent display of the holo. Positioned as he was opposite Caden and behind the optical sensor, she had not been able to see him.

"I've not had much to do with Captain Santani before," he said, "but her record speaks for itself. I think you've made the right choice."

"That's what I thought."

"She strikes me as the sort who will bitch and moan every step of the way, but she'll move the many worlds to make sure you do what you need to do and come home safely."

"Let's hope she doesn't need to move anything quite so massive; it was difficult enough when she only had to take me somewhere. Anybody would think she was paying for the fuel."

◦ ◦ ◦

The entire command deck of the Hammer thrummed gently as her reactors shifted through their powering cycles, almost ready to propel her once more through the eternal dark.

"Status?" Santani asked.

"Green lights across the board, Captain," came the reply from the COMOP station. "Ready to detach."

"Release umbilical, and prepare to clear moorings," Klade instructed.

"Aye Sir."

Outside, in the cavernous docking area, the tunnel connecting the ship to the station interior released its latches and withdrew. Anchor gantries also released their grip, and swung back towards the inner surface of the dock. The sounds travelled through the hull of the ship and reverberated up and down her corridors.

"Detaching," said the officer at the helm. The floor shuddered briefly and the view of the docks began to drop in the forward view ports.

"We're clear of the berth," COMOP reported.

"Under way. Coming up to port speed, beacons are thirty seconds away," said Helm.

"Take her out gently, Helm," Santani said. "The harbour-master at Kosling is a serial complainer."

"Entrance beacons are *forty* seconds away." Helm corrected, dialling back the power to the manoeuvring thrusters.

"Better."

"Standing by to take over gravity functions," said Klade.

"Final confirmation from harbour control; the way is clear. Exit profile has been received." COMOP said.

"Take us out."

Hammer left the pier behind, passed slowly from the docking area into the egress channel, and slid onward towards the exit. The darkness ahead grew wider with each passing second, fringed with the guide lights of the aperture and the blinking entrance beacons, until the boundary passed by the view ports and abruptly disappeared astern.

Helm looked up from his station. "We are clear of Fort Kosling. Laying in a course to the rendezvous."

Klade ordered the ship to take over from the station's directional fields. "Gravity normalised."

Santani stood and walked towards the view ports, scanning the space outside with her eyes. The star field wheeled gently before her, slowly at first but with gradually increasing speed as the battleship nosed towards her destination.

Following the direction of the turn, she found what she was looking for: three silvery splinters, hanging hundreds of kilometres away in space. The rest of the task force, awaiting the arrival of *Hammer*. Clearly Admiral Pensh's reinforcements had arrived as scheduled.

At first it was imperceptible, as *Hammer* began to push with her main engines and started to close down the distance between them. But after a while the three slivers were growing noticeably larger. As the gap narrowed, distinct profiles could be made out. There was *Sai,* also a heavy battleship, albeit the Huntress-class and much more modern than *Hammer*. Beside her ran the *Dagger*, a relatively broad destroyer bristling with gauss guns and point defences. Beyond them both, slightly above their plane but partially eclipsed from Santani's point of view, the graceful lines of a carrier's double hull revealed the third ship as the *ICS Stiletto*.

Santani smiled, admiring the small task force.

"Message *Stiletto* Actual, Captain," COMOP said.

She walked back to her station and flipped her holo into position. "Open the channel."

"Aker, good to see you again."

Santani saluted briskly and her posture stiffened. "Admiral Pensh, I didn't realise you would be joining us."

"Try not to sound so disappointed, Captain."

"Apologies, Admiral. I didn't mean to sound ungrateful. We're lucky to have you alongside."

He smiled. "At ease Santani, before you do yourself a mischief."

"Thank you, Sir."

"We will be making a bound jump from here to

the gate at Aldava, then an unbound relay jump to our final destination. See to it that your crew are prepared for the last leg; it's quite a distance to make in one jump but I don't intend to delay us by hopping the entire route."

"Of course, Admiral. We're fully prepared for some turbulence, in fact we're quite getting used to it."

"Good form. Jump interval at Aldava will be one hour, barring the unforeseen."

"Yes, Admiral."

"As you were," he said, and the channel closed.

Santani drummed her fingers on the armrest of her chair. "That sneaky son-of-a-bitch."

Klade raised an eyebrow. "Captain?"

"Caden. He didn't tell me the admiral would be heading this expedition."

"Would he have known?"

"Yes. Oh yes, I'm sure of it. I suppose he thought that would be incredibly funny." She balled her fist, then raised her voice to call out to the helm. "Bring us into formation with the others. Ready for jump."

Klade gestured at his holo to send a ship-wide message. "Now hear this. All hands, prepare for jump. I repeat: all hands, prepare for jump."

The other three ships now dominated the forward view, and *Hammer* moved to position herself alongside *Sai*. The four began to accelerate, moving as one, headed for the Kosling gate.

In an empty expanse of the system, far removed from the plane of Kosling's five planets, the gate began to stir. Its formation lights were drowned out by the glow of the luminous strips that indicated a wormhole was forming. Vast collimator rings vibrated with the invisible surge of building power, focusing their energies and channelling them into the gravity needle that jutted out and away towards dead space.

For a moment, nothing happened. Then a spark in the blackness, tiny, barely noticeable against the cosmic backdrop. The spark became a burning crack, then a network of cracks, writhing and smouldering and ripping outwards, the space itself tearing open between them.

The light faded, and the barely perceptible perimeter of a perfect disc remained. The event horizon rotated, and through it subtle parallax made the distant constellations appear to shift.

The ships continued, wheeling around to meet the wormhole head on, and still in formation they crossed the event horizon.

Their journey to the Deep Shadows had begun.

◦ ◦ ◦

Santani waited for the wardroom hatch to close behind Klade before she spoke. Behind her, filling most of the view port, the murky orb of Aldava crawled by slowly, scant strips of dirty green the only indications of habitability.

"So," she said. "Tech and Systems. Were you able to speak to them before Eyes and Ears stepped in?"

"Yes, Captain. My contact was able to look over the sensor data and pass her findings back to me."

"Which were...?"

"Unfortunately she wasn't able to do much more with the data than I did myself. The results were ambiguous, to say the least."

"Anything new to add?"

"Not really. She said it was impossible to determine what caused the spike in the readings. As I suspected, irregularities in the power flow could be to blame."

"But what if they weren't? Did she offer an alternative explanation?"

"Exactly what I told you initially: if those readings were genuine and accurate, there was something in the Herros system when we arrived. Something with immense mass, which jumped away as we jumped in."

Santani pursed her lips thoughtfully. She was not yet sure what the full implications of this information were. Certainly it would seem there had probably been a vessel of some kind near Herros prior to their arrival, but why? If it had been involved in the attack, why flee when *Hammer* arrived? Presumably, whatever it was, it had been more than a match for the small fleet that had been tasked with defending Gemen Station. *Hammer* then should not have posed much of a threat to it. If conversely it was just a scout, left behind to see how the Empire reacted to an attack, why flee instead of hiding to observe? And why would a mere scout have such a large mass profile? None of it made any sense, and that troubled her greatly.

"What are the chances of readings like this occurring again, assuming they were caused by random power fluctuations?"

"Well it's the first time I've ever seen them," said Klade, "and I've served on *Hammer* for five Solars. So I'd give a very low estimate indeed."

"Can you use the readings as a template to prompt an automated alert from the sensors?"

"I'm not sure I follow, Captain."

"What I want is to be alerted immediately if the sensors ever provide similar readings."

"Yes, I believe that should be fairly straightforward."

"Excellent. Make the necessary changes as soon as possible."

"I'll see to it at once."

"Thank you Mister Klade, that will be all."

"Ma'am," he said, and left the compartment.

∘ ∘ ∘

Caden had left Eilentes and Throam conducting their weapons drill in one of the training areas on a lower deck. With only an hour between the jumps, he had not wanted to spend such valuable time doing something he was quite confident with. Besides, in his opinion there was not much he could do in the space of an hour to gain any real lasting benefit. He suspected that the other two were only doing it out of boredom. That, and the fact that at every turn they seemed to be finding opportunities to spend time in each other's company.

He reached the quarters he had been assigned, and entered. For some reason nobody had bothered to explain, they were different to the ones he had been given during the Herros mission. He was not surprised to find the compartment followed exactly the same layout and shared precisely the same décor and furnishings.

He sat down in front of the guest access holo, identified himself to it, then tapped in the commands to request routing through the local gate. After a long pause the holo replied that it was now linked to the Aldavan network. He tapped in a unified comms address, and waited for the network to relay his call via micro-wormhole.

When the call was picked up, it was a much younger man who stared back at him from the shimmering display. Younger, but noticeably tired-looking.

"Midget," Caden said.

There was a slight delay before the reply came. "Ugly. Where are you?"

"Out near the Deep on a mission: same old."

"Of course you are. Anything to stay away from here, huh?"

Ah. So it was going to be one of *those* conversations. Caden kicked himself mentally for believing that just once, his brother might seem pleased to hear from him.

"You know how it is, Lau. I have a lot of responsibilities out here."

"Yes, and I have a lot of them right here at home."

Caden ignored the barbs on that comment. "How is she?"

"How do you think she is? The same as usual."

"Is there anything you need me to send?"

"No, we'll do fine. The proconsul's people are mostly living up to their word. The visits have stopped, but we get looked after."

"Well that's good," Caden said.

"Is it?"

"If it isn't, then just say so."

Lau stared back at him for a long moment, then sighed. "What do you think it's like being left behind to look after a grown adult?"

"Not this again. We've been through it before Lau. You don't have to stay."

"Don't I? Do you think she'll be looked after properly if I leave it to someone else? Do you think she'll be happy?"

"I don't think she ever knew *how* to be happy."

"Shows what you know."

"I know her better than you do," Caden said, now irritated. "You don't know what it was like when Father was away."

Lau's face dropped yet further, and Caden felt instantly ashamed. His younger brother had been conceived shortly before the Battle of Chion. Lau had never known their father.

"Sorry," he said. "I didn't mean that."

Lau pursed his lips. "Well I did. I've probably spent more time with Mother than you ever did, definitely longer as an adult."

"I'm not getting drawn into another contest."

"It's not a contest, I'm just stating the facts. Sometimes she's happy. You're just never here to see it."

"I can't help that and you know it."

"Why not? Come and spend some time on Damastion."

"I can't. At least, not right now."

"She asks me where you are, and most of the time I don't know what to say."

"Okay, I get it. I'm on mission right now, and there's nothing I can really do about that. We'll have to talk again when I'm done."

"Promise you'll call."

"Yes, of course."

"Good. How's Rendir?"

"He's the same as always."

"You've not broken this one yet then."

"I've never broken a counterpart, Lau. It wasn't my fault the last one was a psychopath."

"Well you say that, but remember I've lived with you before. I know what it's like listening to you day in, day out."

In the corner of his eye Caden saw a flash in the distance, far off to starboard. He looked out of the port hole and saw a new wormhole forming outside Aldava's orbit. The holo display flickered for a moment, then stabilised.

"We're about to depart," he said. "I should go."

"Don't forget," said Lau. "When you're done, call me. It's high time you came home."

"I will."

The stars began to swing across his view as *Hammer* and her companion ships turned to face the distant event horizon.

"Heard it before, Ugly. Try to keep your word this time."

"Take care of yourself." The screen blinked out as he was talking; Lau had cut the connection from his end.

Caden lay on his bunk in preparation for the jump. He could tolerate only so much discomfort in the space of an hour.

– 09 –
An Empty Echo

Caden stepped off the ramp of the shuttle and trod the crumbling earth of the furthest planet to which he had yet travelled. CC-60125-E, less formally known as Colonisation Candidate Echo; the fifth planetary body out from the star catalogued as 60125. He had already agreed with the others that they would just call it 'Echo' for the sake of simplicity. If anyone ever did terraform this godforsaken place, they could argue over more appropriate names for it on their own time.

The land was dry and inhospitable, desolate and plain. Small turbid seas supported a primitive microbial ecosystem, which in turn managed to supply breathable oxygen to the atmosphere. Save for the flat endlessness of it all, the landscape reminded Caden of the plateau he so frequently visited in his dreams; only the inoffensive sky and the lack of distant mountain ranges were markedly different. He shivered.

A rushing noise sounded in the air, and he looked up to see the MAGA lander that *Stiletto* had deployed to the surface in support of his mission. The dropship swept down at a low angle, swooped over the landing site, then circled before coming to rest not far from his shuttle.

Caden watched as its outer hull skinprinted to mimic the surrounding landscape. Olive, cream and khaki patterns — left over from whatever planet the dropship had last visited — were replaced by dull browns, ochre, and greys. Vapour hissed from an exchanger to the rear of the craft, and the main hatch was popped from the inside.

Boots crunched on the powdery surface as soldiers of the Mobile Air and Ground Assault forces filed from the landing craft, fanning out in groups of four. Caden lost count at fifty, and guessed that an entire platoon had come down to the surface to support them. Talk about overkill. After the last of the riflemen and squad sergeants had jogged down the metal ramp, a disinterested-looking lieutenant strolled casually after them.

It was not the lieutenant who drew the eye, even with his oddly stiff bearing and world-weary expression; it was the Rodori who towered more than head-and-shoulders over his human comrades, cradling a general purpose machine gun as if it were a sleeping puppy.

Caden had never worked with a Rodori before. He had seen them, certainly, but never so close. From his school days he remembered that although they superficially resembled the reptiles of Earth, they were not truly the same in any biological sense; except of course for the fact that they were cold blooded.

He took the opportunity to study the alien while the sergeants barked orders and organised their squads. The most obvious thing about the Rodori was the sheer size of it; he — at least, Caden presumed it was a 'he' — was not just a solid third taller than all of the humans, but much more heavily set. The slow, deliberate movements were suggestive of dense bone and muscle, of huge weight being pushed around by tightly coiled strength. He noted that the adapted MAGA armour was thicker and more complex than that worn by the humans, which contributed to the overall impression of bulk. The weapon the Rodori carried was generally only used by men while mounted on a tripod, yet the alien lifted it effortlessly.

When the troops moved closer he got a clearer view. The Rodori's broad face was split by a wide mouth, which bristled with neat, narrow teeth. His large black eyes had orange irises, with pupils which were elongated laterally. The head was much larger than that of a human, hairless, and covered in scales. Not leathery or horny, but the smooth, iridescent lepidosaurian scales of a snake, in hues of brown, tan, and red wine. He saw there were larger scales on the crest of the skull, while those on the face and throat were paler and so tiny as to appear almost as a continuous surface. Stencilled on the breastplate of the Rodori's armour, on the left hand side, he could make out the word 'Bruiser'.

The Rodori began to talk in a series of long guttural consonants, and even before its link translated for him, Caden realised he had been staring.

"Something I can do for you?"

"Excuse me, Private. I've just not been up this close and personal with a Rodori before."

"Most people keep a safe distance." With that the alien rumbled past, slinging the machine gun on to his shoulder as if it were a stick.

Caden became aware that Throam and Eilentes had also left the shuttle, and were standing behind him. He turned to Throam and pointed after the giant. "That guy makes you look *tiny*."

"Doesn't count if it's not a human, Caden."

"Always counts if they're MAGA, Tiny."

"Cheeky son-of-a-bitch."

Caden chuckled to himself at Throam's indignation while Eilentes ducked behind the counterpart, trying not to let him see she was smirking.

"Shard Caden?"

Caden turned to see that the lieutenant was looking at him expectantly. Behind the officer the platoon had split into squads and fire teams, now spaced wide around the landing zone.

"Lieutenant...?"

"Lieutenant Volkas, Sir. First Platoon, Bravo Company—"

"I just wanted to know what to call you, Lieutenant Volkas."

"As you wish, Sir."

"What's your game plan?"

"Establish a base of operations here, before sending probes to scout the target location. Once we have eyes on the target we can correlate current features to mapping, and think about establishing a perimeter."

"Can I just stop you there?" Caden's tone indicated he definitely would anyway.

"Well... yes."

"*Hammer* already scanned the site from orbit, and we've both of us performed a fly-by. The place is empty. In fact just look around you: this whole planet is totally uninhabited."

"It is my understanding, Sir, that the purpose of this mission is to establish the presence of enemy forces."

"Involvement, rather than presence. I know it's close, but it really isn't the same thing."

"Be that as it may, I have to assume a hostile force is in occupation."

Caden closed his eyes in exasperation, and counted to three silently. He sensed in this soldier's manner a reluctance to break with protocol, a desire to be seen as competent and capable, the need to secure a reputation as being a safe bet. Not just for his superiors, but for the men under his command as well. Chances were that this was a newly promoted officer and he was determined to make his mark quickly.

"Okay. Good luck with that." Caden turned on his heel and walked back towards Throam, who immediately tossed him a Moachim assault rifle. Caden did not even bother to check the clip before mag-tagging the weapon to his armour.

Eilentes saw the cue and ducked into the rear compartment of the shuttle, returned carrying a long range rifle, and closed the hatch.

"See you when you arrive," Caden called to Volkas.

"The three of you are going ahead alone? Are you insane?"

"No. Just really, really impatient."

Volkas could only gape as the three walked away from the landing zone, towards the artificial structures cresting the horizon.

As they trudged across the dusty plain, Caden heard shouting behind them. One of the troopers with Bruiser was yelling "Sarge, he's doing it again!"

He looked back to see the Rodori lumbering after them, his fire team clearly unsure what to do about it.

"Stop him then!" Their squad sergeant bellowed.

"Begging your pardon Sarge, but *you* try to fucking stop him."

"Been there son; I'm not making that mistake again."

Volkas was turning red, although Caden was too far away to tell whether it was with anger or embarrassment. Either way, he was impotent in the face of the Rodori's decision to come after them. The lieutenant trotted towards the fire team and waved his arms at the leader. "Corporal, just... just go with them, yes?"

"Yes sir!"

Not quite so by-the-book then. Or at least, not sufficiently authoritative to put the entire book into practice. Caden smiled. It might have been nice to have a whole platoon with them, but they would have most likely just got in the way. A few extra eyes and hands and magazines would be perfect.

The fire team caught them up after a few minutes, and the leader beamed at Caden from under his tactical helmet.

"I'm Daxon, Corporal Brokko Daxon: fire team Charlie. These reprobates are Brohidder and Norskine." He nodded towards the other two humans.

The first touched two fingers to the rim of his helmet. "Call me Bro."

The second thudded her fist off the centre of her chest and flashed a quick smile.

"Who's your insubordinate friend?" Eilentes asked.

Daxon, Norskine and Bro passed a look between each other and smirked. A second passed before the Rodori's link fed out the translation.

"I am *The Bruised Heart of Faith in Others*."

"That's quite a name," Eilentes said.

"He's quite a guy," said Norskine. She gave Eilentes a wink.

"These ones call me Bruiser."

"And you live up to your name, don't you big fella?" Bro said.

"Indeed I do." Bruiser revealed his teeth.

Caden could not help himself. "Is that a smile?"

Bruiser turned towards him, and his mouth opened even wider. There must have been hundreds of teeth in it.

"Yes."

"It's really awful."

"Your face looks just as hideous to me. So why don't you kiss my cloaca."

"Classy!" Throam said.

○ ○ ○

They had seen the first signs of damage even when they were still some distance away. Now, at the perimeter of the site, they could appreciate the full extent of it.

The compound comprised dozens of low buildings, mostly pre-fabricated plasteel modules which could be erected quickly yet withstand the trials of weather and time. Around the outside of the compound ran a continuous wedge-shaped deflector designed to reduce the damage from sand storms. Its smooth curve was broken in only one place, where it buckled upwards into the air and formed an arch that framed the compound's only entrance. Or at least, it was supposed to form an arch. A hole had been punched through the top of the structure, so that the seared arms of the deflector reached raggedly up into empty air on each side of the entrance.

Even from outside the site, they could see the damage. Windows were cracked and smashed, walls peppered with holes, and two of the nearest modules were completely burned out. Pieces of equipment were strewn across the ground, most of them smashed beyond repair as if thrown and then trampled underfoot.

"Looks like you were right," Throam said to Caden. "This place has been hit hard."

"Not very much like Gemen Station, is it?"

"Not at all. That place looked like they'd spent a week cleaning up after themselves."

The seven of them stood before the entrance to the compound, all rifles at the ready. Caden did not anticipate an ambush, and he was not particularly eager to credit the overly cautious Lieutenant Volkas with being completely right, but at the same time it was not his intention to take any chances.

"Let's do this," he said. "Throam and Norskine on me. Eilentes in the watchtower. Bruiser and Bro with Daxon."

The two groups moved forward, entering the compound in silence. When it became clear that the entryway was as abandoned as it looked, Caden gave a signal and Eilentes moved away from the others. She mag-tagged her sniper rifle before scaling the ladder of the watchtower nimbly. The simple structure was only two stories high, nestled up against the inside of the deflector wall, but from the raised platform she would have a good view over the entire compound.

Once she was in position, with her rifle and scope balanced on the guardrail, Caden gestured to Daxon. The corporal nodded and veered off to the right with Bruiser and Bro.

Caden went left, Throam and Norskine keeping formation with him while he padded as quietly as the compressed grit would allow.

Here and there were the tell-tale signs of conflict: scorch marks on walls and containers, ugly rents in the sides of modules, windows that had shattered and thrown jagged glass in all directions.

He came across a module with a curving line of shallow holes in its outer surface, the dents angled steeply away from him. He brushed his fingers over the indents, and looked down. On the ground at his feet were several small metal cylinders.

"Breakers," he said. "From a geo-survey field kit, by the look of them. They were trying to fight back."

Norskine screwed up her face in a way that spoke half of disdain, half of pity. "They were shit out of luck if this was the best they could come up with."

"I think they might have been more prepared than that." Throam jerked his head at something out of their view. "Check this out."

Caden and Norskine moved up to where Throam had positioned himself, covering the end of the module and the paths beyond, and peered around the corner.

"Well I'll be a world-less wanderer..." Norskine said.

"Viskr," said Caden. "No doubt about it."

The planet Echo had not been kind. The corpse was desiccated, its flesh dried and eroded by weeks of exposure to the harsh sun, the dry winds, and a steady onslaught of coarse sands. But it was unmistakably a commando of the Viskr Junta. The remains of the uniform, the brown of the exposed bones, the ridges and protrusions of the skull, the shape of the hands: they were all of them dead give-aways.

The body was slumped against the rear of the module, leaning to one side as if the commando had sat down to rest his eyes and never woken up. Only the painfully awkward angle of the head and the two visible vertebrae suggested otherwise. The neck had been snapped, and viciously so.

Throam spat on the dry ground. "Looks like someone fought back quite well."

Caden's link chirruped.

"Daxon here. Nothing moving on the east side of the compound. We have two dead Viskr: one with a dented skull, one with a crushed chest."

"Acknowledged," said Caden. "We have one here as well. Broken neck. Finish your sweep and we'll rendezvous back at the entrance."

"Sir." The channel closed.

Throam eyed Caden quizzically. "You're not expecting to find much else, are you?"

"No."

"Want me to call it in? *Stiletto* should let Brant know what we've found."

"Do it. If we find anything else of note we can update them as and when."

"Consider it done."

○ ○ ○

You have no idea what is happening the horizon swinging violently from one side to the other, back again, *You'll fail and people will die* a sickly yellow-white aura clinging to the periphery of his vision, nauseating and disorienting, always there with eyes open or closed, burning and distorting whatever he looked at, *Don't even try to understand* and the humming sound, all at once distant and nearby and... everywhere.

Caden waited it out, and after what felt like

hours found himself kneeling in the dirt. He felt as though he could retch, but nothing came up. His vision was still swimming, his ears rang, and he could not yet stand. This had been a particularly bad one, although it was mercifully short-lived.

He remembered thinking about the vulnerability of the scientists, how the Empire had essentially left them to their fate. He had felt a pang of regret, almost a vicarious stab of guilt. Then nothing else coherent, just the flashing, noisy episode that had assailed his senses. The visual and auditory distortion, and the ground swinging from side to side, the stumbling, and in amongst it all — as he had half seen on Herros — a figure standing before him.

There had been boots, he remembered those. Black military grade boots such as might be worn by anyone who was on the planet right now, or on the starships waiting patiently high above him. Then combat pants, again black, with empty webbing and mag-tags, large pockets, a canvas belt. Again, those could have been worn by almost anyone who had arrived with Admiral Pensh's task force. Then began the abdomen, the torso — a charcoal base layer and black under-armour flexible panels. Combat gear. That narrowed it down to, oh say just two thirds of all those people.

The body had melted into the creeping black morass at the centre of the hallucination, as it had done during his episode at Gemen Station. He had seen more of it this time; instead of just a pair of legs that fused with living shadow, this time he had seen legs *and* a body. He still had no idea who it was, or what it meant, but it was progress of a sort.

The thudding at the back of his skull was subsiding, and he took stock of his surroundings. In front of him stood a row of stone cairns which he had constructed himself; one for each of the expedition members lost on Echo. Even one for Amarist Naeb, since she could barely be said to have survived.

The others had watched for a while when he started working on the first cairn, then helped find stones which they piled nearby as he began on the second one. When they realised his full intentions they drifted away, presumably finding better things to do. Caden had continued to build while they waited for Volkas to deem the compound safe for occupation by his platoon.

Caden was not especially interested in anything Volkas had to say about the site. The lieutenant could secure and record whatever he wanted; Caden already had the essential answers he had come for. The Viskr had played a part in the extinction of this facility, and nobody had been here to stop them.

Except maybe for one being. The dead commandos had not been shot, cut, or stabbed; they had been battered. Caden had formed his suspicions quickly, and he had tasked Bro and Bruiser with searching the entire compound for a particular system. They had found it in a module right next to the compound's organic produce regulators: a bio-charger station, used for powering combination technology. The compound staff had undoubtedly had some kind of android among their number; most likely for maintenance or difficult manual tasks. It made sense, with them being a geological survey team. Presumably someone had been able to relax some of its behavioural protocols, and then turned it loose upon their attackers.

He had shuddered when he realised this. The idea of having body parts crushed by a deliberate blow from a machine was unsettling at best, grotesque at worst. Exactly where the android was now was anyone's guess.

He heard the crunch of boots on dusty gravel behind him; someone was coming. Someone real, with real boots. Wiping the sweat from his brow as subtly as he could, he rose slowly from the ground.

"Are you okay?" Eilentes said.

"Bit of a migraine," said Caden. "It's so dry here."

"You do look pale." She stared at him for a few long seconds, and he got the sense that she was weighing up his explanation. He wondered what she saw when she looked at him. Were his eyes red? Was he swaying?

"Well, we'll be leaving for Aldava soon enough," she said. "Brant has been apprised of the situation and he's passed it along to Eyes and Ears. We've got everything we came for."

"Nothing more of note from the compound?"

"Just one small thing."

"What's that?"

"Volkas had one of his men dig out the researchers' inventory. They should have a small stock of xtryllium here. It's gone."

Xtryllium, the so-called divine currency. The material was extremely difficult to manufacture, yet its unique properties meant so very much to the galaxy. Among other applications, it allowed artificial gravity and wormhole invocation. Caden wondered why they would have needed it here. "It *is* very valuable. It would have been stupid to leave it behind."

"It would be at that," Eilentes said. She gave him another lingering look. "Are you sure you're okay?"

"I'm fine," he said. "Let's get back to the others."

He turned as if to leave, to walk back to the compound, and stopped when he realised she was not following. She stood motionless, staring thoughtfully at the cairns.

"This would be a very lonely place to die," she said after a long silence.

"The loneliest," he agreed.

"What do you think happened to them?"

"I have no idea. But Amarist Naeb somehow found her way back; perhaps the others will as well."

As Caden started walking away, she turned to follow him.

"I hope so."

○ ○ ○

Elm had been waiting for the whole day, although to his young mind it might as well have been for a century. The light outside had faded hours ago, and throughout the centre of the house the safety lamps had turned themselves on to illuminate the corridors and hallways.

He rolled back the covers and clambered down from his bed. Treading softly amongst the discarded paper and presents that were scattered across his bedroom floor, he once more went to the window and looked out upon the grounds.

Below, the softly lit grounds were empty and still. Two rows of small solar lanterns described the graceful curve of the main driveway, leading away to the gates of the estate. As before, there was nobody there.

He sighed and went back to his bed, scooping up one of his new toys. It was a destroyer much like the one Brehim had, for which Elm had felt such a strong sense of envy. He made it soar through the air, firing its inert missiles at the bed covers.

It was actually much less fun than he had expected. So much time spent in longing, for what was essentially a piece of plastic. Still, it would be fun to finally be able to play with Brehim on a more even footing.

For now though it was a hollow experience. He felt a yawning chasm over his stomach, and pushed the loneliness down as hard as he could. Crushed it into a single point and hid it way down deep, before it could do the same to him. Father had to be home soon, and then everything would be better.

He had been promised that Father would return for his birthday. He did not know the time, but he knew it was late, and the promise was starting to look like it might go unfulfilled. He could not help but feel disappointed; Mother and Father were traditionalists, so much so that they still observed the Solar year for birthdays. It was incomprehensible to him that Father would not have moved the many worlds to ensure he was home in time.

Maybe Father had come home and Elm had simply not heard. Father might have decided it was too late to come and wake him. After all, he would not have known that Elm was still awake. He got back out of bed and put on his dressing gown.

Elm padded quietly along the top corridor in his slippers, heading for the main staircase that led to the grand hallway. As he reached the top of the stairs, he could hear the faint sound of music drifting from one of the reception rooms. At least one person was still awake then; perhaps Father was back after all. He hurried down the stairs and crossed the grand hallway, moving towards the only open door. Light and warmth spilled into the hall invitingly. When he reached the door, he stopped and looked in before entering.

The room was still littered with decorations, the remains of the party that Mother had organised for Elm and his friends from school. Other than Brehim, he did not really know any local children. Those few who were fortunate enough to live in the prestigious area were, for reasons quite beyond him, not welcomed by Mother as companions for her boy.

Mother was sitting in a chair across the room, her head hanging towards her chest. He could not tell if she was awake or asleep.

She brought her arm up from the side of the chair, and Elm saw she was holding a tumbler. Ice clinked as she brought it to her mouth. As she raised her head to drink, she saw him standing in the doorway.

"What are you doing out of bed, dear?" She said.

"Is Father home yet, Mother?"

"No dear, he's not."

Elm pouted. "You said he'd be home to see me."

She took another swallow before replying. "Well he isn't. He'll be back, just go to bed. When you wake up I'm sure he'll be home."

"You said! You said he'd be back!"

"It's not up to me." She gestured towards him

with the tumbler. "Learn to be patient, Elm. Worlds know I have to be."

"I waited all day."

She smiled, sniggered, and despite his youth Elm realised that it was not a kindly expression of humour. He did not know why.

"All day? Well aren't you just the definition of endurance."

"Why hasn't he come home yet?"

"I don't know. He's serving on a battleship, dear. There could be any number of reasons."

"You shouldn't have promised."

Her eyes flashed darkly and he realised that for some reason she was now angry with him. "I didn't plan this, Elm. Just go to bed."

"I want to stay up and wait."

"No! GO TO BED!"

He reeled with shock. Mother had never shouted at him like that before. He turned and walked wordlessly back to the stairs.

Back in his bedroom, he sat up in bed and drew the covers up around his body. He would wait here, he decided. Mother could not force him to sleep.

In the pit in the middle of his belly, the loneliness and disappointment jostled for position. They burst outward and expanded into him, no longer under his tight control. He did not try to squeeze them down this time; it was their legitimate moment, after all.

Hours passed before he awoke again.

The room was dark, lit only by the faint glow from the gardens. Something had woken him up, but he did not know what. After a moment he realised there were voices coming from downstairs. Two voices.

He leaped out of bed and went to the door, but as he opened it he realised that the tone of the conversation drifting up from the ground floor was not a happy one. He opened the door wide and waited, listening.

"It's hardly my fault," a male voice said.

Father!

"You could have let me know." Mother.

"It wasn't possible. We made port after a jump from the line. It was already the middle of the night here."

"I still think you could have found a way," she said. "If not for me then for your son."

"You're lucky I'm back at all. The war isn't exactly going well."

"Lucky? I'm *lucky*? I should feel lucky to have a husband who wants to see his son?"

"You know what I mean, Chia. Don't put words in my mouth. I meant it's lucky I was able to get shore leave at all, lucky the *Curtailer* rotated back to the worlds when it did."

"Oh yes, I feel sooo lucky. Lucky, lucky me."

"You're drunk. I can't talk to you when you're like this."

"That's right, run away. Why don't you run back to your ship? You're obviously happier shooting at Viskr than you are looking after your family."

There was a pause. "That's not true and you know it."

"Funny, because that's how it looks."

"But that's not how it *is*. I'm going to bed Chia. I will spend the morning with Elm, and we'll have this conversation when you are sober and reasonable."

"I am fucking sober."

"You aren't, and I don't intend to stand here arguing about it."

Elm heard a door close downstairs, then another opened towards the rear of the hall. Father must be going to the guest quarters.

"Useless shit."

He decided not to brave a trip across the grand hallway to see Father, given that Mother was obviously in a bad mood. It was enough for now to know that he had come home at long last.

Elm returned to bed and tried to sleep. The loneliness and disappointment now wrestled for dominance with a third force; a feeling of confused separation. He did not feel he had the strength to intervene, to try and crush them down into the tiny dark spot where they could be imprisoned and rendered impotent.

It was a long time before sleep finally took him.

– 10 –
Eyes and Ears

March Bel-Askis waited patiently while the other invigilators filed in to the conference hall, their hushed conversations echoing softly around the circular chamber. Considering the urgency of the meeting, they certainly did not appear to be in any great hurry to get under way. Well, he had had to wait almost a standard day for them to convene in one way or another; he could wait a few minutes more.

They had come from far and wide — in person or by remote — each of them representing the topmost cells of the organisation. From across the great expanse of the Empire's territories Eyes and Ears had chosen to converge here, at Ramm Stallahad. His home.

He felt a swell of pride. In all his long years working to protect the Empire, it was only on occasions such as these that Bel-Askis felt he received any real recognition. To host the meeting was to lead the discussion; to lead the discussion was to influence the future. Even those old fools who made up the Home Council rarely encountered opportunities such as this.

He realised with a start that most of the delegates arriving in person had now taken their seats.

Those who were more distant flickered into existence as holograms, shimmering and silvery, the data compressed at source and routed to Ramm Stallahad through the local Herses gate.

He rose awkwardly to his feet. "The time has come to acknowledge that, in all likelihood, the Imperial Combine is under attack."

As he had expected, an urgent murmur ricocheted around the table.

"In the past month, the Navy has lost no fewer than six patrol vessels. The latest report states that five of our gates are failing to respond, two of them only refusing to do so in the past week. Four of our more isolated outposts and research stations have gone dark. All of these incidents have taken place along the fringes of the Deep Shadows, between the Orion and Perseus arms of the galaxy."

Silane Creid, the invigilator for the Shalleon system, raised his palms as if to hold back the tide of revelations. "Are we certain these are not simply accidents or technical issues?"

"That's a good question. Yesterday I received confirmation from Fort Kosling that our facility on Herros has been breached. All personnel are currently missing, as is the task force charged with defending them."

Another urgent murmur.

"And the weapons?" That question from Sashan Geneve, the delegate from Sol. Bel-Askis had all the time in the world for the young woman. As politically naïve as she could be, she was strategically gifted and beyond enthusiastic.

"I regret to report that all the weapons were taken, as were all research materials pertaining to them. In light of this, we can only assume that these other blackouts are also the result of hostile actions."

This time the response was clamorous. The delegates seemed to forget themselves, expressing their shock loudly and abandoning the comportment that Bel-Askis felt befitted the occasion. He found himself waiting for their attention again.

After a few moments, his patience began to wear thin. He was getting far too old to waste time so easily. "Please, compose yourselves. We have decisions to make."

Creid began to speak, and the remainder of the background chatter faded to silence as the delegates realised they might miss crucial discussion.

"I believe my question still applies," he said. "I admit we can infer a hostile agent from the attack on Herros, but confirming one incident is not the same as confirming the others."

"Agreed," chorused several of the invigilators.

Creid looked around as if he had not expected any support, then went on. "We are in the business of demonstrating our conclusions with evidence. What evidence has been collected?"

Bel-Askis sighed. "The Navy has found no trace of its missing ships, and the hundreds of automated probes sent to investigate have all failed to return any telemetry whatsoever. These facts indicate an active opposing agent. At this time, Admiral Pensh is leading an expedition to investigate one of our silent stations in person."

Creid laced his fingers and rested his hands on the table. "I see. I have to wonder why the Navy has only sent probes to check the unresponsive gates."

"A hangover from the Perseus conflict." Geneve said.

Bel-Askis was impressed. She must have studied the multi-volume analysis of the last war carefully. "Almost certainly."

"I don't follow," Creid said.

All eyes turned to Geneve. "In the early days of the war, our biggest military mistake was to send entire battle groups to investigate severed comms and distress calls. Enmeshment accounted for almost half of all fleet losses in the first year of the war alone."

Bel-Askis grimaced. Of course he knew the facts, having read virtually every report compiled on the matter — he had even written a good number of those reports. But there was something so much more visceral about hearing the words spoken out loud.

Creid remained stony-faced. "I'm sorry, but my speciality is knowing who is where, and when. You'll have to explain what you mean."

Geneve continued, looking more than happy to share her appreciation of tactics. "When a destination gate can't be reached, usually it means the system nexus is also inaccessible. Ships have to jump in blind, through an unbound wormhole. They have very little control over exactly where they will emerge, and no idea of what's waiting. Even something as innocuous as a small rock can trigger a catastrophe if a ship emerges into the space it's already occupying. The Viskr exploited that; they laid traps."

"I see. So are we to understand that the admiralty is unwilling to throw ships at these star systems, on the off chance that they could be blundering into ambushes?"

"Exactly. Drawing the enemy is a classic Viskr tactic."

"You really ought to know these things, Invigilator Creid."

Bel-Askis smiled faintly to himself at this comment from Quisten Leksis, the invigilator representing the Cerina system's twin planets. It was no great secret that she thoroughly enjoyed a professional rivalry with the Maidre Shalleon delegate. Appearing by hologram from thousands of light years away, she seemed more willing to poke fun at him than she would have been in person.

"I'm sure I'm not the only person at the table who appreciates clarification."

As amusing as it was, Bel-Askis felt the need to nip this distraction in the bud. "The point does stand. The admiralty is concerned that this series of incidents could be a ruse to fragment the armada, to make us move essential defence fleets outside the Six-K radius."

"If it is a ruse, who is responsible?" Geneve asked.

"From what you have just shared, I would have thought the Viskr are the prime suspects," Creid said.

"Invigilator Leksis?" Bel-Askis looked across the table at her holographic avatar.

"Our listening posts have in fact reported unusual activity along the border. Viskr forces are being redeployed almost continuously, although I should say we can't make head nor tail of the patterns. Their fleets are all over the place—"

Gordl Branathes, his hologram being routed from Fort Kosling, interrupted her. "If I may?"

"Yes, Monitor," said Bel-Askis. "Do go ahead."

"I've just had a preliminary report cross my desk, literally this very moment. Admiral Pensh's expedition has uncovered direct evidence of a

Viskr attack on CC-60125-E."

Creid leaned back in his chair and threw his arms out. "There we go then."

"It would seem our research station on that planet was attacked within the past month or so. Three dead Viskr were found at the site, but all of our staff are missing. The only exception is a woman called Amarist Naeb, who was found at Gemen Station on Herros. She appears to have suffered a trauma, which has robbed her of her memory."

"Direct evidence *indeed,*" Creid said.

The room fell silent, and Bel-Askis knew why. Most of the people called to this conference had been in the intelligence corps for years, and if they had been paying attention they would almost certainly have worked out what was going to come next.

"You probably all realise that I could have sent you these reports electronically, without inviting discussion. You are present in this meeting because we must provide the admiralty with an interpretation, and to provide such an interpretation requires a vote."

Again, the murmur. Only this time it was very quiet and very short-lived.

"The incidents we have discussed are likely intended to draw our fleets apart and reduce defences in the core systems. With the exception of Herros, which is of course under investigation due to the loss of specific high value assets, there is a good argument for simply ignoring them and instead preparing a large scale defence of the border systems."

Geneve gasped. "But we have people out there relying on us to help them!"

"Fleet Command won't help them by sending our ships to their destruction," said Creid.

Bel-Askis looked at Geneve with an expression that mixed guilt and grief. "I'm sorry, Invigilator Geneve, I really am. But you have clearly studied the last Viskr war, so you will know we simply cannot save everyone in these situations. We must act decisively to protect the colonies we *can* protect."

"They are probably already dead, in any case," said Creid. "It's not like it would take very long to wipe them out."

"The border worlds are not densely populated." Bel-Askis nodded gravely. "I believe the average population is somewhere in the order of a hundred thousand. Even the systems with their own gates generally have fewer than a million inhabitants."

"I can hardly believe I'm hearing this," said Geneve.

"But it needs to be heard," said Creid. "Pretending that a small number of colonials on the frontier might have survived what is almost certainly an invasion? We'd be kidding ourselves. And I might point out that any attempt at rescue will be for the admiralty to decide on, not this council."

Leksis hurriedly brought the conversation back on track. "Where is this going, Invigilator Bel-Askis? I believe you were about to say."

"As I said right at the start, all of the incidents we are aware of occurred along the fringes of the rim-ward Deep Shadows. The nearest military force in that direction capable of engaging us in warfare is the Viskr armada. And now Admiral Pensh has found physical evidence that they have certainly attacked us once, and probably attacked us twice."

"I take it there has been no diplomatic contact?" The question came from one of the invigilators who had as yet remained silent.

"No, as usual they ignore our messages."

"So then... war has not been declared?"

"Why should it be?" Geneve asked. "No agreement was signed after Chion; they just stopped mounting their attacks. Technically and legally, we're still at war."

"Ah."

Bel-Askis went on. "The question before you all is simple: are you satisfied that the Viskr Junta is most likely the party responsible for the loss of our ships, the communications blackouts, our unresponsive gates, and the attack on Herros?"

Silence.

It was a long, long moment before Invigilator Creid spoke. "Shalleon votes yes."

"The Kosling system votes yes," said Branathes.

"High and Low Cerin vote yes," Leksis said, without much hesitation.

Creid's vote has given the others moral permission to agree, Bel-Askis thought. Even Leksis has not taken this opportunity to contradict him.

"Earth—" Geneve said. She stumbled on the name of her own home, cleared her throat, and started again. "The Solar system votes yes."

The vote passed around the table quickly after that. Broher, Meccrace, Amuthion, Kementhast; all 'yes'. Firachi and Shuul-Ind, Kol Pent and Bennethium. System after system, all fell in line.

Bel-Askis suddenly felt older than he had for a long time. Even as he spoke, he could imagine future history writing itself with wrathful spite. In a thousand years, scholars might look back at this meeting and label the gathered invigilators with a term both evocative and unkind.

"The vote is unanimous. We interpret the reports as being indicative of an invasion, or planned invasion, by the Viskr Junta. The admiralty will be so advised."

And once they are advised, he thought, they will surely act.

– 11 –
Tabula Rasa

Occre Brant hurried through the starkly lit white and grey corridors of Fort Kosling, anxious to return to medical as quickly as he could. He could not say why exactly, but the conversation he had just shared with Gordl Branathes had really made his skin crawl.

Earlier in the day Brant had received grave news via *Stiletto*: on the planet Caden was now calling Echo, he had found clear evidence of a Viskr offensive against the Empire. It was a troubling revelation, and Brant had sent it forward to Branathes' holo at once, knowing that the monitor was already in session with most of the invigilators of Eyes and Ears.

It puzzled Brant that the target had been a tiny geological survey team on a practically worthless planet. It concerned him that one of the people missing from that practically worthless planet had later turned up on a secret research station, from which all data, personnel, and experimental weapons were now missing. It worried him that a secret research station had been breached in the first place, even more so that afterwards it had looked for all the world as if the staff there had simply downed tools and walked away. And as for the missing ships, which had been assigned to guard the planet and its secrets... it was deeply disturbing that they had vanished without any trace. Not even debris had been found.

But Branathes had seemed delighted to hear the findings of Caden's expedition. *Delighted!*

Maybe he was simply relishing his temporary role a little too much. With the invigilator for the Kosling system otherwise engaged on Earth, Branathes was acting up in her absence to ensure routine duties were taken care of. Those duties had included attending the emergency meeting at Ramm Stallahad, even if it was just by hologram, and Brant could well imagine the lowly monitor experiencing something of a thrill as he conferred with the gathered invigilators. Especially when it came time to advise them of critical intelligence; Branathes had always enjoyed being seen as the man in the know, that much was certain.

Even so, that did not really explain his reaction. Delight? When Brant had received the communiqué from Throam, which had included images of the dead Viskr commandos, he had felt a chilly sensation that instantly tightened his scalp. Even with his poorly suppressed suspicions about the intrusion at Gemen station, having Viskr involvement confirmed was still a startling experience. It meant that now he had to consider the context for these events, and that context was almost certainly going to be aggressive military action from an old enemy. War seemed likely.

Perhaps Branathes actually wanted to see war. He would not be the first armchair warrior to imagine that large scale conflict was exciting or entertaining.

"We'll beat them back again, just like we did

last time," he had said after the meeting. "They won't stand a chance, the sabre-rattling fools."

Brant did not share his enthusiasm: the last war had cost the Imperial Combine dearly, and that cost was much more of a reality to people in his line of work than it was to people like Gordl Branathes. The monitor would just get the final figures, all neat and clean and bloodless, innocent little numerals over which he could hold his brow and bewail the insanity of war and tell himself he felt very sad. It would be Brant who had to trawl through the list of the dead to tabulate Kosling's losses; there would be names and biographies and file images.

That was, he reflected, not even his only concern. Branathes had given Brant no tasks. The monitor had come away from the conference carrying the knowledge that the Viskr were probably preparing to launch an all-out assault, and he had not yet required one single action of his operator. Even assuming that Caden would be successful in his mission, and that the Navy would muster their fleets in time to meet any advance forces, Branathes was being sloppy. The Viskr Junta would not be playing games when their fleets arrived, so it would have been good to know there was some kind of preparation going on.

There was not much he could do about it. Branathes was his senior officer, and if he was not going to give his operator any orders then that was the end of it. But what Brant *could* do was continue to learn. Right now, down in medical, there was a woman who was quite probably a piece of material evidence.

He quickened his pace.

○ ○ ○

The admiral is a difficult man to read, thought Santani. Despite the length of their working relationship, she had never quite managed to spot the difference between his expressions of concern and excitement.

His face was a mask of either emotion. Or possibly neither of them; she really could not say. Not even his tone was giving her any clue.

"You won't be completely alone; I'll leave Bravo Company in your care. The 951st will barely miss the lazy beggars."

"Thank you, Admiral. That's... appreciated."

"I'd like to say I will miss having *Hammer* running alongside me," he said, "but I think we both know it's a bad idea for you to come to the rendezvous."

"Sir?"

"Come now Aker, the Commodore-class is seriously dated."

"Dated she may be, but she's mine."

"I know you love the old girl, but your reluctance to take a new command is now keeping you away from the line."

"The only way I'll leave this ship behind, Admiral, is if she's smashed into a million pieces."

"Spoken like a true captain. Well I can't say I blame you; she's a design classic."

"She is at that." Santani was vaguely aware that this was one of the longest conversations they had had for a good while, and it was essentially going nowhere. Anything to dance around the great big elephant on the command deck.

Pensh looked at someone out of Santani's view, and nodded. "The MAGA transports are on their way to you now. Four platoons — don't say I never give you anything."

"Thank you." There was a long pause. "Admiral..."

"If it doesn't need saying, Aker—"

"—then don't say it." She completed the sentence for him. "Good luck."

"And to you," he said. "I hope that Shard and his mission are worth something, because I get the sense our time is running out."

"I know the feeling."

Again, someone out of view of the holo passed a message to the admiral. He nodded, and told them to prepare the ship for jump.

"It's time. The armada awaits. Until next we meet, Captain."

"Until next we meet."

The channel closed. Beyond the four tiny dots of the MAGA landers, which closed steadily on *Hammer,* the other ships of the task force manoeuvred slowly towards a newly formed wormhole. First *Sai* and *Dagger* jumped away, then *Stiletto,* disappearing into the event horizon like knives dropped into a dark pool.

Despite the conversational murmur that always permeated the command deck, Santani felt very alone.

○ ○ ○

"I've not seen anything quite like this before."

Doctor Vella Laekan stood close to Amarist Naeb, her patient now lying on a bed in a private medbay. The psychiatrist held a holo in one hand, and leaned against the edge of a cabinet with the other. She looked at Brant with an expression that suggested his guess was as good as hers.

He had seen a lot of that particular expression this past day, and his own opinion was that his guess would certainly *not* be as good as hers.

"What do you make of her?"

"There's an old term from classical psychology," she said. "*Tabula rasa*. That's her."

"I don't know what that means."

"Sorry, it's a very old language. It means 'blank slate', and that's essentially what she is."

"Go on..."

"Everything that makes her *her* appears to be gone. Or at the very least, it's inaccessible. Motivation, behaviours, emotion, in fact her whole personality; they all appear to be — for want of a better word — absent."

"She looked like she was whispering something earlier on."

"It's possible her memories are intact, and her mind is playing through them randomly. Or there might be conscious thoughts going on in there, and that's how they're being manifested. I really couldn't say at the moment. I need to get her under a scanner and take a look at what's happening in her brain."

"Help yourself," Brant said.

"Are we aware of any next-of-kin? I'd like to know if there are any similar conditions in the family history."

"Not that I know of. I'll look into it."

"Thanks, that would be a real help."

Brant cast his eye over the quiescent patient, noting the fixed expression on her face. Her eyes stared blankly at the ceiling, and her mouth was now still. Only the slow rise and fall of her chest and the occasional blink indicated that she was still among the living.

"You removed her restraints?"

"I don't think she really needs them, do you?" Laekan said. "She's not about to leap out of bed and start dancing."

"You're the expert."

"Serious error in judgement, if you ask me." The voice came from behind him.

Brant turned to see Tirrano slouching against the wall of the medbay, just inside the isolation hatch. Her arms were folded across her chest, and she gave no clue as to how long she had been behind her colleague.

"I asked you to stay away from her," said Brant.

"Exactly: you *asked*. You didn't *order*, and you can't because we're the same rank."

"She's part of my case, Peras. Not yours."

"Which is why I've not interfered," she said with a thin smile.

"Give me strength." He muttered it under his breath.

"Funny, isn't it? I called her the Blank Woman, and the expert says she's a blank slate. Common factor? Blank. Rasa. *Rasa*. Oh, I do like the way that sounds. She's a Rasa."

"She's a person," said Brant. "You could do with getting that into your head."

"Person or not, I don't trust the Rasa bitch. Not one little bit."

Brant sighed, exasperated. Ever since Tirrano had arrived at Kosling, he had begrudgingly accepted that she was in fact quite brilliant at what she did. It was just a shame that she was so awful as a person, and that he was the one who constantly had to tolerate her. "Did you come here for any specific reason?"

"Not really."

Brant turned away. The apparently airy, carefree persona did not fit Tirrano at all, and he had not taken long to figure out that it was one she adopted when she wanted something. It had also not taken him long to figure out what that *something* was. He grimaced.

"Doctor Laekan," he said. "I'll make myself available if you find anything new."

Laekan did not peel herself away from her work at the holo, but waved him off without looking. "I'll let you know."

Brant headed for the exit, passing straight by Tirrano. As the doors parted and he left the medbay, she followed him into the maze of Fort Kosling's corridors.

"Why so grumpy?" She said.

Grumpy? That was a term that suggested frivolity was in play, that she was teasing him gently. Not for one moment did he believe she genuinely operated on that level.

"I'm not grumpy, I'm busy. You do know the Empire is possibly on the brink of war, yes?"

"I'll believe it when I see it," she said. "A heist and a Rasa do not an invasion make."

"What's your alternate hypothesis?" He asked, knowing full well he was being drawn into a conversation he need not have.

"I'll grant you the Viskr connection," she said. "Three dead commandos is a big hint. As for the hit on Herros, we can infer they want our tech, but we can't infer what they plan to use it for. As Admiral Betombe once said, 'capability is not intention'."

"Capability is not intention," Brant echoed. "It sounded grand when he said it at Brankfall. In this context it just seems naïve."

"It could be they're fighting someone on the rim-ward side of the Perseus arm. Our listening posts can't see that far. Perhaps they're already at war, and they're desperate."

"I don't think so. The latest intel shows the bulk of their armada deployed along the core-ward border. Our border."

"It's only 'the bulk' if you consider the fleet numbers we know about," she said. "We have no idea how busy the Viskr shipyards have been in the past two decades."

"True."

"In fact, that would be just like them. Get their asses handed to them at Laeara and Chion, then slink off to devote an entire generation to shipbuilding."

"Hmm, less believable."

"They *are* governed by a military junta."

"But they'd be insane to devote decades of resources to a retaliatory strike."

"Who's to say the Junta leadership isn't insane?"

"Touché. But what about the Rasa?" He mentally kicked himself for using the term Tirrano had coined in medical. As apt as it was, it sounded so derogatory.

"Whatever role she played, clearly she got herself dumped. Maybe her usefulness ended."

"That we can both agree on," he said, "as it's pretty clear the operation was far too clinical for a mistake as big as leaving someone behind."

"But you're otherwise still not convinced?"

"No. Not with other ships and gates going silent."

"Very small numbers though," Tirrano said. "Could be just coincidence."

"You don't seriously believe that?"

"I think I'm going to wait for a proper reason to

discard the possibility."

They had reached the doors to Brant's office, and he stopped dead. He turned as if to see her off. "Well, this is me. Lots to do."

She inclined her head slightly. "Need any help?"

"No thanks, I'm good."

"Let me know if you change your mind."

Brant smiled weakly as Tirrano turned on her heel and tossed her hair. Before she was even out of sight down the corridor, he had entered his office and secured the doors behind him, isolating the compartment from the rest of the station.

"Fuck that!" He said.

○ ○ ○

Rendir Throam was boiling up inside, for two reasons. The first was that he had taken a very large dose of his pre-workout mix, and not left quite enough time since his last intake of protein powder. The combination was remarkably productive, and he kept having to belch away the excess gas. The hot prickly face and feeling of floating slightly above his own body he could deal with. But the gas was making decisions for him about what he was going to do with his diaphragm and his lungs and his shoulders, and as a natural consequence of this subterfuge it was playing hell with his form.

The second reason, the one voted most likely to give him a peptic ulcer, was the gaggle of idiots who seemed intent on ruining his gym session.

He could not really say or do anything direct, for the idiots were *Hammer* crew. If he smashed one of them to the deck for getting in his way he would not only end up clapped in irons for the rest of the mission, but Caden would probably be lecturing him for the duration. He could rage quietly to himself though, and nobody would be any the wiser.

There were three of them, clustered around the squat rack while they chatted, with one standing within it as if about to spring into action at any moment. That one was flicking through screens on a wearable holo while he talked to his buddies. He sprang nowhere.

Funny how the squat rack seemed to be the equivalent of a water cooler on virtually every planet, station, and ship where Throam had visited a gym. He could explain away the behaviour of these guys as a means of combining light exercise with a bit of social interaction. They were, after all, stuck on a starship which provided a reasonably Earth-like gravitational pull, but few chances to meet new people. Maintaining both fitness and friendships was very important if your duty rotation was measured in months rather than in days. He knew this full well, having spent a year on the *Embolden* when he was still attached to the Fearsome 310th.

Okay, so he had himself not spent that much time socialising in those days, because he had had Euryce Eilentes' bunk to dive into at the end of each of her shifts. However, he *had* spent enough time in the well-equipped 'workout hall' on that fine, majestic carrier to see that it was — for other people at least — a social hub of sorts. Had he not had his own specific goals for his body at the time, he would nonetheless have still been in there every day, maintaining his strength and speed and cardiovascular performance along with everyone else. Like them he had a responsibility to be fit for his duties, but at least he also had the benefit of enjoying it. He could understand why others did not; why they saw exercise as a tedious necessity, and why they combined it with their friendly diversions whenever they could. He just did not agree with them.

On any other day it would not have bothered him so much; he would have just concluded that these particular idiots were unmotivated. But today was leg day, and he needed the squat rack. He knew exactly what would happen when he started to try and split his sets between the squat rack and the leg curl: whether it was malicious or subconscious, whichever piece of equipment he was using, at least one of those guys would drift over to monopolise the other, until eventually he would either be asking them to move every time he switched exercises, or he would go insane and kill them all or himself or everyone else or combinations thereof.

He could do it. He was boiling up inside. He was boiling up inside, and he had *training*. He could definitely do for them all.

Fantasising about violence was one of Throam's most useful coping mechanisms. He rarely, if ever, enjoyed actually *being* violent, except for those occasions on which he was able to utterly destroy something inanimate. Destruction was fun. It was only in his mind's eye though that he allowed himself to get carried away with the living.

He would be the first to admit that pharmaceuticals were a large part of it. The medi-training cycle he favoured was excellent for building and maintaining muscle, but the excess testosterone could be a real bitch. The start of every cycle also included a run of methandrostenolone, which not only caused a rise in blood pressure — contributing no doubt to the sense of boiling inside — but also tended to short-circuit his emotions. He found himself angry at nothing, angrier still at things that should not have made him angry, and angriest of all at things that would usually make him slightly annoyed. When anything happened which on a normal day would make him fly into a rage, he would have to go and lock himself in the head for a while. It was safer for everyone that way.

Today, near the end of the first week of his latest cycle, was a *very* bad day to annoy Rendir Throam.

He was using drop sets on the leg curl, and racked up the weight to increase the resistance on his muscles. It took literally seconds to move the pin, nowhere near enough to fill the thirty seconds of rest time he was allowing himself between these sets. He watched the idiots some more.

They were *still* chattering away. The one standing in the squat rack had not yet moved in any way that looked like an exercise. Two of them had quite defined chests, and reasonable enough arms considering they were serving on a starship rather than in a MAGA unit, but every one of them had skinny legs.

Quads? Thighs? Calves? Nah brah, curls and bench press! What day is leg day? *No fucking day*, that's what day.

And they had the nerve to stand in the squat rack.

Twenty-eight, twenty-nine, thirty. Rest period finished. He started the next set, pulling the weight away from the deck plates by contracting his hamstrings. The movement up was explosive; on the way down, he allowed his quads some benefit by lowering the weight slowly, controlling the descent.

Out of sheer surprise, he nearly lost his rhythm when he saw the one in the squat rack lift up the barbell that was suspended between the stands. Surely he was not truly removing weights from it? Yes, and his friends were helping him. Throam knew from the colour of the weights that they had taken eighty kilos off the bar, leaving twenty behind.

Twenty kilos. Even with those skinny legs — and even though I would normally advocate pushing just beyond your limit, not doing ego reps — have some self-respect man. A child could squat more than that!

He nearly spat out his own tongue when the curling began. Biceps curls. With twenty kilos. *In the squat rack.* More than anything in the many worlds, he now wanted to break a skull.

Once upon a time, it would always have taken chemical assistance to make Rendir Throam this angry. His mothers had raised him to be the stoic, the reed that would bend in the wind. These days though, truth be told, his rage was not just a combination of pharmaceuticals and the provocations of skinny flight deck officers. He had for a few years now secretly found it easy to get angry at almost anything, ever since Thundercunt had left with his son.

What a *bitch*.

He used the anger to fuel the next contraction, and the padded roller bashed hard against his glutes. Perhaps a little too much fuel, Rendir.

He could not bring himself to use her real name any more. Thundercunt seemed perfectly appropriate, given the circumstances, and the more he thought about what she had done the more he favoured it over her real name anyway.

Again, foam rollers slammed against his glutes.

The boy was not even a year old when Thundercunt had spirited him away to some desperately obscure world near the Orion arm's coreward fringe. Throam had been on a three-day training exercise at the time, and he had come home to a written note. It was just over half a page long.

Rollers slammed against glutes.

Caden had wanted them to go and confront her together, even if he was just there for moral support and did not actually get involved. He was good like that. "I had my father in my life for just about twelve Solars, and that wasn't nearly enough," he had said. "You owe it to your boy to do whatever you need to do." But the time was denied to them. No, the answer came, your mission will be here, until then. And after that, you will do this. And so on.

Rollers, glutes.

It was not even as if she did not know what she was getting at the time. Throam had hardly changed while they were seeing each other, and he was much the same near the end of their relationship as he was at the beginning of it. If the strict requirements of his duties bothered her so much, if she resented the time his gym sessions stole from her, if she found him even half as distant as she claimed, then she might have said something about it *before they had made a fucking baby*.

Rollers.

There was a hand, which magically intervened, and the foam roller slapped against the palm and fingers instead of his buttocks. He looked back over his shoulder to see Eilentes smiling down at him, the corners of her mouth turned up sweetly and her eyes narrowed with those tiny little creases in the corners, the ones he had always thought were cute. Ten Solars had somehow failed to deepen them.

"Getting carried away?"

"Euryce, I didn't see you."

"No, I guess not. You were off in your own little world."

He smiled like a boy who had been caught out. "You know me." He unhooked his legs from the curl and swung them around to sit on the bench. "I love my own little world."

"One day you won't come back," she said.

"I'll always come back, as long as you're here."

She smiled knowingly, tipping her head to one side, and walked off in the direction of the cross trainers. As if she had just decided on a reply, she paused half way and turned around. "When did you suddenly decide that?"

"As soon as I saw you aren't wearing a sports bra."

Eilentes gestured rudely at him, but her expression betrayed her. She clearly approved of his observation skills.

She started up a cross trainer, and her arms began pumping back and forth, legs swinging on their plastic cradles in opposite time. Throam could not take his eyes off her buttocks. He was transfixed.

"Hey Euryce," he shouted.

She looked over her shoulder and raised her eyebrows inquisitively.

"Fancy a fuck?"

Her smile was his answer.

– 12 –
Operation Seawall

Stiletto and her companions sliced out of the bound wormhole purposefully, still in formation. The Laearan gate had done its job perfectly, drawing the terminus near and tightly dampening the turbulent churning of the spatial passage.

"Report," Pensh said brusquely.

His COMOP, a young woman in her mid-twenties, flicked her eyes up from her holo. "All systems normal, Admiral. Good jump."

"Good jump indeed," he said. "The other ships?"

"*Dagger* shows green lights. *Sai* reports she has taken damage: minor enmeshment event."

"Serious?"

"It's coming through now, Sir." She studied the data that the injured ship was sharing with *Stiletto*. "A small breach in their auxiliary life support system. Not critical, but it will need attention sooner rather than later."

"Instruct *Sai* Actual to make dry dock at Fort Laeara immediately. I want that ship battle-ready again as soon as possible."

"Aye, Sir."

He rose from his command chair and stepped fore, towards the wide view port that fronted his carrier's command deck.

The vista was breathtaking. *Stiletto* was on a direct course for the fortress, headed away from the blindingly white Laearan star. Ahead, the massive bulk of Fort Laeara sat squatly and obstinately dead centre in Pensh's view. But it was not the station that was so impressive.

Between the carrier and the station lay the Second, Fourth, Fifth, Sixth, Ninth, and Eleventh fleets of the Imperial Combine's naval armada.

Set in the inky dark backdrop of intra-stellar space, ablaze in the direct light from the star behind him, the hundreds of ships reflected enough light back at Pensh to make him shield his eyes. He was not sure if it was the view port compensating or if he simply became accustomed to the glare, but either way within moments he was able to look again. The scene had lost none of its impact.

He saw frigates and destroyers, corvettes and carriers, battleships and dreadnoughts. Here and there were variants — light hulls, heavy hulls, even the ungainly torpedo boat modification. Glistening like so many shards of a splintered diamond, they meandered slowly around the star in sympathy with the nearby fortress.

In amongst them all drifted Guardian Shields, each a vast, roughly hewn dish propelled by a long drive module stemming from the centre of the aft surface. No two of the Guardians were exactly alike.

"Incredible," he murmured.

And there, near the middle of the armada, his attention was drawn to a heavy dreadnought, easily twice the size of the next largest ship. Across its dorsal surface he saw a pink blob, and knew even at such great distance that it was a huge painting of a clenched fist. It could only be the *Love Tap,* Groath Betombe's irreverently named flagship.

The moniker made Pensh wince every time he heard it mentioned — especially at high level meetings — but Betombe's ship-naming policy was tolerated by Fleet Command, if only on the basis of recognising his contributions to liberty and security. There were much more colourful and dubious names in the Fourth Fleet. Betombe might well be a strategic genius, but Pensh suspected quite strongly that the old coot was also barking mad.

"Contact the fortress." He turned briskly to face his COMOP officer. "Find out where Fleet Admiral Betombe is, and whether or not he expects to see me in person."

"At once, Admiral."

○ ○ ○

Captain Santani had changed her whole attitude toward Caden willingly, the moment she heard about the bodies of the three Viskr commandos. That tiny ball of rock at the edge of the Deep Shadows had turned out to be significant after all. He had been right, about Herros as well as Echo. She hoped he had not taken any of her earlier objections to heart; after all, she had only been looking out for her crew.

Now, in the wardroom of her beloved *Hammer,* she waited with quiet patience as the Shard discussed his mission with — for some reason she could not fathom — a minor intelligence drone based back at Kosling.

"Any luck with the examination of Gemen Station?" Caden was asking.

"Nothing of any real use," said Brant's hologram. "We got plenty of DNA and fingerprints, but all of them from people who were supposed to be there."

"The computers?"

"They knew what they were doing: wrote over the record blocks with multiple passes of gibberish. Even the holographic storage couldn't survive that."

Caden sighed. "Well, the link between Echo and Herros is pretty clear, even if we don't understand quite what it means."

"Agreed. My seniors have been apprised, and they've informed the admiralty. Fleet Command have started mobilising already."

"I gathered; we already said goodbye to Admiral Pensh. He's been ordered to rendezvous with Betombe in the Laeara system."

"Things are moving quickly."

"Too quickly. We've been down this road before, and so have the Viskr. You'd think everyone would have learned their lesson by now."

"Apparently a few people missed that day at school."

"You know, the sooner the fighting starts, the sooner those weapons of yours will be deployed. I could really do with knowing what the worst case scenario might be."

Brant was silent for a few moments, and Santani found herself wondering if the holographic projector had frozen up. But no, his eyes closed and he exhaled slowly.

"Assuming just one warhead were to be deployed against any given target planet, the Viskr could erase our Perseus arm colonies in a matter of months."

"What are they?"

The Shard's tone was flat and edged with ice, his lack of patience now so brittle and demanding that he was unable to hide it. Santani gathered from the context that Eyes and Ears had been keeping information from him. She found herself leaning forwards in anticipation, but no answer came.

"Brant, *what are they?*"

"You know what will happen to me if anyone finds out I told you."

"I know the risks. But then I also know the Empress. Whatever your supervisors have to say about it, they'll be over-ruled."

"You'd better be right about that."

"I guarantee it."

Brant flashed a half-hearted smile, but his face dropped again as he gave his explanation. "Their short name is Atmospheric Dispersal Warheads. They're designed to introduce biotoxins into a planetary ecosystem."

Santani finally leant her voice to the discussion. "Is that all? Biowarfare? That's been around for centuries."

"Not like this," said Brant. "*Nothing* like this."

"Go on," said Caden. "You told me before these were chemical weapons, not biological. I'm guessing the other shoe is about to drop?"

"Yes. The warheads themselves aren't biological. But they *do* contain a unique chemical substrate. It's that part that's the real innovation. What makes them so terrible."

"What does this substrate do?"

"It protects the payload. Many of the most virulent and horrific diseases are also desperately fragile when they're exposed, when they're outside the body. This system shields them from damage.

"The warhead enters an atmosphere and cruises at altitude until it has dispersed the substrate as a fine mist. The payload remains insulated from the environment. Wind and rain spread it far and wide, letting it percolate down through the entire ecosystem."

"Worlds..." Santani breathed.

"And what exactly would this 'payload' be?"

"Well that's just it," said Brant. "It could be practically any biological agent. But whatever the warheads are loaded with, by the time it's detected it will already be attacking aggressively, and impossible to contain. These weapons were designed to create persistent ecological catastrophes, not just local infections. Global wildfire."

Santani felt ill. The spectre of viral genocide was much more than she had expected to hear about when she came to the wardroom with Caden. Just push a button, and below you a world dies in slow agony. The idea was appalling, and she paled. Give her a straight ship-to-ship fight any day.

Caden however had remained as stone while Brant finished describing the weapons. "No wonder the Navy is acting so quickly," he said. "I imagine Command will be willing to burn entire worlds to ashes if it will bury this monster. They're not going to wait long for me to find out where those weapons are; the armada will make a preemptive strike while it still can."

"It's like the saying goes," said Brant. "When you steal from the devil, you had better be ready to stand and fight."

"It's the fighting I'm worried about. If the Viskr have these weapons, if they *know* what they have, they'll be galvanised by that."

"We have lead time. They'll need to figure out how to deploy them, propagate their payloads, and actually get the things to their targets."

"Get rid of those first two stages," Caden said. "They have our data and our scientists. Let's assume their understanding of the weapons is a given, and also that they had biological agents ready and waiting before they launched this attack."

"Then they still need to reach their targets."

Santani had some colour back in her cheeks now the conversation had moved on. "What's to stop them opening a wormhole directly in the path of a target planet, and dumping a warhead through it?"

"Range," said Caden. "Our gates won't respond to theirs, so any wormholes they open will be unbound. Firing warheads through an unbound wormhole would be like shooting while blindfolded. They'd never hit the target."

"If the warheads got through at all," Brant added. "The longer an unbound wormhole is, the more violent the passage. Chances are they'd break up in transit."

"I see where you're going with this," Santani said. "The trick then is to use our fleets to press their borders; deny them the close range they would need to use offensive wormholes."

Caden nodded. "Exactly. That way we only have to worry about defending the colonies from launches made from ships, which are much easier to detect ahead of time and present us with larger targets."

"Well I'm glad that's all sorted out," said Brant.

Caden glared at him. "I take it Admiral Pensh knows all this?"

"I'm not sure, but Betombe will. I'd bet my life

he's already planning a line of defence."

"You'd be betting *all* of our lives," Santani said. "Once we're done here, ensure that you check."

"You want me to speak to the admiral myself?"

"If you leave it to me or Caden, it will be obvious you've told us everything."

"Good point, Captain, good point."

Santani rubbed her eyes. It had been a long, long day already, and this revelation about the apocalyptic conflict they might soon face was certainly not helping. She longed for the comfort of her bunk. The sheets were fresh on that morning, and she could hear it calling to her.

"Is there anything else?"

"Yes," said Caden.

Damn the man. Yes he was smart, and yes he had been right. But didn't he love the sound of his own voice? "Go on."

"As far as I'm concerned, my mission is still current. It would be in everyone's best interests if I carried on."

Brant looked hopeful. "What do you suggest?"

"I'm basically back at square one, aren't I? The only real lead is out of her head. That being said, there's nothing to suggest the weapons have yet left Imperial space."

"True, but how does that help?"

"I don't suppose it does. Let's go back to basics."

"I'm all ears."

"Brant, I want every starport, station, dock, ship and government facility between here and the edge of known space on the look out for anyone who worked on either Echo or Herros. Use names, DNA, medical records, even personal links or holos they might have registered with a city network;

anything. And don't just wait for news as it's happening, check back two months as well."

"I can do that," Brant said. "Don't even need to run this one by Branathes. In fact I can submit those queries right now."

Santani drummed her fingertips on the desk while she and Caden watched Brant work, the operator biting his lip as he tapped and swiped at his holo.

"Done," he said at last. "I've passed the search on to the gate network. It'll be routed through to all exit points as each gate forwards its next databurst."

"Thanks," Caden said. "Let's hope it turns something up."

Brant was about to reply, but stopped and flicked his eyes down. Caden had heard his holo chime faintly over the comms channel.

"I've got a result back already."

"Don't keep us in suspense," Santani said, with the slightest hint of sarcasm.

"Ignore me. It's just telling me about the Rasa. Of course we know she's at Kosling."

"The Rasa?" Caden was puzzled.

"Oh, yes; Amarist Naeb. That's what we're calling her now, apparently. Well, it's a term for her condition. Because she's blank."

"Fair enough."

Another faint chime sounded, somewhat distorted. Brant's face blurred momentarily as he read from his holo.

"Doctor Danil Bel-Ures," Brant said. "Project supervisor at Gemen Station. She arrived in the Meccrace system two days ago. Must have left Herros just after they sent their last databurst."

"Any idea what she's doing at Meccrace?"

"It's where her family lives."

"Still," said Caden, "worth following up on. If I were you I'd have some of your field agents bring her in."

Santani stood up. "This could go on all night. If I'm not on the command deck, I'll be in my quarters."

Before she had begun to move, a third chime sounded over the comm. Brant's eyes flicked back and forth, then widened.

"Oh. Oh *shit*."

Santani sat down again. "What is it?"

"Medran Morlum," Brant said. "He was one of the geologists on Echo, a physical chemist."

"What about him?" Caden said.

"Oh, fuck me sideways! Caden, he arrived on Aldava *after* the attack on Echo. He's been where you are right now!"

° ° °

"Make no mistake, Operation Seawall *is* an act of aggression," said Fleet Admiral Groath Betombe. "As of this moment the Perseus theatre of war is once more considered active and hostile."

From the moment he had been ordered to the rendezvous, Pensh had had no other illusions. The Laeara system was not just the ideal place from which to protect the Imperial worlds along the Viskr border; it was also the perfect staging area for an incursion into Viskr territory and, if necessary, for the invasion of Riishi itself.

The bright white star sat near the inner edge of the Perseus arm, a stone's throw away from the Orion arm and just at the point where the two dense stellar bands started to run parallel. It flanked a pinch point which could be used to bar access to the colonies downstream on the Perseus arm, with the added benefit that reinforcements for the upstream edge of the Orion arm could be easily arranged, should the Viskr attempt a retaliatory incursion of their own.

Betombe certainly knew what he was doing, Pensh reflected. But then, as far as the Laeara system went, this was not his first rodeo.

"This operation is the first part of a vital campaign, which will ensure the safety of our Perseus arm colonies. Now, as to why you are all here: it is my intention to enter Viskr space, and to force their fleets to pull away from their own borders."

There was a very brief murmur as the officers summoned by Betombe reacted.

"Operation Seawall is intended to drive the Viskr armada away from the border worlds. We believe we know their objective, and this effort will deny them the opportunity to achieve it. Without that opportunity, Commander Operations believes their forces will back down. For now, at least.

"The Eyes and Ears listening programme has provided us with the latest intelligence on Viskr movements along the border. I will be splitting this armada into a number of task forces, which will make co-ordinated incursions, to herd the strongest enemy fleets deeper into their own territories."

"And what if they don't back off from us?"

The woman standing next to Pensh looked incredulous, as if Betombe had asked her to do something impossible. Perhaps she is right, he thought.

"Captain Riese, a fair question. I would imagine it's one that has occurred to everyone here. Thank you for asking."

She took her seat as he gave his answer.

"If they don't back off, then we will begin to hit civilian targets until they learn to be more cooperative."

A ripple of disquiet spread amongst the gathered officers.

"I should add that we don't expect it will come to that. The listening posts have monitored unusual movements for the past few weeks. Viskr border forces appear to be moving almost randomly, breaking apart and redeploying without any perceptible strategic goal. As a defence force, their movements give them the appearance of being ineffectual. It is the opinion of Commander Operations that the Junta has appointed an incompetent to oversee those fleets.

"We've seen this before. The command structure of their navy is shaped more by nepotism from above than merit from below. In this case it certainly looks as though there is no forward planning involved in the border patrols. The ship commanders will be at the limits of their patience already, and we will exploit that."

It was clear from her expression that Riese remained unconvinced. "How exactly will we be exploiting it, Sir?"

"We will be decapitating every fleet we come into contact with. Your primary targets are capital ships and command facilities. Cripple them, scatter the remainders, and then move on— Admiral Pensh?"

Pensh had raised his hand. He felt all eyes turn to him. "The Gousk battle station will surely take some decapitating?"

"Very true, which is why *Love Tap* will be leading the task force that hits the Gousk system."

"Admiral." Riese's tone conveyed plainly to Pensh that she did not share Betombe's optimism. "How confident are you that their forces will withdraw?"

"Command projects a high probability, based on past experience. Also, take into account that the border worlds are relatively low in value. The Junta would rather consolidate its defences than spread them thin. Historically, the Viskr have been very consistent in this regard. I'm sure our downstream colonies would attest to that."

A chuckle passed through the room, but Riese took no part in it. "When we hit their command points, the rest of their border fleets *will* retaliate."

"You will of course defend yourselves. Our objective is to make the border regions as hostile as possible for the Viskr forces."

"I see. In other words we will be picking fights, knowing full well that they will respond."

"Basically yes."

"What's to stop their gates from interdicting against our withdrawal?"

"Nothing at all. If they attempt to interdict, make the gate your primary target. But my suspicion is that they will not wish to prevent our forces jumping away."

"One more question, Sir, if I may. Why exactly are we opening this old wound again?"

Betombe hesitated before he answered, fixing Riese with a hard stare. "Because Command believes the Viskr have acquired a significant weapons technology, which they intend to use against us."

Pensh saw a perplexed look flash across Riese's face, but she appeared to have run out of questions. Either that, or she had decided she was coming dangerously close to disputing a fleet admiral'-s strategy in front of a room full of flag officers.

"Rest assured, Captain, that the show of strength the Viskr Junta likes to advertise is as much for its own people as it is for us. It's smoke and mirrors, by and large. In battle they are no more capable than you or I."

In Pensh's opinion, Riese looked as though she were already resigned to the fate Betombe had prescribed her. He knew her better than that though; she would keep the rest of her misgivings to herself until something went wrong, at which point she would be making angry representations to Commander Operations.

"Before we move on to commands and assignments, are there any other questions?"

Pensh looked around the briefing hall, and saw dozens of unquestioning faces staring back at Betombe. Unlike Riese, the other captains apparently had no issues with this operation.

Things were certainly about to get interesting.

– 13 –
Unassuming Aldava

In some ways, Jasamma was almost exactly like Damastion. But in others, Elm had found quickly, it could not be more different. All the colours here were bold and vivid for a start, the weather could change at a moment's notice, and he could do things here that were — for whatever reason — forbidden on his homeworld.

Banks of pure white stratus interrupted the deep indigo of the planet's sky, turning what might have been an oppressive canopy into an appealing, ever-shifting canvas. Far off in the east, dim vertical bands betrayed the rain that a cumulonimbus leviathan unleashed onto distant foothills.

Here though it was still dry and warm, and Elm played in the shallows of the serene lake just a stone's throw from where Father had erected their tents. Unlike the Damastion freshwaters near their home, the inland waterways of this part of Jasamma's temperate zone held no dangerous predators. Elm had been free to make as much mischief as he could in the clear, warm waters.

Father was laying on a recliner while he read from his holo. He had claimed he was only bringing fiction with him, but soon after they had arrived Elm had spotted him reading what appeared to be a map of the border territories. He had chided Father in the precocious manner of young children, not understanding the reason for his own objection. For him, it was simply enough that Father had said one thing, and done the opposite.

"You're right," Father had said. "I did say I wouldn't bring work with me."

"We're supposed to be on *holiday*," Elm had persisted.

With a smile Father had turned off the holo and picked up a towel. "How about a swim?"

That had been almost two hours ago, and Elm was now alone in the water, pale and wrinkled. Father peered over the top of his holo occasionally to check that Elm was still within sight.

Elm decided that for now he had experienced all the entertainment the water had to offer, and splashed back to the shore with exaggerated, sloshing steps. When he reached dry land he ran with arms waving, shaking off the water, until he was free of the sandy bank and the brilliant emerald of waxy native grass was beneath his feet. He found the towel that Father had left for him, and draping it around his slight shoulders he ran back to the camp.

Father placed his holo in his lap and smiled. "Had enough?"

"I got bored." Elm shivered. "I'm really hungry."

"That's hardly surprising; you've been jumping around all afternoon."

Father got to his feet and tossed the holo onto the recliner, then went over to a ring of soot-smudged stones that surrounded the remains of their last fire. He took twigs and broken branches from the pile nearby, and arranged them inside the ring.

"Can't we use the grill?" Elm asked.

"No, let's do it properly," Father said, "otherwise we might as well be at home."

"But it will take *ages*."

"You won't die of hunger, Elm."

Sure enough, he managed to survive long enough for the fire to take hold, and Father cooked them both fish from the lake. Elm was given the task of finding leaves and berries, specially selected from the list of safe and edible plants that Father had downloaded from the local network. They sat on a log that someone had once dragged down to the shore, looked out over the glassy surface of the silent lake, and ate.

When they were done, Father was quiet. Elm looked at him expectantly, hoping that his customary war story or anecdote would follow the meal. But Father stared out across the waters, as motionless as they were, as if he were a world away.

At length, Elm broke the silence. "Father, tell me a story about a battle."

Father looked at him and smiled wanly. "Not now son."

"Why not? I want to know about the war."

"Because I need to talk to you about something else."

Elm recognised what he thought was sadness in Father's eyes. The man looked tired all of a sudden.

"Your mother and I have been talking about separating," Father said. "We aren't good for each other any more."

Elm felt a silent explosion go off in the top of his head, *pop*, the shock of what he had heard jarring his comprehension. He did not know how to react.

"I want you to know that we both still love you."

"Are you leaving?" Elm was almost shouting.

"It makes sense for you to stay with your mother. I'm going to be away most of the time anyway, as long as this war carries on."

Elm was speechless, and a cold, empty hollow formed in the place where his stomach should have been. A sharp blade of pain stabbed upward from it, and lodged in his throat. There was nothing he could do but cry.

"It will be okay." Father put his arm around him. "In some ways it won't be any different to the way things are now."

Elm pulled away sharply, ducking his shoulders under Father's arm. "No it *won't* be okay! Why would you leave?"

"You'll still see me just the same as you do now, Elm."

"It won't be the same. You're leaving me!"

"I'm not, I'm leaving your mother. Believe me, it will be much better for the both of us this way."

"How will that be *better*?"

"You'll understand when you're older."

"I don't want to understand when I'm older, I want to understand now. Why would you leave me?"

"Please believe me son, I have no intention of leaving you. It's your mother and I who have the problem. It's your mother I'm leaving, and I will love you just as much as I do now."

"Why can't I live with you?"

"You know that's not possible," Father said. "I'm going to be back on the *Curtailer*, on the front lines. Families aren't allowed on warships."

"You're just saying that," Elm sobbed. "You don't want me with you."

"It's not allowed."

"Then don't go back."

"You know I have to go back, Elm."

"No you don't," he shouted. "You don't have to go back, you have to be a father."

Before Father could reply, Elm leaped to his feet and stormed away, tears stinging his eyes. He picked up speed, not caring which direction he was headed in, and ran into the tree line.

Under the canopy the air was still and humid. Here and there clouds of insects buzzed around each other in a complicated courtship dance which heralded the twilight of their short lives. Elm was oblivious to them, and clambering through low branches and undergrowth he tried his best to find a place to hide.

After a short time he came to the base of a huge tree, its hulking roots creating sheltered wedges, and he sat down heavily on rubbery moss and a litter of crimson leaves.

Deep inside him, in the place where he kept the bad feelings, he could feel the inevitable stirring. Something was twisting inside him, trying to expand. He had long ago learned to bury the emotions that hurt him, pushing them down into a single point and forgetting all about them, but sometimes they fought back. Sometimes they clawed their way out of the pit, emerged from the emptiness to confront him.

Today was one of those rare occasions when he was not strong enough to keep them down. The gates burst, and the feelings escaped. Leading the offensive came resentment, abandonment, and worthlessness, riding on a foaming wave of personal affront.

He wrapped his arms around his knees, buried his face in them, and cried.

It was some time before he ran out of tears, and the light was beginning to fade. In the distance he could hear Father's voice, his name being bellowed with increasing urgency. He put his hand on one of the great roots to help himself up, and almost immediately felt a tickling followed by a sharp stabbing sensation.

Elm yanked his hand back, cradling it protectively with the other, and looked at the root. On its back, close to where it had rolled when he pulled his hand away so sharply, a long white creature writhed and flexed its centipede legs. Vivid pink striations stood out against its milky, segmented body, and Elm remembered reading that this was the warning colour displayed by so many of Jasamma's venomous fauna. His hand was already starting to burn, as if the blood itself were boiling.

He backed away from the creature — which was already righting itself — and ran from the tree, heading back the way he had come. He ducked beneath branches, leapt over stones and fallen trees, snapping twigs and churning up the carpet of fallen leaves as he barrelled through the woods in the direction of Father's voice.

By the time he reached the tree line, his vision was starting to swim. His ears rang, and a dull, throbbing pain filled his head, elbowing out everything else. He staggered the rest of the way, every thought breaking apart and becoming difficult to hold on to. He was vaguely aware of Father catching him just before he fell to the ground.

There were flashes after that. A voice here;

Father's urgent message to someone on the holo. A picture there; his own hand, swollen and bruised, held up in front of him while Father examined the bite. But mostly there was the molten hot pain, and the deafeningly noisy churning void of delirium.

Most of the experience was mercifully rejected by his memory. But in months to come, he would remember that he had awoken to hear the shrieking roar of air jets, his bones shaken painfully by the forces of a rapid descent. While his vision swam and the shape of things around him seemed to bend and warp, he had realised that he was looking at the inside of a medivac lander, bound no doubt for some Jasamman emergency ward. Before he lost consciousness again, he had felt the vehicle shake hard and veer off sharply to one side —

° ° °

—the deck swinging one way then the other in response to the turbulence.

Eilentes' voice crackled over the comm. "Heads up, this is going to get rough."

Sure enough, the forward deck bucked hard as the nose of the lander rammed into a bank of high pressure, and the aft compartment immediately followed suit. Caden was glad for the padded restraints and headrest.

The blast shields were down over the view ports in the rear compartment of the MAGA lander, and in some ways he was glad of that too. With Eilentes at the controls, the traversal of Aldava's violent atmosphere was intimidating enough even without a good view of the approaching ground.

"If we survive this," Bro shouted, "I'll never

step foot in another lander again."

"What makes you think this is survivable?" Daxon shouted back.

"Hope. Pure hope."

"She's just showing off her skills," Norskine yelled.

"Showing off? Skills?" Bro shouted. "You can't polish a turd, sister."

Caden saw that Throam was grinning at him, and smiled inwardly. They both knew the troops had certainly experienced much more violent descents than this one; the banter must have been for their own benefit, seeing as Eilentes could not hear them from the separate flight compartment.

The only one of them whose expression of consternation looked entirely genuine was Bruiser, and he could be easily forgiven for it. His size made it impossible for him to fit into the standard safety seating, and he had lashed himself down with the same webbing that secured the cargo crates.

"Bruiser, you good?" Caden yelled it over the din of rushing air and vibrating bulkheads.

The Rodori bared his rows of sharp teeth and approximated a thumbs up. "Still here."

The angry roar of atmosphere faded away without warning, and Caden felt the seat pushing against him momentarily. The lander had decelerated hard.

"Ninety seconds to ground," Eilentes said over the comm.

"Thank fuck for that!" Bro said.

A grinding noise rang through the outer hull, and Caden saw that the blast shields were retracting from the view ports. He unbuckled his restraints and carefully made his way to the port opposite, holding on to the safety bars to keep himself upright.

Outside, the dismal grey skies of Aldava stretched as far as he could see. Only when Eilentes banked the lander did he see anything of interest, and it had barely been worth getting up for. Beneath them, on the floor of a wide valley, the city of Barrabas Fled pooled and sprawled like mould. Clusters of low buildings hunched together, separated only by virtually unmarked roads. Even allowing for the morning haze, there seemed to be almost no underlying order to the conurbation.

The city was pale, drab, and seemed almost totally colourless, even more so as the lander plunged into the shadow cast by the valley wall. The closer they came to the ground, the worse the visibility seemed to get, until finally on the approach to the outlying starport — such as it was — the air seemed to hang thick with dust.

When Eilentes delivered them safely to the ground, Caden did not bother waiting for the sergeant to get his men organised; even the prudent Lieutenant Volkas had agreed that a squad of four fire teams was more than sufficient for this visit, and that they would accompany Caden's team only as a precaution. He had already spoken to the sergeant — a grizzled lifer called Chun — before *Hammer* had dropped the lander into Aldava's atmosphere. Chun, as it turned out, was the same squad sergeant who had so loudly declined to stop Bruiser following Caden across the surface of Echo, even after ordering someone else to do the very same thing. He had the same view of the situation as Caden: his squad, Bullseye One-Three, would keep a low profile unless and until they were needed. That is, he had suggested, as low a profile as could be achieved with a Rodori and a bunch of excitable children in the mix.

Caden disembarked with Throam and surveyed what apparently passed for an arrivals and customs terminus; a long spur of a building stretching from the central hub all the way out to the landing area. Most of the walls were glass, and he could see that there was nobody inside. Nobody was waiting at the entrance to the terminus either, nor at the edge of the landing field itself. He wondered what was to stop anyone from just walking off in another direction. Looking around, the explanation was probably that Barrabas Fled was marginally more interesting than a wasteland full of scrub. Nobody on *Hammer* had been able to explain to him why the capital had been built in a dusty and unappealing part of the planet, when this continent supported a perfectly good tropical band just below the equatorial. He did not quite care enough to go find out whilst they were on the surface.

The hatch popped in the side of the cockpit, and Eilentes swung herself out of the lander, using the recessed rungs in the hull to climb down to the ground. She jumped the last metre and grinned at Caden and Throam. "On the ground, safe and sound."

"Had every faith you'd keep us safe." Throam smiled back at her.

"But you might take some flak... from those in the back." Caden kicked himself for rhyming.

Chun appeared, circling around from the rear of the lander. He left his troops checking over the first of two Kodiak armoured vehicles they had rolled down the ramp.

"Might as well take Charlie fire team," he said.

Caden was happy enough with the suggestion. "Good idea, we're already acquainted."

"Well yeah, but what I meant was that you can take them off my hands. DAXON!"

Brokko Daxon was there in an instant. "Sarge?"

"Corporal, take your clowns and accompany Shard Caden into Barrabas Fled. I'll be holding this position. Any problems, you shout up immediately."

Daxon saluted in an almost comically sloppy fashion, before moving off to round up his team. "Yo Bruiser," he shouted, "saddle *up*! Norskine, where the fuck has Bro gone?"

○ ○ ○

It was very easy, as conspicuous as the group was, to forgive the locals for staring. But no matter how many times Caden saw someone stop and gape slack-jawed at the passing soldiers, the feeling of being watched stubbornly refused to go away. It was not just that they *were* being watched; no, as crazy as it sounded even in his own head, he had the peculiar sensation that they were all of them being subjected to cold, calculating scrutiny. Something did not feel right about this town.

"These people are creeping the fuck out of me." Throam muttered in his ear as they walked.

"So it's not just me then," Caden said. "I can't put my finger on exactly what is wrong here."

"It's literally too quiet, for starters."

Caden realised the counterpart was completely right. Barrabas Fled was for all intents and purposes a combination of frontier town, transit hub, and trading centre. By all rights it should have been a boisterous and obnoxious calamity of sound and shoving and sweat. But the people on the streets seemed mute and evasive, and they were surprisingly few in number. Most of the shops and houses Caden and his companions passed had shutters or curtains closed across the windows and entrances. Instead of an ever-changing nebula of charcoal smoke and perfumes and the scent of cooked food, there was a moist, dirty odour, hanging in the air like a thin musk, the smell of mould and stagnation.

"Stay alert buddy. I don't like this any more than you do. Something is telling me we shouldn't be here."

"You and me both."

Apparently sensing the tone between Caden and Throam, Daxon leaned in. "What's going on?"

The corporal had been keeping pace with them both. Bro had taken point out of habit more than anything, with Norskine between him and the others. Bruiser trudged along in the rear, somewhat predictably drawing the lion's share of the stares and undeniably holding them for longer.

"This place is fucked up," said Throam.

Caden rolled his eyes. "We were just discussing the oddness of the locals."

"Yeah, I'd noticed. I don't think this place gets many visitors."

"It's supposed to be a gateway planet." Caden made it sound more like a question than a statement.

"Once upon a time maybe," said Daxon. "I guess demand for stopover towns ended real quick when the gate initiative ran up against the Deep Shadows. A lot of the planets along the edge are like this; only the systems with busy prime gates seem to attract new people."

"Doesn't explain why *these* people are all so

weird," Throam said. As he spoke, a woman carrying a bundle of blankets hurried out of their path and into an open doorway. Once over the threshold she turned and stared at them for a moment before slamming the door closed.

"They probably get left alone, for the most part. We march through the town with our big-ass guns and our big-ass Bruiser; that's bound to draw some attention."

Caden grunted his agreement, and stared at an elderly man who sat on a stone bench encircling a fountain. He was tanned and leathery, deep wrinkles lining his mouth and eyes while he squinted at the outsiders and smiled pleasantly. As they trudged closer, and began to pass by, he started to hum. Slow and mournful, the tune seemed to tug at something in Caden's memory, something which refused to surface. It was not a melody he remembered ever hearing, but somehow it was one that he knew.

The man turned his head as they passed, continuing to peer at them, smiling his faint smile and humming the same refrain over and over.

Caden was still feeling unsettled by the strange performance when they reached their objective, a large building on the edge of town furthest from the starport. It was what must have passed for a high class establishment on Aldava, the alcove-dotted walls lavishly festooned with conspicuously foreign display plants. The sound of gently dripping water betrayed an otherwise concealed irrigation system; expensive to run in this climate. A single portico entrance was walled on each side with elegantly wrought iron — not in a thousand years were those made on Aldava, Caden thought — and cornered with slender white pillars. A single step up into the portico area led onto a tiled mosaic floor, almost cold where the shade fell across it. As far as could be achieved in the city of Barrabas Fled, the premises were tastefully presented.

As he walked across the portico, a soft chime rang out in the entrance lobby. Within moments, the sounds of fluster and hurrying began to approach.

"Are these the premises of Joarn Kages?" Caden said, when the hurrier appeared.

The man the chime had summoned was huffing and puffing across the lobby, overweight and red-faced, a sweaty sheen on his forehead and upper lip. His fair hair was cut very short, presumably to hide the enthusiastic spread of his bald spot, and his fat fingers were over-burdened with gold rings. But the neglect he showed his body was not evident in his dress; he was as tastefully presented as the front of the building, adorned carefully and without ostentation. The clothing spoke of money, but money spent in just the right way.

He smiled expansively as Caden asked his question, threw his arms wide, and took a deep breath as he gave the shallowest of bows. "Welcome one and welcome all, indeed these *are* the premises of one Joarn Kages, and I have no doubt that you will find here everything you seek."

Caden raised his eyebrows. "Will I really? How very convenient."

"Why yes, even here in the doldrums of the galaxy there are answers to be had. Why go anywhere else?"

"Why indeed. Tell me, where is Mister Kages?"

"I myself am the dutiful servant of that particular obligation, Sir. And you... you are a Shard, specifically Elm Caden, the incarnate will of Her Most Radiant Majesty, the Empress Ecoria Faustrathes Maerane, may the light of a thousand suns shine down upon Her."

As carefully as he had selected the fine fabrics for his clothes, and the skilled people who had cut and stitched them, Kages did not seem to have the same aptitude for assembling modest sentences. Caden forced himself to be patient with the man. The dramatic affectation alone was worth a backhander across the jaw, but he had never yet struck a man for being florid, and this was not the time to start.

"You already know who I am?"

"Anyone with any sense of self-preservation knows the faces of the Shards, Sir."

"I see. As it happens I have come here only for information, so there will be no need for self-preservation."

"But of course you have," said Kages. "That is why *everyone* comes here. Why else would anybody visit an information broker?"

"You had a visit from a human recently, a male. I need to know why."

"Ah, that is not the sort of information I sell. I simply can't confirm anything like that."

"It wasn't a question, Mister Kages. You *did* receive that visitor. Also I should probably mention at this point that I have no intention of buying anything from you."

"Sir, with or without payment, I do not provide information on my clients. In my line of work that would be suicide; in both the business sense, and the more obviously personal one."

"We didn't intend to give you the option."

The smile finally dropped from Kages's face,

and he cast a belatedly wary eye over Caden's companions. At Throam, glowering darkly with his arms folded; at Eilentes, hands on her hips as she tilted her head to eye him suspiciously; at Norskine, Daxon and Bro, all hanging back, their careless stances revealed as a sham by the way they held their rifles before them. And lastly at Bruiser, towering above even Throam and holding an enormous machine gun as casually as a child might hold a stick.

Kages swallowed emptily. "Perhaps you would care to discuss this somewhere more private?"

– 14 –
In Low Places

It had been remarkably difficult to get to the surface without being detected, far more so than Castigon had expected. He could not for the life of him fathom why the Empire cared so much about security on this crowded and tedious planet. Surely they had far more people wanting to escape than they had people wanting to sneak in? Low Cerin was known as an unrepentant dump even across the foreign worlds of Lemba and Gomlic space.

But he was here at last, and his major concern for the moment was only to put enough distance between him and the starport to guarantee that he would not be caught. When the tech he had bribed port-side finally got around to reporting he had 'found' a breach in the perimeter, Castigon intended to be very far away indeed. Sure, getting back into space might be a little trickier this time, certainly more difficult than it had been from Fengrir, but he would cross that bridge when he came to it. For the moment, he was actually doing quite well.

That being said, Firenz had been relatively easy to despatch, and it would not be wise to get carried away with such an early success. Her youthful counterpart had been as green as green could be, and Ider herself had been taken by surprise. Word of her death would have reached other Shards by now; they would be much less easily ambushed. Kulik Molcomb, for example, was paired with a very capable counterpart, and he had always seemed ready for anything.

Perhaps 'ready for anything' was doing Molcomb slightly too much of a service. Others might say he was constantly on edge — in fact they *did* say that — and those who were less polite would call him a crazy-eyed, paranoid stim junky. But none of the nicknames or whispered insults actually made him any less dangerous; he *would* be alert to threats and he *would* see Castigon coming. This one would need to be special.

Once, a long time ago, Molcomb had told Castigon one of his war stories, a tale of the grim days he had spent on the Perseus Front. At the height of the war, Molcomb had been one of many Shards sent by the Empress to — in his own words — 'royally fuck the enemy until they bled out of their asses'. As charming as the mental image was, it was not the reason why this particular story had stuck so stubbornly in Castigon's mind. No, the reason it was so indelible was because it contained clues that might help explain Molcomb's knack for survival; lessons for life and its preservation.

"We weren't expected to ever come back," Molcomb had told him. "She knew what She was asking us to do, we all did. Me and two others I know of, we came home. You know what She said to us? Nothing, the ungrateful bitch."

Castigon had been mesmerised throughout by the way Molcomb's tongue appeared to be too big for his mouth — a remarkable illusion of proportion considering that his jaw must have been one of the widest in the galaxy —and his teeth were like tombstones. His eyes too; they seemed to bulge out of the sockets as if they were intending to venture forth on their own at any moment. The Shard always looked grubby, as though he had come directly from a hiding place in a ditch somewhere. Streaks of grime and dusty sweat emphasised the bright blue ice of his irises and the whites of his giant eyes.

Distractions aside, Castigon had managed to pay enough attention to memorise the salient points of the tale.

"Ressingale was the end of the line," Molcomb told him. "We all knew it. Didn't expect anything but a fucking quick death. Detachment of Tankers got dropped in before us: supposed to smash back through the lines from the rear. Poor bastards were pulverised. And I mean *pulverised*. The Viskr were using hordes of skulkers."

There had followed a short intermission in which the Shard tried to explain to Castigon how a skulker worked, and Castigon tried to explain that he knew very well it was an autonomous robot sentry designed to rapidly deliver traumatic wounds to as many moving organic targets as possible, thank you very much. Even though that was essentially correct, Castigon still had to sit through a detailed explanation with lots of wild gestures thrown in for emphasis. He had started to suspect at this point that Molcomb was a lot more drunk than he was letting on.

"You can imagine what we thought when we 'chuted in. Tankers are supposed to be the heavy duty beasts — were then, still are — and we were up to our ankles in what was left of them. What the fuck were *we* going to do that they couldn't?

We weren't sappers and we weren't human juggernauts either.

"But we know there's no way off-world, right — no air support at all, for them or for us; too dangerous — and we know we have to finish the job. Ressingale has the only xtryllium production facility for a hundred light years that we have a chance of taking back, and Command says we can't win the campaign without xtryllium. As far as we're concerned it's liberate the planet, or die in the mud.

"So we dig in behind their lines, and every second of every day we're expecting to be torn to pieces by skulkers. We dig in and start laying our booby traps across their supply routes, and never know from one moment to the next if a cloud of whirling blades is about to come rolling across the ground and dice us.

"Imagine it. One day, two days, three... a week goes by, during which we have crawled, *crawled,* across fields of dead, black mud and rotten crops. Not just flat terrain mind; we're in and out of craters and ditches, and trenches too, up and down, and even climbing over bodies when we have to. Humans and Viskr alike, the ones who couldn't be recovered. We've not washed, barely slept, and eaten minimal rations. Only the stims are keeping us moving. Everything is wet. And every few minutes we're freezing where we are, waiting to see if that slight noise was a buddy moving out of time, or an enemy machine that's zeroed in on a heartbeat.

"And just when we think we're about to finish what we set out to do, just as we are about to lay the final traps, they change their pattern. They bring in an early resupply, and BAM! Up go our charges, our mines, our snares, BAM BAM BAM, popping all the way along the enemy lines, and there are Viskr running this way and that, firing at smoke and shadows, rounds zipping past our faces, mortars coming down every which way, and the fucking skulkers are going bat-shit *insane*.

"The Viskr were easy enough to pick off, most of them that weren't blown apart by our traps or killed by their own mortars, but the skulkers were vicious. Fuck knows how many they had, but those metal bastards were *everywhere*, whirring and whistling and slicing. We couldn't run, or they'd have had us; chopped us into little bits if we gave them the chance. So all we could do was dig in again.

"Five days we lay there, in the mud and the rain. Just dug right in, literally hollowed out the earth with our hands and boots, wriggled down into the ground as best we could. Two were killed where they were, this skulker that wouldn't give up. Kept chopping back and forth across the ground like it was determined to kill something for what we'd done. Never seen a machine behave like that motherfucker did, never in my life. I swear, when it found Jaias and pulled out her insides it was actually enjoying it. You know they build those things with vocalisations? It fucking *laughed*."

At this point, Castigon had realised that the rumours of Molcomb's prodigious appetite for stims were not in the least bit exaggerated. Everybody knew that skulkers were just dumb machines responding rigidly to specific stimuli. Yes they made noises, but they could not gloat or crow or scoff, and they certainly were not programmed to enjoy.

The story had meandered on for a while longer,

but he could not quite remember how the rest of it went. Most likely he had stopped listening by then, or Molcomb had rapidly become incoherent as he was wont to do when he drank. The bits that mattered though, the parts that gave an insight into the way Molcomb's brain responded to mortal danger, were still safely filed away.

Before long, Castigon would know if they had been worth holding on to.

○ ○ ○

Kulik Molcomb had been as amused with being sent to Low Cerin as ever he was with being sent anywhere, although to be fair to his keen sense of injustice it was true that the world offered plenty to complain about.

It was not just the planet he despised though, with its densely packed cities, lack of amenities, and widespread poverty; it was the ultimate pointlessness of his purpose here that made him burn with resentment. Nobody *cared* about the Coalition that much these days, and those who did sympathise with the movement were rarely invested enough to risk being charged with sedition.

Observe and report? Pah!

This was not, in his opinion, a job for a Shard. Eyes and Ears should be running this show, and not even officers — field agents would be perfectly adequate to the task. There must have been much better things he could be doing right now than scouring the dingiest corners of the Empire for people who had the nerve to not accept that their lives were basically awful. He had survived both Tochi *and* Ottomas, for goodness sake, and before them the entire Perseus conflict. How had it ever come to this?

He trudged through a narrow alleyway, covering his mouth and nose when his path was partly obstructed by a midden, which over time had been poured out of one of the overlooking buildings. Garbage and effluent, dumped directly onto the street. Nice. Insects crawled over the sprawling mound, foraging amongst the rotting scraps. The familiar orange and turquoise mottling of a powdery Blight plaque encrusted much of the oldest matter, and it reminded him not to linger in the unsanitary passageway for any longer than was strictly necessary. The plaque and its spores were not a threat to him, but the last thing he wanted when the time came to leave Low Cerin was to be stuck in quarantine awaiting decontamination. Decontamination was *never* fun, and when it came to the Blight it always seemed to take forever.

The sooner they got off this filthy planet, the better. He had already exhausted all of the potential leads that he came to the capital with, and failed to find any more. Big surprise. It was not that he was treating the endeavour as a box-ticking exercise, or doing the bare minimum he needed to do before he could honestly but inaccurately claim to have completed the mission. It was just that there really were no Coalition interests being advanced in the city. Each of the contacts he maintained here had looked at him as if he were mad when he asked about political dissidents. It was time to collect Rupus and go to the next city.

He had left Rupus Dyne drinking and whoring down-town, much to the counterpart's great satisfaction. Neither of them had felt it particularly important that they stick together, not on this assignment and not on this world. Molcomb had said Rupus would just get in the way if they went to meet his contacts together. Rupus had agreed, and said Molcomb would just get in the way if *he* came to the bordello.

They had split up.

Molcomb was beginning to regret it. If they had stayed together, he could have been on his way to the starport by now. Instead he was weaving his way through the cramped and dirty streets of the Empire's least impressive capital city. Next time he would—

He whirled and dropped at the same time, pivoting his body into cover while turning to face the threat. A single shot had been fired from the opposite side of the street, some way ahead of him, and he had felt the air being displaced when the bullet sliced past his cheek. He put his fingers up to his face, and they came away sticky and red.

People were screaming, panicked, running in the street like headless chickens. Except for one man, who walked towards him casually with a rifle and a grim smile. It was a man Molcomb had once hoped never to see again for as long as he lived.

Although he had not got his wish, he suspected immediately that it would probably not be an issue for very long.

○ ○ ○

Rupus Dyne woke up the very second his link started to chirrup. Groaning at the suddenness of the awakening, he shielded his eyes against the full daylight that streamed through the window. Akasi's arm was still draped across his chest, her forehead resting against his shoulder. More than anything, he wanted to stay right where he was. After all, he *had* paid.

Silently cursing Molcomb, he plucked his link from the night stand and placed it to his ear. When he clicked the button and answered, he was almost deafened by a staccato blast of automatic weapons fire. In a flash, he was off the bed and sliding into his trousers. Akasi rolled on her side and propped her chin on one hand, her elbow resting on the mattress.

"Who are you talking to?" She said.

Dyne ignored her. "How the fuck have you managed to get into a fight on this nothing planet?"

He slapped his holo onto his wrist, and brought up Molcomb's location. "I'll be there in six minutes."

"You're going? Come back real soon honey."

Dyne continued to ignore her as he scrabbled under the edge of the bed for his pistols. "Well it's not really my fault is it? You're the one who let me go whoring. You know how much I love whoring."

He mag-tagged the pistols to his outer armour, and grabbed his rifle from where he had slung it behind the door. "Yeah, well until I get there, just try not to die, okay?"

Akasi was pouting by the time he leaned across the bed to kiss her on the forehead.

"Thanks," he said.

◦ ◦ ◦

The situation was not great. Molcomb did not like being exposed one bit, and after finding such a great place to lie low he had already forced himself to move once by contacting Rupus. This new hidey hole was good, but much less ideal than the last one. If only he had found them in reverse order.

In the gloom of the stairwell, his holo was far too bright. He turned it off.

A scraping sound came from below, and he peered cautiously over the railing. Beneath him, in the entrance lobby, a figure was advancing slowly into the lobby: Castigon must have seen him enter the building, damn him to the Deep.

The figure was out of his line of sight again before he could get off a certain kill-shot. Molcomb withdrew silently, before Castigon could look up and spot him.

The last he had heard, Castigon had been serving hard time on Urx. Nice of the authorities to let him know the guy was being released! If indeed he was supposed to be back in the worlds.

Truth be told, after his initial relief that Castigon had been sent down, Molcomb had started to miss the crazy bastard. It had been very uncomfortable indeed to give evidence against his former ally. It occurred to him, what with the shooting and all, that Castigon might be a bit annoyed he had done it. That was a shame, because Molcomb had not really had any choice about testifying, and his part in all of that hard hardly been worthy of a deathly vendetta. But then Castigon had been away for a long time. And on Urx, of all places. What a shit-hole.

Even as a veteran of the last war, he was acutely aware that Castigon was a much better shot than he was. And a better blade, and a better fist, and at this point in their lives, he probably had better legs and lungs as well.

Rupus had better hurry the fuck up, he thought.

○ ○ ○

Castigon sighed to himself as he worked his way along the ground floor corridor. He had always expected Molcomb to go to ground, he had just hoped he would do it in a less complicated setting. But then, a Shard was hardly going to make things easy for him.

Most of the doors along the corridor were locked, and those rooms that were insecure were for the most part empty. The old apartment building was without utilities, and the rooms that were occupied were invariably tenanted by squatters. Some of the most wretched people Castigon had ever seen, in fact.

Eventually he came to the stairwell at the far end of the corridor, and rounded the corner of the first flight of steps carefully, his rifle at the ready. There was no way he was going to use the lift in this decrepit building; he had an acute sense of self-preservation, after all. In any case, in all likelihood it was without power.

There was nobody in the stairwell, and he emerged on the first floor corridor. Further down, perhaps some six rooms away, a thin figure with long hair was leaning against a wall. A drug-addled squatter, judging by the movements.

Ignoring the civilian he advanced along the corridor, checking rooms as he had on the ground floor, until he reached the far stairwell. Unbeknown to him, he walked through the very spot Molcomb had stood in when he watched Castigon enter the building, and followed the Shard's exact route up to the next floor.

Two identical floors later, he exited the stairwell and came up against a makeshift barrier. Someone had tried to create a barricade with furniture dragged out of the nearby rooms.

As defences went it was pretty poor, and he was able to push it over almost in one go. But the moment he had made a gap large enough to step through, the shooting began.

Rounds whizzed past him, sinking deep into the cheap plaster of the wall behind, some of them making hollow popping sounds as they passed through the flimsy furniture in the barricade. He had no real cover to speak of, just a few bits of wood and plasteel that screened the view from the corridor, so he returned fire on automatic.

The shooter was down the corridor, near the far end, and the gloom and range made it difficult to aim true. Luckily, what was so for Castigon was so for his opponent. Unwilling to stand firm in the line of fire, the figure hopped into the stairwell at their own end of the corridor, and ascended.

Castigon punched and kicked the remains of the furniture out of his way, and barrelled down the corridor towards the stairwell, all the while wondering why Molcomb — and presumably it *was* Molcomb — had gone up, not down. When he reached the end he saw why: the descending flight was blocked by what appeared to be discarded filing cabinets. The whole stairwell smelled of urine. He bounded up the stairs.

There were no more corridors, just the roof access. He exited cautiously, knowing full well that he was probably about to step out of a position that was entirely exposed on all sides.

Wherever Molcomb was, he had not hung around to take advantage of the fact. Castigon advanced quickly until he hit the tall side of an environment control module, and hunkered down into cover.

Where in the worlds had he gone?

Then, as if to answer that very question, there was a scrabbling sound off to his left, and someone whispered *"Shit!"*

Castigon mag-tagged his rifle, and creeping cautiously to the edge of the roof he peered over the safety rail, pistol first.

Molcomb was hanging from a cable that ran along a narrow ledge, less than a metre below the edge of the roof. The clips that should have held the cable flush against the wall were beginning to twist away under his weight, slackening it. He was trying to dig the toes of his boots into the wall as if that would take the weight off the cable.

"Hey," said Molcomb.

"Hey."

"Long time no see."

"Whose fault is *that*?" Castigon asked, and shot him in the face.

Moments after Molcomb's body hit the ground, so soon after that Castigon was still looking over the edge, another figure ran towards the crumpled mess. Castigon heard shouting from the ground, strained and anguished, and the figure looked up towards him. It could only have been the counterpart. A weapon was raised, but the aim was terrible. Whether that was due to the distance or the counterpart's apparent distress, Castigon could not say.

He waved cheerfully, and stepped back from the edge.

– 15 –
The Battle of Gousk

"Brace for impact!"

The entire superstructure of *Love Tap* shuddered, distant clangs and crashes reverberating savagely through his corridors. Somewhere along the length of the immense ship, a metal slug had penetrated his hull at a low angle and ripped through bulkhead after bulkhead. Alerts blared across the command deck.

"Helm, what are you *doing*?" Betombe shouted. "Keep us angled into the station's field of fire, nose first. Give them the smallest target possible."

"Yes, Admiral."

"COMOP, damage control teams to whatever sections we just lost."

"Already on it, Sir."

The battle had already passed its most furious point, Betombe knew. Unless the Viskr could shore up their defences they had already lost. All he had to do now was keep grinding at them until they broke: he knew it, and they almost certainly knew it too.

What they probably did *not* know was that try as they might they would not be getting any reinforcements. Operation Seawall should be making sure of that: all the Viskr fleets in the neighbouring star systems would by now be engaged in similar skirmishes of their own.

Until they realised it though, the Viskr at Gousk would fight to the last ship. Betombe had little chance of putting them to flight, since they would never abandon their permanent battle station to the mercies of an invading force.

"Sir, *Surprise Entry* reports critical damage to primary engines. They're fighting fit, but down to manoeuvring thrusters."

"Have *Hard Times* move in to provide additional cover."

With thick blast shields covering all the view ports on the command deck, much of the compartment was given over to a holographic master map of the battle, centred on the battle station that long ago had been the keystone of the Viskr border defences. Parts of the hologram flickered in and out of cohesion — the Viskr were flashing the Imperial ships with their lasers as quickly as they could, hoping to knock out enough sensor palettes simultaneously to create a moment of opportunity. The Imperial ships were doing the same thing right back at them, and the space between the opposing forces was criss-crossed by an ever-changing lattice of almost invisible beams.

The lasers were of little concern to the dreadnought. He had so many sensor palettes dotted across his hull that the Viskr could not hope to block them all. Even with the rest of the fleet half-blinded, for most of the time *Love Tap* could see well enough to guide them all.

The gauss guns however were a very real threat. So very many of them were mounted on the battle station, and more besides on the vessels that guarded it. Betombe had already lost two ships, and even the beloved dreadnought had taken several nasty hits before his flak curtain really started to take shape.

It was the station's ordnance that presented the greatest problem, Betombe reflected. Deflecting something as you pass it by is easy, he had thought. After all, you just need to give it some more energy, to get it moving along a vector angled away from you. But a slug coming straight at you? You either move your own ass, or you supply the slug with enough energy to fully oppose its momentum. The triple-fire C-MADS turrets that defended the Imperial ships were good at what they did, but their designers had unfortunately not equipped them to work miracles.

Still, they had made short work of the drones that the Viskr ships had launched early on in the fight. Unmanned, unshielded craft did not stand much of a chance against high velocity mini-guns. The enemy had not launched any more drones after the first wave, and had yet to send a single fighter against the Imperial fleets.

The Viskr fleet though had not allowed itself to be drawn away from their base, so it could not be fought safely out of range of the battle station's weapons. And so a dilemma had arisen: Betombe's fleet could either stay in a wide orbit of the station, just at the effective range limit of their weapons systems, or they could get close and personal while presenting the smallest target profiles they could get away with. The former choice would mean offering the largest possible targets to the enemy for the long time it would take to chip away at their defences; the latter carried the risk of much more serious damage for every hit they took. In either case, combat effectiveness would be reduced.

It was not the kind of choice Betombe liked making. Dilemmas in general annoyed him, and in his professional opinion this specific one was really quite shit. So, in the manner that had won him both battles and infamy, he simply created a third option.

His twist on the flak curtain was not really a new idea, as such, but he was pretty sure it had not been used before in quite this way. Or at least, what he had come up with was definitely not a tactic taught at the War College or the Imperial Flight Academy. Sometimes the most effective idea was just so simple that nobody could slow down their brain enough to think it up.

The Imperial ships' C-MADS defence turrets had all been re-tasked. They were no longer trying to deflect the slugs being fired at their own hulls, as their engineers had intended. They were firing to protect *other ships*.

Betombe's battle group was arranged around the Viskr battle station, the starships hanging in space and converging slowly on the station as they fought with its defensive fleet. Only brief bursts from manoeuvring thrusters kept the Imperial ships in slow lateral orbits, their noses always pointed at their ultimate target as — excruciatingly slowly — they spiralled fatefully inwards.

Try as it might the station was unable to fight them off; every time one of its metal slugs streaked towards an Imperial ship, the neighbouring ships' turrets would deflect it with a rapid barrage of smaller projectiles. Each time a true anti-ship missile came close, it was detonated prematurely by a burst from a gigawatt laser.

Betombe knew that the Viskr crewing the opposing ships would now be wrangling with almost the same dilemma his own fleet had faced when they first entered the system. But there was no chance they would derive the same solution; the Viskr were desperately dependent on battle computers — to the point of being almost strategically illiterate — and no battle computer he had ever heard of would think to use its point defences to protect something other than itself. In a way, it was almost funny.

"Sir, message *Sleeper Hold* Actual: be advised there is a gap in enemy fire cover, five-zero degrees from your heading."

"Acknowledge the message. Tactical, get on it. Show me this gap."

"Aye Sir," the tactical officer said. She flicked her hand across a holo at her station, and within seconds she was passing the data to the central battle map. "I believe I've found it."

Betombe studied the enemy ships, watching the way they moved and reading off the information that *Love Tap* had gathered from them.

"This one is listing." He pointed to a corvette which was moving further and further out of formation. "These two frigates should be filling the gap, but they're each trying not to expose themselves."

"Plug the gap with a battleship, you could do a lot of damage," Tactical said.

"My thoughts exactly. COMOP, contact the *Gorgon* and have them do just that."

"Incoming volley," a voice yelled from the starboard consoles.

The entire command deck jerked hard enough to make Betombe brace himself against a guard rail. It must have been a significant impact indeed if it was enough to jar the entire ship.

"Damage control, what just happened?"

"Combined fire," an officer called back. "Three destroyers; gauss guns firing in close order along a shared trajectory. We've lost the forward hangar."

"They're adapting," Betombe muttered. Somehow their damned battle computers must have figured out how to confuse the targeting systems on the C-MADS turrets. That would not do at all. "Return fire. Everything you can manage. I want those ships pulverised for their efforts, before their friends copy the idea."

"Aye Sir, tracking to targets." Tactical's hands danced across her holos, and *Love Tap* responded with immediate violence.

Invisible against the inky backdrop of space, metal slugs streaked towards the trio of Viskr vessels that had attacked the dreadnought, accelerated hard along the guide rails at the core of the ship's lateral gauss guns. *Love Tap* was already swamping the enemy sensor palettes with laser light, hoping to knock them offline just long enough for his projectiles to get inside the flak boundary. Steel flechettes accompanied the slugs, simple decoys which would reduce the chances of the real ordnance being knocked aside by point defences.

The destroyers broke their tight formation, two of them protecting the third with their broadest sides. Defence turrets sprang into life along their hulls, spinning and pivoting rapidly to track the incoming fire, spitting tungsten interceptors venomously in a near constant stream. Hundreds of bursts of heat and light revealed the many projectiles that were deflected from their targets.

The two ships were peppered by small explosions, deeply pitted craters appearing in the smooth metal of their outer hulls. Gouts of burning atmosphere erupted from the breaches, and the vessels seemed to reel under the assault, pulling away from *Love Tap* as if shielding their exposed flanks instinctively. Another volley, and both ships took more hits this time. The first wave had damaged too many of their defence turrets.

Inevitably, the closer ship took the brunt of the attack. Before the next volley had even made contact, secondary explosions were ripping through its structure. A great yellow and white flower burst open from the ventral surface, folding and tearing the metal in its path as if the plates and crossbeams were nothing more than dry leaves. Geysers of fire sprang from the hull one after another, streaming out into the cold void, taking the ship's innards and crew with them.

The final volley battered the doomed destroyer mercilessly, and life boats started to launch from her aft hangar. A blinding light flared in the darkness. Seconds passed before the shock wave contacted *Love Tap,* plasma and metal debris slamming against the dreadnought's hull, causing his corridors and compartments to ring and shake with the clamorously alarming noise of a violent machine death.

On the command deck, Betombe added his voice to a cheer that faded with the explosion. The second destroyer was limping away, ignoring the life boats that had fled its late companion. Judging by their uncontrolled rolling, not one of the pods had cleared the destroyed ship in time. Either their navigation systems were fried, or concussion had killed the occupants.

You can run, Betombe thought, but your companion's fate will also catch up with you. And you have revealed your command unit.

He looked to the unscathed ship of the trio, now a good deal more distant than it had been when *Love Tap* first returned fire. The way the others had moved to block the line of fire... whatever military unit the three ships belonged to, they were all of them beholden to that third ship's commanding officer.

"COMOP, have *Shrike* and *Fury* concentrate their fire on that destroyer. I want it burned out." He pointed into the battle map, picking out the command unit. "Notify all other Sixth Fleet commanders to harry enemy battle groups, and watch for signs that they are protecting specific units from our fire."

"Sir."

"Tactical, hit that damaged destroyer with a ship-to-surface missile."

"Admiral?"

"They were formulating a response to our tactics. If they shared it with their friends, then I want to *strongly* discourage the other commanders."

"As you wish, Sir: firing ship-to-surface."

An audio alert pipped twice, and Betombe watched a red streak leave the representation of *Love Tap* that shone brightly at the heart of the battle map.

Outside the ship, in the funereal silence of space, the missile bore down quickly on the already damaged destroyer, evading the enemy ship's flagging defence systems with ease. The warhead, designed to level an entire city from orbit, was rammed into the fleeing craft's engine cluster. Explosions burst through the hull one after another, faster than the eye could follow, ripping bulkheads and decking and armour plate alike. The destroyer was completely obliterated.

COMOP did not wait for the celebration to die down. "Admiral, message *Gorgon* Actual: enemy resolve is crumbling at his location, requesting more units to press the advantage."

Betombe evaluated the master holo. "They can't hold their lines. Redirect all Sixth Fleet ships; have them join *Gorgon* in forcing the issue where the Viskr formation is weakest. Fourth Fleet ships will maintain the flak curtain."

"Aye Sir, sending instructions."

"Tactical, this is it. Prepare all forward cannons for a fusillade. Target the battle station: command centre, engineering levels, primary reactors. I want it utterly disabled."

"Understood, Admiral."

On the battle map he watched *Gorgon* and her compatriots working together to widen the gap in the Viskr defences. As more and more Sixth Fleet ships arrived, the hole grew bigger and bigger. Viskr ships began to abandon other parts of their perimeter to reinforce those being pushed to retreat. Their line was falling to pieces.

"Helm, ahead one half. Get us to a good striking distance."

The ship's conventional drive flared, and the faintest of vibrations trembled through the command deck. With the blast shields down, that barely detectable reverberation was the only indication the dreadnought had begun to move.

"Brace for impact," yelled Tactical.

The corridors leading to the bridge rang with the deafening sound of metal hammering against metal, painfully loud and uncomfortably long-lived. When it followed, the rapid clacking and heavy *whir-thump-thump* of the responding C-MADS turrets was so close it could be heard through the intervening decks. The station must have been trying to knock out the ship's command deck. An explosion rumbled through the superstructure and an alarm began to sound; somewhere above and aft of them, *Love Tap* was losing atmosphere. Red strips now illuminated on every bulkhead, and pressure hatches began to close throughout the primary decks.

Tactical shouted over the din. "Target has locked on to us; they're retraining all primary weapons."

"Ready on forward cannons. Have Fourth Fleet hit their sensor palettes."

"Sir, most of them have already come about to intercept enemy fire."

"They can do both. Send the order."

The battle map became a bright network of lines, each one connecting a warship to the enemy station. Every line represented a sensor being blinded, a chance to strike without being blocked. More and more of the lines appeared.

"Tactical; fire at will."

Each of the main forward auto-cannons fired in turn, one after the other, shaking the deck. The discharges were so violent that the momentum dampeners could not absorb all of the spare energy, and sound and motion escaped into corridors and bulkheads and compartments. Lighting strips crackled and flickered. Rack shelving and webbing tipped and rolled precariously, threatening to spill their contents. Dust leapt from every surface, catapulted into the air by each sudden jolt.

Hit by dozens of sabot rounds, the battle station came off quite a lot worse.

The entire upper section imploded on the side facing *Love Tap,* and a hole was blown out through the opposite hull. Vapour billowed out of both wounds, taking with it hundreds of objects too small to make out. An intense burst of light and flame jetted from the docking aperture — somewhere inside the structure, a docked ship must have gone up.

The lower section, a huge rotating habitat structure, had taken a number of hits itself. Globular blooms of gas escaped from the hull in every place it was shattered, burning out almost immediately in the cold void of space, and the rotation of the entire section became jarring and irregular. A few point defences on the hull were still trying to respond, spinning randomly as they tried feebly to lock on to incoming ordnance. The station was mostly firing on its own debris.

"Hold fire," Betombe said. The cannons stopped. "Assess damage."

"They've lost command and control, co-ordinated firing control, launch capability, and spin regulation. Their weapons lock has lifted from us. Secondary explosions detected throughout the entire structure. Distress beacon has been triggered, and already failed. Primary reactor appears to have shut down."

"In other words, we fucked them up real good. Any chance of them salvaging it?"

"Unlikely Sir. Looking at these readings, the place must be torn to pieces inside; hull breaches, zero gravity, fire, explosions, pressure variations... they'll be lucky to evacuate survivors, if there *are* any."

"Good, I'd call that mission accomplished."

"The remainder of their defence force is disengaging from our ships," Tactical said.

"Have our units pursue them aggressively. Damage rather than destroy; I want them able to jump out of here, but no longer equipped to fight. Make them a burden for the enemy."

The Viskr were defeated, and they knew it. The ships that had so recently mounted a furious defence of the battle station were now in disarray, most of them frantically attempting to find a defensible orientation, to put distance between themselves and the battle.

Betombe cast his eye over the battle map one last time, and clasped his hands behind his back. "Open blast shields," he said.

When the heavy shielding retracted from the view ports, he turned to look out to starboard at the retreating ships. Their carriers had already moved well out of range, and wormhole apertures began to form beyond them. Destroyers, corvettes, and a handful of battleships limped after them, chased down by the Sixth Fleet.

The admiral watched with satisfaction, proud that even after so many years without a real engagement his crew were still battle-ready. Not just his crew; all of them. It had been some time since any of these ships had been involved in anything more than war games.

A large explosion erupted into being out in the black, bright and pale, out-shining the other fiery sparks of ship-to-ship conflict. He was already shielding his eyes against the glare before the view port compensated. Something out there was not right.

"Tactical, what ship was that?"

"Sir, I'm afraid it was the *Gorgon*. Massive systemic damage. I see no distress signal."

"How?"

"I'm now showing additional enemy contacts, multiple signals."

"The wormholes?"

"Yes... the wormholes aren't an exit route; they're delivering reinforcements."

"But that's impossible," Betombe said. "From where?"

– 16 –
Ex Caelo

Joarn Kages wore his discomfort openly on his sweaty face. You could not really blame him, Caden thought. He was almost a prisoner in his own office, surrounded by people whose disposition he was only guessing at, and the purpose of their visit — although probably not quite entirely clear to him yet — was obviously down to him doing something he ought not to have done.

"There was a man," said Caden. "Medran Morlum. He would have come through here within the last few days. I don't know how many times he visited you, but he linked in once while he was here. He made a payment to your personal account, from his own."

"Oh *him,*" said Kages.

"So you know the person I mean?"

"Oh worlds yes, I would never forget someone that strange. He wasn't alone either."

"Someone else was with him?"

"In a manner of speaking. A droid of some kind. He called it... Prem, I think it was."

"Penvos Robotics," said Eilentes. "They have a whole line of maintenance and worker models."

"That would fit. Go on Kages, what did he want from you?"

"Oh I can't tell you *that*, Shard. I'm sorry, I thought we were already quite clear on that point."

Caden fixed the corpulent information broker with a steely gaze, and waited.

"I won't crack," Kages said after an uncomfortable interval. "I'm not going to betray my client's confidence and potentially put myself and my livelihood at risk, just because you stared at me."

Caden smiled. "Okay, well I certainly respect your integrity."

"Thank you."

"What if Mister Throam were to kick you through a window? Would that help?"

"I beg your— what?"

"I said, 'what if Mister Throam were to kick you through a window?' It's a simple enough question."

Kages gaped stupidly at him. He blinked twice, then seemed to regain his composure.

"You're just trying to intimidate me."

"That is certainly a component, yes," said Caden. "But don't think you won't be going out of that window if you carry on being unhelpful."

"You can't do that, it's just ridiculous! You represent the Throne."

"Yes I can; I can pretty much do anything. Especially when it comes to the security of the Imperial Combine. As you said, I represent the Throne. When I complete my mission to preserve it, nobody is going to care that you were kicked through a window."

"Do it then."

"Well, there *is* the inevitable inconvenience of having to come outside to retrieve you before we can continue," Caden said. "Perhaps it would be easier to just tell everyone in the city that you assisted the Viskr and their allies by providing them critical information."

"That isn't true!"

This time, there was a plainly visible flash of fear across Kages face. Whether it was concern for his professional reputation, or the thought of what the other people living on this border world might do to him if they heard he aided the Viskr, was not entirely clear. Chances were it was a little of both.

"Isn't it? It *sounds* true. That's what matters. And to be quite frank, it remains to be established whether or not you're a traitor. Unless he's being coerced I think it's likely that Morlum has fallen in with the Viskr Junta somehow. And his coercion wouldn't carry over to you: if you gave him what he wanted, then you gave the Viskr what they wanted, like a good little traitor."

"A traitor—"

"Of course, we have no way of knowing if you have sold out your own kind to an invading force, because you won't tell us what information you gave to Morlum."

"I would never betray the Empire—"

"I can't confirm that. Our civilisation is spiralling towards open war, Mister Kages, and all I know so far is that you have been selling information to anyone with the money to pay for it."

"All right, you've made your point."

"Are you going to tell me what you sold him?"

"Yes, but there is one thing."

"Which is...?"

"Well, the information I sold him... I don't know if you'd consider it treason or not."

"I'll be telling you that pretty much straight away."

"Yes, but the thing is... I don't really want to die."

"I'm on a schedule, Kages. I don't have time to run you in and have you charged, tried, convicted, and sentenced to death."

"Oh thank you, thank you."

"So I'll just do as I promised and tell everyone."

"Please, I didn't betray the Empire. I just gave him the codes."

"What codes?"

"The lockout codes... for Woe Tantalum. He wanted to go to the surface."

"Woe Tantalum?"

"Illegal colony planet out in the Deep," said Daxon. "It was a terraforming disaster. Whole planet went geo-toxic — everyone died."

"And you're telling me Morlum *wants* to go there?"

"That's right," said Kages. "There's a quarantine security network around the whole planet. He purchased the codes to bypass it."

"That's all?"

"That's all. Oh, well no... he wanted the location as well. He seemed to know Woe Tantalum exists, but not where it is."

"Anything else?"

Kages's eyes flicked up and side-to-side as he tried to recall his dealings with Morlum. "No, I don't think so."

"Right then."

"Are you satisfied?" Kages asked.

"Well it certainly wasn't worth getting kicked through a window for, was it?"

"No, not at all. Thank goodness you saw sense."

"Throam," said Caden.

Kages's eyes widened. "Oh... don't!"

Throam kicked him through a window.

° ° °

"This is way outside my area of expertise," said Laekan.

Brant stared at the images that were lined up neatly on the holo, side-by-side slices of the inside of Amarist Naeb's head. He had no idea what he was looking at, for the most part, but even with his limited knowledge of medicine and biology he could see that the scans had revealed something unusual. Human brains were not supposed to look like *this*.

"Do you know what it is we're looking at, Doctor?"

Gordl Branathes had deigned to come and visit the isolated medbay, finally showing some interest in what his operators had been dealing with since Elm Caden first arrived at Fort Kosling. He too had been instantly transfixed by the scans Laekan showed him.

"I'm afraid not," Laekan said. "What I can say with certainty though is that these... *structures* are new. The scans run during her last routine medical, before she went to Echo, were all normal."

"What the hell are you?" Brant murmured.

"A threat," said Tirrano. "It can't be a coincidence that this *Rasa* just happened to appear during the start of a new Viskr offensive. Balance of probabilities says she's some kind of weapon."

"Maybe so," said Branathes. "What would you propose we do about it, Peras?"

"Kill her and be done with it, before she does whatever it is she's meant to do."

Brant was appalled. "Are you kidding? She's a citizen. If this was done to her deliberately, then she's also a victim. We should be trying to help her, not talking about killing her."

"Oh okay, we'll just let her complete her mission then."

Brant stopped himself from replying in kind. He knew this game well. Peras wanted to draw him into a childish squabble before she delivered her killing blow. Not this time, not in front of their superior. He counted to five in his head.

"Even if she *is* a weapon," he said, "which is by no means certain; killing her would be stupid. We should take the opportunity to learn as much from her as we can."

"She's not telling us anything. We can surely learn as much from a dead Rasa as a live one."

Branathes had been looking from one to the other, waiting while they argued. Brant found he could not tell what the man was thinking. Odd, he was usually quite easy to read.

"We're not killing her," the monitor said. "You're quite right Occre, this 'Rasa' could turn out to be an invaluable source of information."

Great. Now Tirrano had Branathes saying it as well.

"Well I'm glad you settled that," said Doctor Laekan. "Are there any other patients in medical you'd like to consider killing?"

"Apologies, Doctor," said Branathes. "My staff did not mean to offend you."

But some of them might have been indifferent to whether or not they did, Brant thought to himself. Tirrano was standing with her arms crossed, stony-faced. She had said nothing since her plan to terminate Naeb had been vetoed, and would probably stay that way until she was alone with Brant. She would make her feelings very clear, then there would be a gap of a couple of hours before she came back to him with a cloying and painfully insincere apology. Her way of getting back into Brant's good books.

At some point, he would have to find a kind way of telling her that she had never had a chance of being in his good books.

Branathes had not finished. "Draft in whatever specialists you need from Kosling, Doctor. Or even from other systems; I want to know what this woman is, and what she means."

"I'll do my best," Laekan said.

○ ○ ○

"And you said it was weird *before*."

Throam smiled grimly. Whatever it was that had changed while they were talking to Kages, it did not bode well. He could feel the difference in the air. He could smell it on the breeze. Trouble. He always knew trouble: he had a sense for it.

The few people in the streets of Barrabas Fled had paid them relatively little attention when they were on their way to Kages's place, other than looking to see who they were and maybe staring for a little too long. Some had watched as the Rodori thundered by, and others had eyed up the weapons they all carried, but none of that was unusual.

Now, matters were different.

Throam could feel the eyes boring into him, everywhere they walked. As they retraced their steps, navigating through the eerily silent streets of the city centre, his skin began to crawl and itch. Something was wrong, wrong, wrong.

And apparently Caden felt the same way, since he had just commented on it.

"Don't like this one bit," Throam said. "Suggest

we lose no time getting off this rock."

"Agreed. I don't intend to lose time anyway," said Caden. "We have what we came for, and Morlum has a head start on us."

They were coming up on the small square containing the fountain and stone benches. As they rounded the corner, Throam saw that the same old man was still there. Only this time he was standing in the middle of the way, leaning awkwardly on a gnarled wooden cane as if he had never tried to walk or stand with it before this very moment. He was still humming the same refrain.

"Did you get what you came for?" He asked, when they were close enough.

"No business of yours, old man." Throam said.

"It's everyone's business."

The humming resumed.

They hurried past, and into the next street.

"You'd better hurry," said a young girl. She had dark shadows under her eyes. She was stick-thin, and stood on a dirty blanket in a niche between two buildings.

"Are you talking to me?" Throam said.

"Or don't hurry at all, and that way you won't leave so soon."

She began to hum as she skipped away, the same refrain, the same melody that had been so alien yet so infuriatingly familiar to Caden.

"Caden, what the fuck is up with this crazy-ass town?"

"I don't know, but something tells me the people here aren't quite themselves today."

"We need to leave, *now*."

"You're telling me."

Daxon was already talking into his link. "Bullseye One-Three from Charlie, come in."

"Go on Daxon," replied Sergeant Chun.

"We're en route to you now. Be advised this city is possibly hostile. Suggest immediate dust-off when we return."

A gaunt man with a bread basket walked across their path. Throam caught the damp, powdery scent of decay, and looked into the basket as he passed by. What should have been a cargo of loaves was nothing but a lumpy carpet of blue and green mould. Specks of it covered the man's hands, wrists, and sleeves. How long had he been walking around with that basket?

"You'd better hope you know what you're doing."

Throam whirled around, and backed away so that he could keep the man in his sight as the group moved on. The old man and the girl were one thing, an adult male was quite another. Who knew what weapons he might be concealing.

The baker hummed his way out of earshot.

They hurried on, all of them now adopting a defensive formation out of habit. Throam could see that everyone in the group felt the same unease, the same sense of not-quite-threatened-but-freaking-out.

The street narrowed. Two mature women rose together from a bench by the side of the way, and stepped side-by-side into the middle of the path.

Throam edged towards the front of the group, inserting himself between Caden and the women without making his intention obvious.

"You don't *have to* do anything, you know," one said.

The other gave a sickly smile. "It's always been much safer not to take sides."

"Who *are* you?" Throam said.

"Why, I'm me dear. I *am*."

The sickly smile widened. "Now be a good lad and tell us what you intend to do next."

Throam shoved through the middle of them as forcefully as he dared, not wanting to knock the women down. Whatever was happening to the people in this part of the city, he did not want to risk harming them if he could avoid it.

The women moved aside easily, and just stood there staring vacantly as the others passed between them. Then the humming started, the very same melody.

"Oh shit," said Bro.

Throam stopped dead when he caught up with the private. The street opened out onto a plaza, and the plaza was full of people. The entire throng was humming softly.

Both groups stood motionless.

"Come on," Caden said. He punched Throam's arm. "We've no time to waste."

"Fuck's sake." Throam darted after him.

Caden was not running but walking briskly, stepping between the people standing in the plaza. Throam did his best to catch up, to stay close, but the lack of space made it difficult. The Shard was certainly not making his job easy for him. He was much lighter on his feet than Throam.

"Caden, wait up a moment."

"Pick up the pace, Tiny."

Then suddenly he was almost falling over Caden. The Shard had stopped dead, and Throam could not see why at first. He came right up behind Caden and looked over his shoulder.

The man in front of Caden, just off to the left, had put his arm up and placed his hand on Caden's chest.

Caden brought his own arm up sharply and knocked the hand away. The man let his arm drop, and stood rooted to the spot.

A woman off to the right took a single step closer, and placed her right hand on Caden's shoulder.

The others were catching up. Throam could hear their voices coming up behind them. "Daxon," he shouted. "Get us evac. NOW."

More people were stepping in towards Caden. Most stood motionless in the plaza, but those nearest were moving closer, aggregating around him as if drawn towards him somehow. Throam lunged forward and pushed them back, one at a time, striking them to the chest with the heel of his palm. They moved back easily; most seemed weak and unmotivated, some bordered on malnourished. But there were so many of them now, still closing in.

The rumble of twin engines filled the plaza, and Throam saw that the throng was thinning out. Somewhere ahead of them, a vehicle was being forced through the crowd.

People nearby began to react, turning slowly to stare impassively at the approaching Kodiak. Throam seized the chance, and grabbed Caden by the arm. He pulled him out of the nucleus, away from the mass of bodies, and propelled him towards the transport.

"Come on," he yelled at the others. "We. Are. LEAVING."

They reached the armoured vehicle, and Throam yanked hard at the heavy side door. The hatch slid back on its runners, and he half-lifted, half-threw Caden into the passenger cabin.

"Watch it, you great oaf."

"You're welcome," said Throam.

He climbed in after him, and the others began to follow. Bro, Norskine, Daxon, and Bruiser piled in. Eilentes brought up the rear.

Throam reached back and grabbed the rail on the inside of the hatch. He began to drag it forwards, and as he did so he realised someone else was approaching the Kodiak. For a moment he thought he had miscounted everyone on their way into the cabin.

The man outside the hatch was one of the city-dwellers. One of the people who was behaving so oddly. Throam continued to slide the hatch, and just before it slammed closed to seal off the outside world, he heard the man speak.

"Fill the silence," he said.

– 17 –
Shadows of the Heart

Of all the people who could have demanded Caden's attention, the Chamberlain was perhaps the least of his favourites. But the call had been deemed so urgent that it had been sent on the Actual-Confidential channel. For the CO's eyes only. Or Shard eyes only, in this case.

"Operation Seawall is a disaster," the Chamberlain said, in a dolorous tone. "A disaster, yes. Admiral Betombe seems to have provoked quite the reaction."

"The Viskr aren't falling back?"

"Not in the least bit, no. Their border fleets have been reinforced three-fold since the operation began."

"We're committed now. We can only try to hold those systems."

"Indeed. Captain Santani will be needed back with the Second Fleet."

"That might be an issue. I've just found our first usable lead, and it's likely we don't have much time left."

"Do tell."

"Medran Morlum — one of the people missing from Echo. It looks like he's working with the Viskr, and he's been to Aldava, sniffing around after the lockout codes for Woe Tantalum."

"Woe Tantalum... why in the worlds would he want to go there?"

"Because nobody else *would*. I did some research. There's no gate in the system, which means no nexus; whatever goes on in the space local to the planet won't be seen from afar. And from orbit, it's virtually impossible to detect what is happening on the surface. It's an ideal hiding place. An ideal staging area."

"Hmm, yes, ideal indeed. What do you intend to do about this?"

"Take *Hammer* and Bravo Company, and go find Morlum straight away. Tear down whatever he has set up."

The Chamberlain nodded slowly, and drummed the side of his face pensively with three long fingers as he considered Caden's reply.

"The Empress was insistent that the border engagement should remain our priority," he said at length. "However, if we recover those weapons, then the Viskr border won't *need* to be held. She will want this matter brought to a swift conclusion."

"I'll head there straight away."

"There is another reason for this call," the Chamberlain said, his voice even more mournful than usual. "Something else you need to know about. Two of your fellow Shards have been killed. Murdered, in fact."

"Murdered?"

"Oh yes, murdered indeed. It would appear from the witness accounts that your former counterpart Maber Castigon is responsible."

"He's escaped?"

"No, released. He went missing immediately."

Caden felt ill. "*Released*. I should have put a bullet in his head while I had the chance."

"It might have been better for all concerned," said the Chamberlain. "But then, without proper justice, where would we be?"

"I don't know," said Caden. "But I know a great many people who would have liked the chance to be there with us."

"Indeed," said the Chamberlain. "Ottomas Endures."

"Until the Last Breath. What are the names?"

"Kulik Molcomb, killed on Low Cerin. Ider Firenz, killed on Fengrir. Both shot in the head."

His stomach sank further still. He had known Molcomb by reputation, Firenz by association. The latter had run a joint op with him; a rare occurrence indeed for Shards, even in those agonising days of the Trinity Crisis.

"And the counterparts?"

"Rupus Dyne was unharmed. I gather he was not actually present at the time of the incident, and will doubtless be called upon to explain why. As I understand it, Mostrum Appatine made a valiant attempt to stop Castigon, and has been disabled as a result."

"Permanently?"

"It is not clear whether he will walk again. I am told he was most fortunate to survive, oh yes most, most fortunate."

"What's being done?"

"Eyes and Ears have started scouring the worlds for him, naturally."

"They won't find him. He will have spent the past few years figuring out how to move around without being seen."

"Indeed."

"When I return from Woe Tantalum, I expect to be sent after him."

"You know as well as I do that that will be entirely at Her discretion."

"Anything you can do to sway Her opinion will be appreciated."

"I shall do my very best."

"There is one thing before I go," Caden said.

"Name it."

"Aldava... there's something wrong with the population. Well, as far as Barrabas Fled goes — I couldn't say what the rest of the planet is like. I don't know if it was disease, mass hysteria, or water contamination, but the people there were *very* strange."

"I will have someone look into it."

○ ○ ○

Eilentes had been awake for almost an hour, and could not take any more. Had she fallen asleep almost immediately, as *he* had, then she would not have noticed the discomfort of the damp bedding. But she had been laid there for what seemed like an age now, with the cold sweaty slick of the sheets clinging and rubbing against her skin. She swung her legs over the edge of the bunk, and trailed her toes on the floor.

Behind her, between her back and the bulkhead, Throam's snores rumbled and sighed. *That* did not bother her, and it never had done. Neither did the heat coming off his back — she never needed nightclothes when he was there — nor indeed the fact that at some point afterwards he always rolled over and slept facing away from her.

No. What was playing on her mind, what was keeping her from getting back to sleep, was that they had more or less picked up where they left off during those last few days together on the *Embolden*. She might as well have been zapped back in time.

Four times now. Four times they had managed to bunk up since they first set off to Herros. Four times, and neither of them had said the words 'relationship', 'another go', or even 'what exactly is this?'

She would not get that from Throam, not spontaneously. She would have to ask. After all this time, she still had no idea if he was just going with a good thing for as long as it went unquestioned, or if it genuinely did not occur to him that it needed to be discussed.

Some things never change, she thought. Some men never change. In fact, show me one who does.

Maybe this was what a relationship was to him. It certainly seemed to have been enough in those long ago days on the *Embolden*. Could she make that work? It was not like she particularly needed him to do anything else right now. Maybe she was going to be sore in the mornings, but at least she knew she would not need to be finishing herself off.

Euryce Eilentes! I'll tell your father!

Exactly as her mother had said it so many years ago, when she had foolishly tried to discuss sex with her that first time, the prudish words now popped straight back into Eilentes' head. She giggled to herself. A woman grown am I, and yet Mama is still my vagina's chaperone.

She rose from the edge of the bunk and walked over to the wash stand. A faint green light shone within the bowl: gravity functions were normal, and flowing water would be happily provided. She cupped her hands under the stream and splashed water on her face, then soaked a wash cloth and wiped downwards. Starting under her jaw, then her neck, shoulders, breasts, armpits.

Well shit, she thought. I might as well have a shower. It's not like I'll wake him.

Throam grunted and spluttered, and rolled over towards her, onto his back. His right arm flopped across the space she had been in, and his hand dangled limply off the edge of the bunk. She was turning back to examine herself in the mirror when he spoke in his sleep.

"Pffff, Gendin come."

Gendin? A man's name! I fucking knew it. He'll hump anything.

Eilentes went back to the bunk, sat down heavily in the space under Throam's out-stretched arm, and jabbed him in the ribs with the merciless fingernail of retribution. His eyes opened groggily, and he raised his eyebrows.

"Morning Tiny," she said. "So who's Gendin?"

◦ ◦ ◦

"I am really sorry," said Caden, "but I'm caught up in something complicated."

"It's always the same story," said Lau.

"This is really important, Midget. I can't say why, but there is no way I can walk away from it."

"It's like you only get in touch when you have a reason to not come home."

"Oh wow," he said. "That is something really special."

Lau shrugged. "I'm just saying what I see."

"Did it ever occur to you that I'm more likely to call when I'm reminded of what I have to lose?"

The image on the holo was flickering and full of grain, but he could see Lau raise his eyebrows. From his expression, he had not been expecting that at all.

Caden had called home almost immediately after speaking to the Chamberlain. If his suspicions were correct, then Woe Tantalum could be a fortress by the time *Hammer* arrived. Going there might well be a one way trip.

It was the middle of the night ship-time, but his holo had calculated it was early afternoon in the city of Galloi. Lau had answered the call within seconds.

"I didn't think of it like that," Lau said after a long pause.

"Of course not: you've never served."

"I've not had the opportunity."

"That's not my fault, Lau."

"Debatable." There was a long, awkward silence. "We still miss you."

"I don't doubt it. Please believe me when I say there's a very good reason I can't be there."

Lau nodded slowly.

"How is she?" Caden asked.

"The same as usual. Hammered most of the time."

"Just don't let her drink," he suggested.

"Really? You think I never tried that? It makes her *worse*."

"How can it be worse?"

"Last time she broke the door off every cupboard I had locked. I found her drinking antiseptic gel."

"I didn't realise things were that bad."

"Well, they are."

"You should have told me."

"You should have *asked*."

○ ○ ○

"For the last time, Euryce; I am *not* seeing anyone else."

"So Gendin is some kind of ex then?"

"What is this obsession you've got with me sleeping with other guys?"

"I'm not obsessed. *You* were talking about him in your sleep, okay? *You*. All I want is to know who he is."

"If you want a threesome, just say so."

"No, I don't want a fucking threesome. If we're going to get back together, I want you to be honest with me about who you've been sleeping with."

"Okay, whoa there... tone down the crazy. That's a whole load of bombs you just dropped."

"Oh right, so I get angry about something and suddenly I'm crazy. Don't patronise me, Rendir."

"You're not crazy for getting angry, you're crazy for getting angry about something imaginary."

"I'm just imagining things, am I?"

"Yes!"

"I didn't imagine you talking to this 'Gendin' in your sleep; that *happened*. I heard it."

"Yes, I can tell. I can hear you shouting at me about it."

"So you're not denying it then?"

"Doesn't look that way, does it?" He pulled back the sheets she had whipped off him and dropped them over his body, then punched some life back into the pillows.

"Oh, you are *not* going back to sleep now."

"Why not?"

"Because we're not done here yet."

"Fine," he snapped. He lurched upright, sitting himself up in the bunk. "One, I don't have any male ex-partners. Two, nobody said we were 'getting back together'. Three, Gendin is—"

"Is what?"

"Is not your concern."

"He's not my concern? Of course he's my concern."

"I just told you, I don't have a male ex."

"What is it then? Male impersonator? Hermaphroditic species? Sex droid? You filthy son-of-a-whore."

"No, you crazy bitch. He's my *son*. Now let me sleep woman, and we'll talk about your insanity in the morning. Oh, and just for the record: it would be two whores in my case."

She did not know whether to laugh or cry. The embarrassment of it all!

Throam wriggled back down in the bunk, rolled his body to face the bulkhead, and pulled the sheets over his shoulders again. But he was not quite done.

"*And* I can't believe you don't want a threesome."

○ ○ ○

Elm was in his Civics class the day his world ended for the first time, the same day he first named *it*.

It was particularly cold in Galloi. The disappearance of the coastal geese and the shortening of the days both signalled the coming of the Damastion winter. Inside the school, however, the classrooms were warm and bright.

"Place understanding before imagination," went the same chorus that started every one of the Civics lessons. The teacher led the children in their recitation of the Principles. "Reality is not beholden to dreams.

"Knowledge is a product of understanding, which is the product of reason. Strive to reveal it.

"Reject resentment. You are not the arbiter of what is deserved.

"Heed not the ego. Your capabilities are a product of your nature, not your desires."

Elm did not need to follow the words on the printwall; he knew them well enough. Mother had made certain of that during those long months in which Father was away on deployment. He glanced around the room as he recited with the others, picking out the ones who were only mouthing nonsense, camouflaging themselves in the group effort.

"Empathise with others. Do not assume that they share your views.

"Fact and opinion are entirely different. Treat them so."

Something began to happen. Another teacher had come to the door of the classroom, one more senior than his own. She signalled the teacher at the front of the class, who in turn beckoned one of the children at the front to take over from him.

"Wealth is not a reward in its own right. Currency must act in order to have value."

The two teachers convened outside the door, and through the glass pane Elm could see them talking. His own teacher stopped, and looked back into the room — straight at Elm. His face was an ashen mask.

"Seek not power over others. To govern is to serve."

When his teacher came back into the room, Elm already knew that he was going to come over. Something in the way the adults were looking at him warned of unusual events. While the others continued to recite the Principles, he was led outside the door.

They told him about the ambush and the skirmish that had followed it. Without being gruesome, they tried to explain how the crippled *Curtailer* had come to a fiery end. They told him as gently as they could that he would not see Father ever again.

His world was a dark glassy bubble, shrinking in around him, and he knew he should shatter it by crying and screaming and becoming inconsolable. But he found himself pushing the feelings down, down into the centre, crushing them into an infinitely small ball that would take up no space at all, and entombing them like all the others he had trapped within.

He had become strong in the past few years. He had learned to keep them deep down and buried, most of the time.

Much to the astonishment of his teachers, he wiped his cheeks on the back of his hand and returned to the classroom, taking up the chant as he walked back to his desk.

"Know well your limitations and your talents. Others will see them more clearly than you do."

He was strong, but it fought against him. The feelings he had side-stepped were threatening to burst forth again, to make themselves felt. He pushed them down deeper, tried to visualise them being squeezed away to nothing, into a volume so small that it went beyond nothing and became void, a hollow shell where once he had stored the emotions he could not or would not manage. The void was true negation, cold and silent and dark.

He called it the Emptiness.

"Above all, bring something new into the world. Wherever you find yourself, light the dark."

– 18 –
The Battle of Woe Tantalum

With a silent gasp, *Hammer* burst from the maelstrom of the wormhole and dropped into normal space, once more bidding farewell to a small scattering of her own pieces.

"Report."

COMOP was already on it, his hands whirling around and through the holos that fed him information from the sensor palettes.

"Minor hull damage. Enemy contact, system interior. Reading nine distinct Viskr signals... and six Imperial transponders, all verified. Last known locations have been pushed to Helm and Tactical. There's no nexus in this system, so account for a five hour delay on those sensor readings."

"Someone already came for them," Santani said. "That should even the odds a little. Helm, time on secondary jump?"

"Generators are ready, Captain. Just waiting on green lights from the safety systems."

Santani's face was grim. Trial by fire; the moment had finally arrived, and now she would find out just how proficient her relatively young crew was. Well, she *had* wanted to know.

She thumbed her holo and opened a channel to

the entire ship. "Now hear this. All hands, this is your captain."

Even those officers and crew working on the bridge listened in, not stopping their work completely but devoting most of their attention to their commander. It was not often she addressed the crew in this way, and even Klade had turned to face her.

"In a few moments, we will be making a short jump to the vicinity of Woe Tantalum, directly into ongoing combat. All crew will report now to their designated combat stations. We will be making a MAGA battle drop immediately upon emergence. The forward hangar will be cleared of all but the most essential personnel.

"I do not pretend to know the precise tactical situation at Woe Tantalum, but I can tell you that *we must not fail*. This day must end with our total victory, for we are out of time. If we do not crush the enemy forces we find here, this war will end very soon, and not well for us.

"I know each one of you will do your duty until the very last moment this ship can support life, and I thank you for it. On behalf of Her Most Radiant Majesty, I thank you. Prepare to jump. Prepare to fight. Most of all, prepare yourselves to succeed."

The channel closed, and a deathly silence fell across the command deck. Long seconds passed before Klade intervened. "Red alert! All hands to combat stations, I repeat all hands to combat stations. Hangar two to lock-down please."

Life returned to the compartment, and the familiar hubbub of voices and gentle interface feedback filled the air again, more urgent now.

"Green lights across the board, Captain. We're

ready to jump."

"Give the word, Mister Klade," said Santani.

"Prepare for immediate jump to system interior. Helm: calculate for Woe Tantalum distant orbital, best guess for vicinity of those Imperial ships."

The Helm officer's hands danced across holos, and a wormhole began to form in the space ahead of the battleship. Blast shields slid into place, hiding the view. The ship lurched forward.

"Jump."

Hammer crossed the event horizon, and the world was plucked into folded leaves of papery light. For an infinitely long moment the walls of reality were undone, and the outside places poured through.

They snapped away again in a time too short to measure, too long to know. *Hammer* slammed into normal space, groaned, and spooled up her conventional drives.

"Contact the Imperial forces," Santani said. "Get me the lead vessel."

"I'm trying, Captain," COMOP said. "No response as yet."

"Captain," said Tactical.

"Use the Act-Con channel," Santani told COMOP.

"*Captain*!"

"What is it Tactical?"

"Ma'am... they're not firing on each other."

"Explain."

"The Viskr and Imperial ships... they aren't in combat at all. In fact they're now powering weapons and coming about."

"What are the Imperial ships doing?"

"I'm *talking* about the Imperial ships... *and* the

Viskr ships. They're all moving to engage us!"

Santani did not miss a beat. "Prime all defences; turrets, lasers, decoys, drones. Ready on damage control."

"Yes Ma'am, all defences are primed."

"Time?"

"Estimating seven minutes to effective weapons range."

"COMOP, are you getting anything?"

"A lot of comms traffic, Captain. Most of it using Viskr encoding, some unidentified. No Imperial transmissions are evident. There is also hard traffic between the ships and the surface."

"Show me, quickly."

COMOP detached a holo from its support at his station, and slid it into the projector in the centre of the command deck. The main battle map switched on, throwing a representation of the planet and its attendant moons into the middle of the bridge. *Hammer* appeared in green, the approaching ships in red.

He thrust his hands into the holographic field, surrounding the ships that were red, and curled his fingers into a cage to tell the holo he was selecting those elements. He pulled his hands apart, and the field of view swept inwards to magnify the enemy fleet.

Now that the approaching ships were larger than insects, Santani could see shuttles and landers moving to and fro between their parent vessels and the planet. Dozens of the smaller craft were heading to the surface, while only a few appeared to be making the return trip. They had been outpaced as the larger craft headed to intercept *Hammer,* and they now seemed to be hanging back, as if uncertain about precisely where they wanted to be. Some came about, and headed back towards the surface.

"Route me to our lead lander," Santani snapped.

COMOP stepped back to his station and patched her through. "Channel open, Captain."

"Lieutenant Eilentes, I'm sending you the current tactical situation. If you want to make the surface you will have to be quick. We will get as close as we can and try to stay between you and the enemy. Be advised that the Imperial ships at this location appear to be hostile."

"Acknowledged, Captain. Just give us the word."

Santani nodded to COMOP, and he suspended the channel.

"Databurst to Kosling, Fort Herses, and the Laeara system. Send them this battle map along with our sensor logs, and advise that we are engaging the enemy. Request immediate reinforcement."

"At once."

"Helm, ahead full. Give me a hard burn for the planet."

"Aye Captain, ahead full."

"Captain," Tactical said. "That will cut down time to weapons range. Estimating... two minutes to contact."

"Understood. Let me know when we reach a safe insertion point."

"Enemy carrier group has split off from the main force, moving to outflank us."

"Correcting course," Helm said immediately, without being ordered. The ship swung slightly to port, but continued towards the planet. "Ninety seconds."

"They're all launching drones. I read two carriers, probably full complements. No fighter wings in the air as yet."

"They won't send fighters at us while we have working turrets," Santani predicted. "Not if they have any sense."

Klade leaned across to the tactical station. "Launch our own drones, and decoys too. Any of their drones get too close, chew them up."

"Aye, Commander." Tactical said. "Captain, I think this is the best insertion point we're going to get. If we leave it much longer our landers will be de-orbiting under fire."

Santani nodded to Klade, and he in turn used his holo to send word to the hangar bay: launch.

On the main battle map, green dots appeared next to the blob representing *Hammer*, one for each of the MAGA landers that carried the four platoons of Bravo Company, 951st Battalion. The dots sped away from the battleship and her pursuers, and accelerated towards the planet.

"All stop," the captain said. "This is where we make our stand. Bring us about, Helm, and let's show these fuckers who we are."

° ° °

Every time the lander jolted, Eilentes was sure they had been hit. She kept having to remind herself; it's not enemy fire, it's just the atmosphere.

Woe Tantalum was a resentful, brooding world, its chaotic atmosphere rent in purples and browns and the darkest of the greys. From orbit, there were only brief, fleeting signs of the surface. Boiling, billowing storm clouds wreathed the whole planet in a violent, electrically charged cloak.

Within seconds of passing into the upper atmosphere Eilentes found herself relying entirely on the automatic navigation systems. Visibility dropped to zero so quickly she would have become disoriented immediately had it not been for the holographic overlays on her view port. All she could do now was trust that her flight holos had enough data about the planet to ensure they properly tracked the lander's descent. The other three landers were completely dependent on Eilentes, not just her own crew. Where her transponder went, they would follow.

The sky opened out into a wide vista, huge banks of cloud separated by an empty gulf that was bridged occasionally by the sudden sharp crack of electrical arcs. The lander dropped from the paler brown cloud above, and plunged headlong into the swirling surface of the purple layer below. Eilentes was blind again.

Lightning forked and reached out at them, arcing across the sky in a network of splintery fingers that were gone the moment they appeared. Dull flashes receded into the distance on all sides, electrical discharges reflected and diffused through sheets of vapour.

More flashes, in series this time. Smaller and more coherent than the lightning, trailing across her field of view. Enemy fire!

The noisome descent through the storm drowned out the sound of whatever kind of ordnance the anti-drop batteries were firing from the surface. Those that detonated were just small bursts of light, dulled and muffled by the thick banks of vapour.

Eilentes was not fool enough to ignore them though. As pitiful as they looked, it might only take one lucky shot to disable — or perhaps entirely destroy — a lander. She hoped to whatever greater powers might listen that there were only the guns on the surface, and no missile pods waiting with them.

"Fire from the surface," she snapped into the comm. "Take evasive action."

On her tactical holo, she saw the other landers reacting. One nose-dived past her, another braked hard and veered off to the side. The last began to spiral, cork-screwing around her descent trajectory.

She gave the batteries on the ground a few seconds to register their evasion, to resume firing. Tracers again sliced up through the banks of cloud, and she waited until they arced close before pulling a manoeuvre of her own.

She veered off to one side, then braked hard to slow their descent temporarily. The lander's nose lifted against the descent, and she felt herself squashed down against the padding of her chair. The cabin rattled and reverberated in protest, and over the rushing, bellowing din of the air outside she could hear the engines making their thunderous objections.

Dive!

Gratefully, the lander tipped forward once more, rolling in its axis as it did so, easily avoiding the streams of fire that tried so persistently to pluck it from the sky. Eilentes barrelled downwards, following a curving path that she tightened and loosened randomly, swinging left and right when the mood took her. The batteries spewed uselessly into the space where they calculated the landing craft would probably be.

And then they broke the cloud cover again, swept into the dismal gloom below, and a desolate wasteland was hurtling towards them. She continued almost straight down, waiting for the last minute to pull up hard and scream low across the twisted nightmare that was Woe Tantalum's scorched surface.

A heavy jolt pushed them to one side, accompanied by a great booming clang. For a split-second Eilentes thought they were being knocked out of the air. Through the thick port-side canopy she caught a glimpse of something sailing past them, tumbling away and towards the ground, twisted metal leaving a trail of thick black smoke and wisps of flame that struggled for life in the wet air. They had lost one of their companion landers.

Orange sparks flashed in her face, scattering outwards, and she realised she was flying straight towards a battery. It was the only way the defences would be able to lock on to a craft moving this quickly so close to the ground, and she was handing it right to them. Before she could change course, the first hits bit into the canopy, chewing out a series of opaque spider-webs that stretched out cracks and splinters threateningly.

The canopy was somehow holding, for that she was glad, but even slamming on the air brakes and dipping perilously close to the ground was not enough now. There had been a rapid series of hollow-sounding hits that immediately followed the line across the canopy, and the port-side intra-atmospheric engine was already coughing and rattling alternately. Her systems holo registered a hull breach, intermittent power, multiple failures in the cooling jacket... the engine was about to die.

She punched the comm. "Everyone back there hold on to something solid. We're about to go down hard."

° ° °

Wind swept across the tortured rock where nothing ever grew, changing direction quickly and without warning, tirelessly vindictive as it plucked and tore at everything it touched.

He pulled his face plate down and clipped it into the jaw mount, shielding his face from the vicious, clawing shrike that was the air itself. Bracing his body against the winds, he leaned first one way and then the other, managing to remain upright as the force of the gale randomly shifted direction. It was simple enough, once one learned to anticipate the wind. He felt as though he had been here many times before.

As far as the eye could see, there was only scarred crust; a desolate wasteland of charred shapes and melted rock, scoured of all life and littered with the twisted statues of melted buildings. The surface of Woe Tantalum was entirely ruined.

The sky above was a nauseating patchwork of purple bruises set against a festering brown, blotched with sickly orange where light struggled feebly to penetrate layer upon layer of cloying, odious cloud.

This was a place that wanted living things to die.

He could hear a ringing sound, almost painful to listen to, and struggled to remember precisely when it had begun. It was at such a high pitch, and descending so slowly, that for all he knew it might have started either seconds or minutes ago. He could not seem to work out where it was coming from.

The sound dropped lower, lower still, descending in pitch until it reached a sonorous rumble that seemed to dissolve into the general chaos of the wind and dust, lending its own strength to theirs. The ground itself trembled.

With an ear-splitting crack, the air tore open some ten metres away. Blackness boiled out into the world, a vertical spill towering over him, reflecting nothing. Wispy tendrils lashed and curled from the fringes, the main body tapering to nothing at top and base, wider in the middle, a rip in the world into which light could enter, but never leave.

There was no pain.

Ever-shifting gales began to fall into order, whipping around, becoming cyclonic. Fragments of charred debris skittered over his boots, bullied across the punished surface by the raging air.

Yet around the deep blackness was absolute calm. Stretching out from it, and almost reaching him, was a region in which no wind blew. It was only in this protected area where wisps of black ash drifted lazily back to the ground, and the cold, dead embers were as still as the gnarled and glassy boulders.

He took a step forward, into the calm.

All at once it was as if the chaos belonged to a world he had simply left behind. An invisible boundary held back the swirling vapour and airborne litter of the planet's tortured surface, and outside in the seething maelstrom he thought he could see blurred figures moving slowly against the wind. In the centre of the silent zone though, eternally patient, waited only the dark formless nothing that was the Emptiness.

You could never have escaped this.

He had already known as he stepped into the calm that this moment would come, that the

Emptiness would have its precious gloating. It had been stalking him for so many years, through so many trials and tragedies, that it had become almost like a toxic old friend.

No! Not a friend, not ever like a friend in any way.

But the only one you will ever be able to rely on, it oozed its poison inside his head.

The shadowy crack in the world seemed to contract, and for a moment he thought it was drawing back into the nothingness it came from. But it was not; instead, it shrank and receded, moving closer to the ground.

He wondered why he had stepped forwards this time.

It was inevitable. It happened because you are weak.

The Emptiness was condensing, its outer edges rolling in on themselves, tendrils shrinking back along their own lengths to become nothing. Vague shapes began to coalesce from its smoky, impenetrable depths.

But now it is time to accept your nature.

The edgeless shape became a coherent form, and he found himself transfixed. Immobile, aghast, he could not move or turn away.

All of it was wrong, different in some way or another. The limbs were elongated and spindly, the teeth needle-like and fringed with crimson stains. The skin was too pale, sallow and without life; the hands were slender with discoloured, horny nails. Worst of all, the eyes were narrow and pale and cruel.

But despite all the differences, despite the part of him that only wanted to deny this abomination, there was no escaping the simple fact that had stepped defiantly into the world before his very eyes.

Starting at the boots, and moving up past the combat pants and the webbing and the base layers and the flexible armour, and ending at the face, which parodied awkwardly a grin of genial triumph, there was no denying that the Emptiness had manifested in the image of its maker.

Make us whole again.

◦ ◦ ◦

The passages and compartments rang with the near-constant vibrations of *Hammer*'s turrets, and with the repetitive clacking of lasers flashing enemy sensors as quickly as they could. The noise was deafening.

On the command deck, Santani snapped brief, concise orders whenever she felt the need to supplement the orderly and efficient battle recipe which Klade and the tactical officer had devised. She was transfixed by the master battle map, totally bemused by what it showed her: whoever commanded the hostile fleet was behaving like an imbecile.

Contrary to her earlier assertion, the turncoat carriers had launched their fighter wings almost immediately, before *Hammer* was even in range. Not only were the Imperial battleship's defences operating at full capacity, but the fighters also had to cross the wide empty space between their parent vessels and their target before there was even any point in opening fire. *Hammer* had torn them to shreds.

There seemed to be no order to the assault that the other ships made, no real coordination between them. Individually they were making Tactical's life slightly difficult, but they were no more threatening as a whole than they were separately.

What are they doing? Santani wondered. This fight should have been over almost as soon as it began. They started with fifteen ships, and we stand alone. We ought to be dust.

Instead, the lone battleship was putting up quite the fight.

"Turret sync failure: forward port quarter,"

"Compensating,"

"Torpedo incoming: aft one-oh-five degrees, firing countermeasures..."

"Hull damage amidships, decks twelve and thirteen. Control teams on standby. Life support assessment?"

"Life support compromised. I'm sealing those compartments."

"Destroyer on intercept, forward three-one degrees—"

"We just lost auxiliary fire control."

Santani's crew were proving themselves more than capable of holding things together in battle, despite the worries she had had.

Hammer released a rapid burst of laser flashes against the exposed broad side of a Viskr cruiser, and followed those up immediately with a volley from her ventral gauss guns. The enemy hull buckled and split, venting gas, flames, people. She began to pull away from the damaged vessel, and when the gap was wide enough she fired again, this time directly at the engine blocks. The cruiser went up like a nova.

She released a swarm of decoys into the path of a torpedo strike, harmlessly detonating the missiles far from her hull. Her forward gun mounts reoriented, and fired on the torpedo boats that had tried to ambush her, tearing easily through their undefended hulls.

Enemy drones streaked beneath her flak curtain, harrying her defence turrets and trying to knock out their control systems. She had sent her own autonomous drones to worry the largest of the Viskr cruisers, to attack its defences in the same way. With enough turrets taken out of action, even a mighty leviathan would be vulnerable to a concerted, focused strike. Fortunately for *Hammer*, the hostile drones were much less sophisticated than her turrets, and were gradually picked off until none remained.

Santani began to allow herself to acknowledge hope. There might be a chance they would get through this battle. Oh, the great ship would be beaten out of shape, but she would survive. They might *all* survive.

She was still holding on to this thought when a klaxon blared its warning. She had no idea what the noise was.

"Mister Klade, what was that?"

He consulted his holo quickly. "The alarm you requested, Captain."

"What alarm?"

"You asked for a prompt for those sensor readings. From Herros. The vast mystery object—"

"Oh, by the worlds," she said.

They both turned as one, and looked at the battle map.

There at the edge of the cloud of ships was a new shape, a craft unlike anything she had seen before, the remnants of an enormous wormhole dissipating around it. The ship was massive, brutally inaesthetic, and it lumbered slowly into the fray, making a direct line for *Hammer*. The other ships scattered like fleas, those too slow to move aside were simply smashed across its already scarred and pitted hull.

"Open a wormhole, Captain?" Klade asked.

"And leave our people vulnerable down there? No, we stay here. We stand together, we will fall together."

"Tactical," Klade barked. "Assessment?"

"Hull configuration is unknown, they aren't transmitting any known Friend or Foe identifiers. Hold on... their weapons have gone hot. They're locking on."

"Lock our own weapons, and fire."

"Sir. Firing now."

Tactical's hands skipped across her holo, and *Hammer* unleashed her full fury on the hulk that bore down on her.

She might as well have been a child throwing acorns at a bull.

The dreadnought was almost upon them when it started to slow and released a volley of its own. Dozens of ship-to-ship missiles erupted from their launch tubes, diverging and winding around each other as they tried to outsmart *Hammer*'s defences. None made it past the barrage of the flak curtain, but another salvo was launching even before the first would have hit. The dreadnought's lasers lashed furiously across *Hammer*'s offensive targeting sensors, stopping her from returning fire.

"We can't win like this," Santani said. Her voice was as grim as her expression. "We either retreat, or we die. Helm, take us down."

"Ma'am?"

"You heard me. Take us into the atmosphere. With any luck it will play havoc with their targeting."

"Understood. Preparing for low orbit, atmospheric insertion."

The deck plating quaked and shivered in response to the conventional engines ramping up to full power. Slowly at first, but with increasing verve, *Hammer* began to come about and dropped quickly towards the planet.

The dreadnought was changing direction too, bearing down on the battleship and still launching missiles from its forward tubes. It was no longer bothering to laser the rear sensor palettes on *Hammer*'s hull. The fleeing ship had stopped returning fire, and only her defensive turrets were active.

The trembling in the deck plates became a rumbling, signalling contact between the exterior hull and the rapidly thickening atmosphere of Woe Tantalum.

"Put us in a holding orbit, Helm," said Santani. "Low enough that we can avoid detection, high enough to climb back out of the gravity well without giving ourselves away."

"Yes, Ma'am. What depth would you say is low enough?"

Klade replied for her. "Assume they have sensors like ours, descend until we can't detect them, then drop half as far again."

The holos displaying the outside atmosphere continued to darken as thick clouds wrapped around the descending ship.

"We're levelling off," said Helm.

"Steady as she goes," Santani replied. "What's our altitude?"

"Based on the archive entry for this planet, about fifteen klicks."

"I take it there's nothing on the surface tall enough to hit us then?"

"There's not much on the surface taller than fifteen metres," Klade said. "Not any more."

"Good, we'll stay hidden down here until we can assess our sensor readings of that ship. We need to come up with a way to retrieve our people and—"

Her words were rendered inaudible by the loudest imaginable noise, a great metallic booming that seemed to fill the ship. The lights on the command deck flickered and went out, and all at once the deck lurched to starboard, the gravity plating failed, and something aft of them exploded violently. *Hammer* was hit, and hit hard.

"Captain," said Tactical, "they've followed us in!"

– 19 –
Sabotage

Vella Laekan rubbed her tired eyes and tried once more to focus on her holos. What she was looking at was difficult enough to interpret without her body failing her. Worlds knew she needed some sleep, but this was important. It was, in fact, possibly the most important thing she had ever set eyes on.

What she had before her was a true scientific mystery: macroscopic changes to the structure of the brain, in a living person, matching nothing she could find in the vast Imperial reference libraries. What was the cause? What — if any — was the purpose?

She had already sent out invitations to several colleagues in more suitable medical fields, asking them to travel to the fortress and assist her. With only her word that they needed to hurry she guessed they would do anything but. Branathes had forbidden her from sending any information about the Rasa via databurst.

'Rasa'. It was interesting that the Tirrano woman had chosen to refer to Amarist Naeb using that term. She was so *angry,* it made a kind of sense that she would feel compelled to categorise people, to pin blame to them with a word. Only in this case she had the wrong meaning of the word. Tirrano thought it only meant 'blank', but that was not quite accurate. In its original context, it meant something that had been cleared of content. Thousands of years ago, people had recorded their musings and calculations and reasoning on malleable wax tablets. To erase those thoughts, they warmed the wax and scraped away the indentations.

Judging by these scans, she thought, and given the way Naeb has been acting, that appears to be a more appropriate translation. But the angry intelligence operator had still jumped on the label despite her faulty association.

Oh, and she *was* so very angry. Laekan had seen her files when she came to Fort Kosling.

Tirrano's mother, Orshan, had been killed at Chion. Captain of the *Crusader*, she had held her ship in the enemy's line of fire long enough to take out the wormhole generators on one of their capital cruisers. The Viskr fleet had been unable to jump away, which was her goal, but *Crusader* had stood no chance of limping back to her own lines. The reactors went up, and everyone died. Everyone.

Laekan had heard Tirrano talking to the others, whenever they were down in medical, or in the mess hall, or even just in passing. Laekan did not need her training to see that she hated the Viskr. *Hated* them, with a passion the doctor found slightly unnerving. In her profession she often came across such tightly bottled emotions, but rarely did she encounter a pressure cooker like Tirrano.

Take the Shard for example. His father died on the *Curtailer*, when it was ambushed at Laeara.

And that ship was not even destroyed outright; Modim Caden was just one of the unfortunate ones who never made it to a rescue deck. But not once had she heard the knife-edge of anger pressing into the Shard's words when he spoke of the Viskr. Either he had long since sorted through his issues with them, or his feelings about the old enemy were wound up so tightly that even he knew nothing of them.

She raised her head suddenly, glanced around. She had been letting her mind wander, and a slight noise brought her back to reality. It was still fresh in memory, her ears still reporting the sensation of sound, yet she had no idea what it was she had just heard.

"Hello?" She called out.

Nobody answered.

Laekan spun around in her chair and got to her feet, picking up a glass mug as she did so. As long as she was passing through the medbays, she might as well get a refill.

Walking to the open isolation hatch, she cast her gaze around. Nothing had changed. There was the Rasa, no, there was *Amarist Naeb*, laying on the bed. Her chest rose and fell slowly, air passing her lips silently.

She carried on, opening the hatch at the far end of the bay. Conscientious as ever, she closed it behind her before walking into the tiny catering compartment that served all the medbays at this end of medical.

The green light was on, so she swilled her cup out in a stream of hot water, and flushed the cold leavings from her last cup of tea down the pedestal sink.

She filled the cup almost to the top with boiling

water, and started the walk back to her work station, thinking about which variety of leaf to have next.

Closing the medbay hatch behind her, she walked across the centre of the compartment, heading for the next compartment and the relative comfort of her work station. She was almost through the doorway when her brain forced her to stop.

Something is different, Vella.

She turned around. For a split-second, she was not even aware that she was having to look over someone's shoulder to see that the bed was empty. Her brain caught up with reality, and she brought her arm up instinctively. The cup was knocked from her hand, and tea splashed across the deck.

Laekan looked down, and saw that Naeb's hand was already crimson. She was not yet registering the pain, but she knew it was coming. She dared not move nor make a sound, and sucked in breath through O-shaped lips. Terrified of what might happen if she let go, she held tightly to Naeb's wrist with both hands.

Amarist Naeb pulled back sharply, and her slick red hand slipped out of Laekan's grasp. A searing, tearing slash of pain stabbed up through her core when the scalpel was pulled out. Laekan gasped and staggered back a few steps, bending double to cradle the deep wound that Naeb had inflicted. She clutched both hands to her abdomen, and felt nothing but wet warmth.

Laekan collapsed to the ground, still gasping, and looked up at Naeb. The woman was impassive, *blank,* and paid her no more attention. Her head turned slowly to one side, looked towards the open hatch that led to the work station. She stepped through the opening.

Doctor Vella Laekan mustered all of her strength, and strained to reach the comm terminal on the wall. Her body resisted, a paroxysm of pain exploding within her, and she collapsed back into a crumpled heap on the floor, moaning with the agony. Gingerly, she peeled her sodden blouse away from her skin, and lifted it. Craning her neck to look down, she saw a deep slash across her abdomen. It gaped at her, and she saw the edges tear slightly wider even as she looked. She could see right into her own body; under the skin creamy blob-like fat cells were dotted around, as if not quite sure what to do with themselves now they had been pulled into the open. Dark tissue glistened beneath them, and she thought she could see a rhythmic pulse of sinuous movement. Crimson blood pumped along the lower edges of the laceration, and ran onto her paling skin.

Killed by a damned Rasa, she thought.

◦ ◦ ◦

Brant had been poring over the battle reports and tactical assessments for hours, hoping to see some single critical flaw. He was coming to the point now where he had to admit that Betombe's strategy was entirely sound; what was at fault was the assumption that it had been based upon, and that assumption was one Brant had had a significant role in creating.

The Viskr were not reacting as he had expected them to, indicating that he was wrong about their intentions. He looked again at the report listing the enemy fleets that Eyes and Ears were able to count. So *many*. Their response to Betombe's offensive looked almost desperate. Did they even have the warheads?

The door chimed, and Tirrano entered before he could respond.

"What are you doing?" She demanded. "You're supposed to be sorting out the extraction of Doctor Bel-Ures."

"I got side-tracked." He gestured at the holos. "It happens a lot."

"Yeah, don't I know it?" She said pointedly. She looked down at the holos and the scattered charts. "You know this isn't our job, right?"

"What isn't?"

"All of this." She waved her hand at everything on his desk. "Commander Operations has a whole department dedicated to campaign analysis."

"I know, it's just that we're sort of involved now."

"So what? Fleet Command won't listen to a word you say, even if you think you've found something."

"You're probably right."

"Of course I am. So stop wasting your time, and make the arrangements to secure Doctor Bel-Ures before someone else does."

"Do you really think she's at risk?"

"The Shard seems to think so." The faintest trace of reluctant agreement tinged her voice. "It would make sense, if she has operational knowledge of what was going on at Gemen Station."

"Probably should have done this already, huh?"

"No shit."

Tirrano had edged her way around the desk, until she was standing next to the seated Brant. She leaned forward, curving her body, and rested her fingertips on the desk as if to peer at a holo.

Brant rolled his eyes while hers were elsewhere,

and rose to his feet on the other side of the chair. He always felt more comfortable with at least one piece of furniture between them.

"I'd best check with Branathes, see what resources he will allow me to tie up with this."

"The order came from a Shard. I'd say that's pre-authorised. What will Gordl do? Overrule him?"

"Good point," he said. "I'll just get on with it."

"It's waited this long," she said. "It can wait another five minutes." She placed a hand on his shoulder, as if to pull him closer.

Oh worlds, he thought. Of all the times to pick, *now* she's finally going to try it on.

He was actually relieved to hear the alarms sound.

○ ○ ○

Calling and celebration and fulfilment
familiar words flowing from all sides
gently flowing

The body that had formerly housed the personality and will of Amarist Naeb ran swiftly and quietly through the corridors, light on its feet, a weapon held down by its hip as if it were just an afterthought.

It had found no difficulty in destroying the work station used by Laekan, in escaping medical, in ambushing a pair of security officers and taking a side-arm.

the song, forever the song, oh by the worlds
by all the many worlds, the song!

waves of faces
white spiral waves
I understand, I belong

It came to a junction, edged carefully around the corner, saw no-one, and crept forwards. A sealed pressure hatch barred the way at the end of the corridor, standing obstinately and confidently between the body and its objective. It cocked its head, searching for a manual release or an access panel with simple controls.

There was nothing on or beside the barrier, nothing that looked as though it controlled it. Any access must have been granted from the other side.

It was turning away to find another route when the hatch opened with a sharp hiss.

yes yes, I feel you yes
and the song is unbroken
forever the song

○ ○ ○

"What's happening?" Brant yelled.

"Evacuate this deck," the security officer yelled back, turning only briefly to give her answer. She kept running.

"There's smoke," Brant said worriedly. "Why is there smoke? What happened to fire suppression?"

"Come on!" Tirrano grabbed his sleeve, and pulled him along the corridor towards a printwall that displayed environmental data and the station's public system messages.

"Fire hatches refusing to close throughout medical," Brant read. "Environmental systems not responding to containment protocols."

"Well; *that* could go really wrong," said Tirrano.

◦ ◦ ◦

"You can't be in here!"

The security officer was answered only with a gun shot, and took the hit below the left shoulder. He collapsed backwards, writhing in pain. Blood pumped between his fingers and he screamed incoherently into his link.

It continued on its way, oblivious to his presence now that he was no longer a threat.

Another pressure hatch barred the passageway, and like those before it this one hissed open obligingly as the remainder of Amarist Naeb approached.

This one opened out onto a broad platform, a huge hangar-like space with maintenance bays marked out on the deck plating. It was close now.

Across the platform, moving swiftly over a narrow cat-walk bridge that connected to another identical platform, a chasm that dropped through six decks just beneath its feet.

On this platform was a shuttle, left with its insides hanging out when the workers had responded to the sound of the alarms. It went around. The pressure hatches in the far bulkhead hissed open. It walked through the opening, unopposed, directly into the vast space of Dry-dock Nine.

Before it lay the sleeping body of the *ICS Hector*.

◦ ◦ ◦

Brant had thought it was chaotic before, with the smoke creeping down the bulkheads and the alarms whining in every passageway. When the lights started to go out, and the entire deck boomed with the repercussions of some heavy impacts elsewhere in the station, his sense of apprehension was lifted to a whole new level.

"What the hell was that?"

"No idea, keep moving," said Tirrano. She steered him around a corner in the direction indicated helpfully by an emergency printwall.

The noise was repeated, and the deck actually warped beneath their feet. Tirrano stumbled into Brant, and a man following close behind them tripped over the edge of a piece of plating that had dislodged from the deck.

The lights went out completely, and it felt like a long few seconds before the emergency lighting faded on. Soft blue draped itself diffidently across the faces of the people who were so dependent on it.

They started moving again, as soon as they were able to walk safely under the faint light. Another booming thud shook the deck plating, and the muffled sound of a huge explosion rumbled up and down corridors a few decks below them. The emergency lighting faded almost to nothing, then came back up to full strength, such as it was. Brant felt the pull of the gravity plating weaken.

They rounded the final corner, and Tirrano ushered people into the deck's survival shelter, Brant first. Only when the last person had ducked through the circular port did she swing the heavy hatch closed behind her.

○ ○ ○

Dry-dock Nine was an inferno. *Hector* pummelled the bulkheads with bitter fury, firing her forward cannons one after another, as quickly as they could reload. Ragged holes had been chewed through to the adjacent dry-docks and repair bays, and searing jets of burning gas poured like lifeblood from severed conduits and pipelines. Nobody else would be coming to board the ship any time soon.

Moving clumsily, the corvette rose away from the docking run, tearing clamps and supports from their housings. The lateral gauss guns spun around and fired repeatedly at the sealed hatches that barricaded the way to the docking channel.

Air began to whistle from the dry-dock: the hatches were breached. A ship-to-ship missile finished them off.

With all the grace expected of a damaged ship with a crew of one, *Hector* limped through the scorched opening and made her bid for freedom.

– 20 –
Light the Dark

Throam came around slowly, his ears ringing, and at first he thought he had gone blind. Then he remembered where he was, and wriggled hard until the dry impact foam around his head and hands broke into lumps and fell away. The inside of the lander was a mess, with containers thrown out of place and a layer of hardened foam coating every surface. The dry tang of electrically burned smoke filled his nostrils.

Groans and shouts came from every direction, the sounds of a slightly dazed and battered platoon recovering from the impact that had silenced the lander's dying engines. Throam punched his arms free, tore away a large piece of the shell-like foam that covered his midriff, and released his safety harness.

The lander was tipped to one side, and he almost had to climb to reach the rear hatch. Others were breaking free of the foam and trying to retrieve equipment or help their squad mates, and he was forced to navigate around them. A simple jostle could have easily sent someone tumbling across the uneven surface, doubtless taking others down along the way.

The inner hatch hissed open when he slapped

the release, the outer hatch was already open. He plucked a re-breather from the bulkhead and pressed it over his mouth and nose.

Outside was a gale, loud and angry. Standing amidst the raging wind was a lone figure, just at the limit of visibility.

"Oh for fuck's sake," Throam said.

He ducked back inside the rear compartment and closed the inner hatch.

"Volkas," he shouted. "Where is Lieutenant Volkas?"

"Over here," came the reply. Volkas waved to him from across the compartment.

"Get your men combat-ready, Lieutenant. We'll be moving out as soon as we are able. We can't stay here."

"You're not in charge of this unit, Counterpart."

"Yeah, we don't have time for that crap. You: Lieutenant. Me: Captain. Either do as I say, or stay here and get killed."

"I'd prefer to not get killed." The voice sounded like Daxon.

"Of course you would," Throam muttered. He pulled on his outer armour. It was remarkably difficult with the deck tipped to one side, and with hardened foam and moving bodies all around him. He felt as though it was taking forever to get kitted up.

Thankfully Volkas seemed to have taken the hint, and he was giving his men utterly redundant commands, instructing them to perform tasks they had already carried out without needing to be told. Whatever he thought of Throam, and whether he intended to follow the order or not, right now he was doing what Throam needed him to do. That was enough.

Finally Throam was done, and he shoved his helmet down over his head. As usual, he wished he had made the effort to clean it out properly the last time he had worn it: the sponge lining stank of musty old sweat.

"Hey buddy," he said. He rapped the private next to him with the back of a gloved hand. "Check my seals?"

"All looks good," the soldier told him. "Helmet seal too."

"Appreciate it." Throam grabbed his rifle from the magnetic rack.

He dived back out through the rear hatch, and into the hurricane.

◦ ◦ ◦

Caden came to with a start, and felt as though he had drifted off in the middle of a concert. All around him was noise and motion, but it was as if he had only just become aware of it, as if he had been somewhere else.

"I said, are you okay?"

He vaguely remembered hearing the question already. In fact, the insistent and slightly annoyed tone suggested it had been repeated more than once.

He turned around to see Throam, fully kitted up and armed to the teeth, stomping confidently towards him over the uneven ground. Caden raised a hand, a half-hearted gesture that was just enough to signal that he heard, he understood, and he was indeed okay.

"What are you doing out here?" Throam was asking.

I wish I knew, he thought.

You do know.

A high-pitched whine descended into a bone-trembling rumble, and a Viskr shuttle soared overhead. It was on a gentle descent towards a building in the distance, a structure as ruined as the others but possibly massive enough to still contain intact levels.

He pointed at the receding shuttle, and raised his eyebrows. "Go that way?"

"We both know there isn't any other plan, so yeah. Guess so."

Two more craft swept over the crash site; one another Viskr shuttle, the second a small Imperial lander. Both were headed in the same direction as the first, clearly with the same destination in mind.

"Better get Eilentes," said Caden. "She won't want to miss this."

"Not now I've crashed the car, anyway."

Throam stepped aside and turned back towards the lander, and Caden saw Eilentes was now standing behind him. She carried her favourite rifle in her arms. Like their armour, the rifle's long barrel and precision scope had skinprinted to replicate the charred surroundings.

"Sorry about the shitty landing," she said.

"You did fine, under the circumstances."

Throam jerked his head towards the rear hatch. "We waiting for our MAGA brothers?"

"Did they look ready?"

"More or less."

"Then we might as well."

You would only fail without them.

"Those guns that took us down," Eilentes said to Caden. "We'll need to disable them before anyone can lift off again."

"Any idea how to find the control centre?"

"They looked like auto-turrets. They'll be autonomous."

"So each one needs to be taken out individually?"

"Exactly."

"Oh great. How many did you count?"

"Difficult to spot them with the cloud cover, but judging by the area they were covering I'd say there are a dozen or so."

"Okay, well we have a dozen squads between the other landers."

"No, we don't. We lost a lander on the way down: Third Platoon is gone."

They'd still be alive if you hadn't brought them here.

"Shit. *Shit!* Okay, Second and Fourth can handle the batteries between them. We'll make a search for the dead when we're done with Morlum."

The dead you made.

"Captain Pinsetti was with Third Platoon."

Caden looked towards the voice and saw that Volkas had now also left their lander. The MAGA troops he commanded were beginning to disembark, filing out of the rear hatch. Some lifted crates and equipment between them.

Caden turned to Throam. "You're the same rank Pinsetti was. You outrank all the other officers who came down with us."

"You know damned well I'm not going to take command of them," Throam said. "I need to be where you are."

"Just giving you the option," Caden said. He turned back to Volkas. "Tell Second and Fourth to sort out between themselves who is going to take the lead. Their objective is to knock out the batteries so we can leave the surface again."

"And what about me?" Volkas asked.

"We're going over there." He pointed to the

building the enemy's shuttles had headed for. "You and First Platoon are going to clear a path for us."

More lambs to your slaughter.

◦ ◦ ◦

"We can't take much more of this, Captain." COMOP was shouting, struggling to reconcile the information his various holos flashed at him so desperately. "I'm getting failures across all systems."

"She's becoming difficult to control," Helm added. Her hands skipped from one panel to the next.

Santani batted away the loose hair that had slipped across her face, and wiped soot from her mouth. It was getting difficult to breathe the air on the command deck now, despite the best efforts of the emergency scrubbers. Deep inside, she knew *Hammer* was losing her battle with the inevitable.

"Can we use another drone as a decoy?" She asked Klade.

"It didn't fool them for long before," he said. "I don't see why it would now. The drones just don't have the power to fake our energy signature."

"Give me options."

"We could fire off all of our ship-to-surface missiles, and hope that they're at least blinded."

"We can't risk it. If we irradiate the surface, we finish off the people we have down there."

"Then I don't think we can do anything but run, and hope they follow."

"No! We need to take them out. As soon as we stop being a threat, they'll move on to Caden and his team."

"We just don't have the weapons for this," Klade said. She heard the defeat in his voice.

"What if we could access the quarantine network?" Tactical asked.

"Explain," Santani said.

"They deactivated it, so they clearly view it as a threat," Tactical said. "But they weren't expecting any interference. What's to stop us turning it back on?"

Klade and Santani looked at each other.

"It might actually work."

"Do it," Santani said. "Then scramble the codes."

Klade barked orders at COMOP. "Make it happen. Bring the orbital platforms back online, and randomise the access codes."

"Working," COMOP said. "You do realise, Captain, that the platforms will fire on us as well? We're well inside the red line."

"Understood," Santani said. "Helm, try to find us a soft spot to put down. But don't make it look like we're going to descend, not yet."

"There are no facilities," Helm said. "We'll lose half the ship."

"We'll lose it all if we stay up here."

Klade was already broadcasting across the ship's comm. "Now hear this, all crew evacuate below decks. I repeat, evacuate below decks. Abandon *all* duty stations at once, and move immediately to deck one. Secure hatches and prepare for emergency grounding."

"Ready for go, Captain. Platforms will reactivate on your command." COMOP's hand hovered over his holo.

Santani looked at him and realised he was hoping for her to change her mind, hoping that they would find some other way. But the dreadnought had followed them into the atmosphere, and despite its huge size it seemed perfectly capable of manoeuvring against the winds in its efforts to find them. It showed no sign whatsoever that it would give them up for lost, and every so often their hull was raked by a hail of slugs, or their over-burdened defences strained to take down the swarms of missiles that could so easily tear the ship wide open.

There really was no other way.

"Do it," she said.

◦ ◦ ◦

"Skulkers!"

Caden dropped to the ground immediately and rolled behind a lump of masonry. In the dusty fog, which seemed to extend forever in all directions, he could not see who had shouted. He was not going to waste time finding out, not with skulkers on the prowl, but it had sounded like Bro.

He heard the sharp rattle of them springing from their hiding places, the hiss and slash of their blade rings meshing past each other.

A metallic whine came from somewhere up ahead, and a scream was cut off as soon as it began. Whoever had been on point had been the first to go.

"Stay down," Throam whispered.

He glanced over to where the counterpart was hunkered down behind another block of charred masonry. Throam quietly removed a grenade from his webbing, and pulled the pin.

Caden heard a grating sound; skulkers were already in the courtyard in front of them. Their drive rings skittered and rattled on the stone surface.

Somewhere off to their left there was another short scream. He tried not to think about the spattering sound that followed, but it had already registered. He shuddered.

In one smooth movement Throam was up, throwing his cooked grenade in a short, tight arc, then back down again in cover. The explosion hurled sharp metal pieces in all directions, some of them clanging against the backs of the stones that shielded him and Caden.

The slash, hiss and rattle of more skulkers filled the air, growing louder. They were not clever machines by any measure, but they were smart enough to investigate when one of their own was destroyed.

An anti-personnel rocket streaked across the space between the buildings, and another skulker was blown into razor-edged fragments. Its two companions whirled towards the threat.

"Hoo-yah! Take that, motherfucker!"

Caden looked up and saw a MAGA trooper in the upstairs window of a half-burned building. He did not know him by name, but recognised him from Chun's squad.

"I've got you covered up here," the soldier shouted. He racked another rocket into his launcher. "They can't reach me. Two more shots and you're clear."

Another rocket fired, and another skulker was torn apart.

"Ready—" Caden whispered.

Shots. Rifle shots.

Caden risked peering over the top of the stone block, and saw figures at the far end of the courtyard, stepping quietly between the stumps of broken columns. They came out of the thick mist in ones and twos, silent but not cautious, moving without any military precision. There was no discipline to their approach, no strategy. It was a basic skirmishing line: sweep and clear.

He wondered why the last of the remaining skulkers had not yet gone up in flames, and looked towards the window. The trooper with the launcher was slumped against the broken sill, a hole through his face.

So much for *that*. He looked at Throam.

"How many?" The counterpart mouthed.

Caden held up both hands, fingers splayed, then wobbled one from side to side. About ten.

Plus, of course, one skulker.

Throam nodded, but whatever he had been planning on doing about it suddenly became irrelevant.

Spent casings flew from Bruiser's machine gun in a steady stream, bouncing and skittering across the cracked flagstones of the courtyard as he came up behind Throam and Caden to walk calmly between them. He focused his fire on the skulker's centre, taking advantage of the precious seconds it took the figures to hurl themselves into cover, and kept firing until the machine's sounds were throaty and erratic. It tried to roll forwards and jammed up, with grinding noises coming from its core.

Bruiser ducked into cover, and gurgled with delight. "Been aching to play hard for ages," his link translated.

Throam unclipped a density grenade. "Ever hear the human expression 'like shooting fish in a barrel'?"

"Never," said Bruiser.

"This should explain it." He hurled the canister towards the far end of the courtyard, with a shout of "Hey fuckers!"

Three of the figures at the far end of the courtyard emerged from their cover, and popped off a few inexpert shots in his direction. The grenade soared high overhead and burst just above them.

They were engulfed in a cloud of fine vapour, which reacted instantly with the air, forming a mound of thick, smoky foam. The three were just visible as dark shapes suspended inside the foam, struggling feebly to work their way free.

"Nice," said Bruiser. He sprayed the foam with bullets.

It did not take long to finish off the others.

"Viskr, *and* humans." Caden tapped one of the bodies with his boot. "They're working together. This doesn't bode well."

Throam slapped a fresh magazine into his rifle. "We're nearly there. We'll find out soon enough what their deal is."

"Let's move on," Caden said.

They filed out of the courtyard, watchful for figures moving in the fog, listening for the tell-tale sounds of more skulkers whirring into life. In the distance he could hear staccato bursts of gunfire, the sounds of Second and Fourth securing their targets. But here, in the immediate vicinity, all was still and silent: as far as Caden could tell, there was nothing else out there for the moment.

They found a road, seared clean of all markings, and moved to the building line. The road led almost directly towards their destination, curving slowly uphill. As they moved, the fog began to thin out.

Caden's link chirruped.

"Caden, Eilentes. I've got you in my sights now. If you carry on along that road, I can cover you most of the way there."

"I think you missed most of the excitement, but thanks all the same." He turned around to see if he could make out her position, but she was superbly well-hidden. If he had not known she was out there, he would never have guessed that he was being watched through a scope.

Caden was about to resume when something made him stop. A noise that was just audible above the incessant wind, repeating somewhere high overhead. A *boom-boom-boom* that could have been accompanied by faint bursts of light, almost imperceptible in the tumultuous cloud cover. The lightning and swirling vapours could play tricks on the eyes, but he was sure he was not imagining those bursts.

He was right.

○ ○ ○

Eilentes watched Caden through her scope with a smile on her lips, chuckling to herself as he peered back towards her.

He's trying to make my position, she thought. Good luck!

She had ensconced herself carefully in the remains of a stone structure which had likely been built as a clock tower. A wide crack had split the stones across one wall, on the side facing towards the force which had devastated the entire continent, and she was using the stones beneath the crack as a hide. A scrim was draped over her rifle; smart fibres woven throughout the material adopted the colouration of the surroundings, in much the same way that her outer armour was mimicking the environment.

All in all, she was pleased with this hide site. The only issue she had with it was the lack of a rear wall. Behind her, there was only a gaping hole framed by the ragged edges of the side walls. Still, there were a few hidden troops guarding her position on the ground below, and the skulkers would never be able to reach her up here.

She adjusted her eyepiece minutely and refocused on Caden. What was he looking at now? He still seemed to be looking at her, but his expression had changed. Now, instead of a faintly quizzical look, he appeared concerned. He was beginning to point. His mouth was opening and closing silently, and others were turning around to follow his gaze.

She strained to hear, as if his words might somehow cross the distance. Of course they did not, but she did hear a roar building steadily in the sky above her.

She rolled onto her back, and sat up just in time to see the clouds forced apart.

Above her, and far too close for comfort, the angry skies which had so recently battered her own craft were themselves ripped asunder by a much larger visitor. A vast, dark grey hulk breached the lower layers, trailing plumes of thick smoke, hurling pieces of smouldering debris towards the ground. Yellow and blue flames hissed aggressively and rippled back along its length, caught between the leaking fuels that fed them and the torrents of wet air that would snuff them out. Small explosions punctuated the roar of the de-orbiting starship.

Hammer was falling to the surface.

"Oh m y worlds, oh my fucking worlds!" Eilentes breathed. She fumbled for her link. "Volkas, it's *Hammer*. She's coming down! Warn the other platoons! She's coming down!"

"I see it," came the crackling reply. "It'll miss them by some distance, I think."

The battleship was whining now, the sound of her engines fighting as valiantly as they could against the gravity of Woe Tantalum, and against the ship's own momentum. The whine competed with the rushing roar of the air that the huge ship displaced as it hurtled heavily towards the ground.

"They're not going to make it," Eilentes said to herself. "They can't *possibly* make it."

The hull came closer and closer to the remains of the town that had once been the beating heart of a young colony world. Eilentes felt a knot of dread building inside her chest. She could not stand to watch this happen, but she could not turn away either.

And then it was happening, and somehow she was still looking, and time seemed to slow down to a crawl.

The gravity spur was the first part of the battleship to hit the ground. Protruding forward of the main engine blocks, angled slightly downwards, it practically invited its own destruction. It jabbed into the soil and rock like a needle striking through to the bone, and convulsed as it buckled and split along its length, bursting apart where it joined the hull.

The support skeleton of the spur tore away completely, taking with it the concentric collimator rings that helped focus its wormholes. They were ripped back and to the side, twisting and unravelling violently, throwing loops of xtryllium out into the air.

The nose of the ship hit next, crashing onto the ground and thundering forwards through already broken walls. Eilentes fancied she saw the whole length of the hull shudder and ripple, an understandable reaction to being smashed in the face with a planet.

The belly of the battleship came down, still sliding forwards, and the lower decks were crushed outright. Hull plates warped and sprang from their mounts, the engine blocks exploded, pieces of metal and jets of flame were forced from the many holes that seemed to appear everywhere she looked.

The wreck hurtled on, levelling everything in its path. Behind it, a wide trough of ploughed earth was littered with the pieces *Hammer* had left behind, and the few large stones her passage could not dislodge.

The sounds of explosions and screaming metal grew gradually fainter, and Eilentes' view was blocked finally by an impenetrable pall of powder-black smoke.

She leaned against the cold stones of the dead tower, and covered her mouth with both hands.

○ ○ ○

"Fuck—"

"Come on Throam, we've still got a job to do." Caden grabbed his counterpart by the upper arm and pulled hard. Throam did not exactly resist, but he was not easy to move at the best of times. "Come *on*."

"Yeah, sorry. Just... fuck! That was the *Hammer*."

"I know, nothing we can do about it. Best case scenario is we now have a short time to act before we get wiped out from orbit."

"Right. Sorry."

"Are you with me?"

"I'm with you. Yes."

"Good. Look sharp, yeah?"

They were with you, and look what happened to them.

"Not now!" Caden muttered.

"What?"

Throam had started back along the road, and looked over his shoulder at Caden.

"Nothing. I didn't say anything."

"Sure? First sign of insanity, you know, talking to yourself."

"I'm sure."

"Wouldn't be the first time."

"Whatever. We need to get up to that structure."

Throam seemed to recognise the tone and became serious.

"There's a breach in the wall. It meets the ground on the left hand corner," he said. "We should head there."

"Fine. And let's double-time it."

Throam signalled to the others, and they all began to jog up the road, still keeping to the building line. There were so many places for people to hide, so many possible ambush points, that it barely mattered what other precautions they might take.

"A chemical works," Caden said when they reached the perimeter fence. He scuffed dirt across the surface of a fallen metal sign. "Should have pretty solid interiors."

"Solid enough to house an operation."

"Chun, bring your squad with us. Everyone else, set up a perimeter."

"Ready for this?" Throam asked.

"Of course I am." Caden thumbed a helmet control. His face plate darkened, and light enhancement sensors switched on. "Let's do it."

They climbed through the tear in the outer wall, picking their way as carefully as they could through the mangled rooms beyond. Water dripped on them from somewhere above, somewhere it had had time to pool and gather rust from the twisted metal skeleton of the outer wall. It splashed across their visors like old blood.

The building was more heavily damaged than it looked from afar; inside the main block, floors were caved in and support beams were buckled and twisted. All that remained of the furniture and the more robust furnishings was in a long, burned pile against the far wall, as if it had all been swept there by a powerful wave of fire.

Caden opened a link channel to Throam. "Looks like it's all admin up here," he said quietly. "I'd bet the levels below are where all the real work went on, and ten to one says that's where the work is going on now."

"Underground plant?"

"Why not? All those wall boundaries we saw out there looked like shops and houses. The town probably didn't plan on having any industry visible on the surface."

"Hmm," Throam said. "Aspiring to Earth's standards."

"If you can't duplicate, emulate," said Caden. "Let's try and find the way down."

Throam gestured to Chun, who in turn had his squad fan out. It was Norskine who linked back first.

"Lifts are out," she said. "But there's a staircase over here that's big enough to roll Bruiser down."

"Fuck that," Bruiser chimed in.

"Knock it off," Chun snapped. "Daxon, your fire team takes point. You all seem to like courting danger."

"Sarge."

Daxon jerked his head in the direction of Norskine, and Bruiser and Bro went after her. They moved stealthily down the wide metal staircase, even Bruiser managing to tread lightly. Caden and Throam followed with Daxon; Chun led the rest of his men after them.

On the landing of the flight below the ground floor, they saw the first light. There was a chain of them, simple maintenance lamps on tripods, slaved together with a power cable. Dim spots of light were visible through the grille panels on the landings, stretching down into the darkness.

"Someone is definitely here," Caden breathed.

It was not until they reached the sixth level down that they saw the first person.

By the time Caden reached them, Norskine and Bro had re-emerged from their hastily adopted cover on each side of the gaping entrance. Bruiser was still in the stairwell, peering around the corner with his machine gun trained on the pale figure.

"What's going on?" Caden asked.

"You tell me," the Rodori's link said. "That human is not moving."

"He's just standing there," said Bro.

"Remind you of anyone?" Throam asked Caden.

Beyond the wide doorway, the light fell off sharply. The gloom was punctuated by another lamp on the far side, which illuminated a similar doorway opposite.

Caden stepped down onto the landing, around Bruiser, and moved up to join Norskine. "Cover me."

"Hell no," Throam said. "I'll go."

"Suit yourself."

Throam raised his rifle and flicked on the light. It threw a tight beam out into the darkness, and he pointed it at the motionless figure. He advanced cautiously, almost sideways on, one foot over the other. Moving to the side, giving Norskine a clear shot, he reached out gingerly with his hand, and prodded the man in the back.

The man moved forward slightly, without resistance, and then tipped back again.

"Just like Naeb," Caden said. "*Exactly* like her."

Throam moved around, and the light from his rifle speared the gloom. It flashed over another pale shape, and another, and another.

"Fuck, oh fuck... they're everywhere."

The counterpart tightened his stance, turned slowly in a full circle. Caden watched the beam of light from his rifle as it splashed over still bodies, one after another.

"Fifteen," Caden said.

"They were waiting," said Throam. "They're all armed. Like they were laying in wait for us until a few minutes ago."

"Creepy," Norskine breathed.

"What do we do?" Daxon asked Caden.

"Follow the lights."

They carried on, quietly picking their way through the throng of statuesque bodies, and passed through the far doorway.

Beyond the doorway was a short corridor, opening directly into a cavernous chamber. The roof was two stories high, and barely visible. Bright yellow markings were painted on the floor, indicating where safety margins and clear walkways should have lain. Whatever this plant had been designed for, it looked as though calamity had claimed Woe Tantalum before the machinery had been installed.

But the space itself was not empty. In the centre of the huge expanse of floor, arranged in neat rows, were dozens of metal racks. Some of them held warheads.

"Jackpot," Caden announced.

Norskine and Bro entered the space, veered off to each side, swept back and forth with their rifles. Bruiser lumbered forward more casually, hefting his machine gun.

"I wouldn't come much closer," came a voice from the gloom. There was a wobble to it, as if the speaker were forcing himself to talk. "I'm not sure how my companion will react."

Throam and the others directed their lights towards the voice, and the beams converged on a gaunt-looking man standing just within the shadows, on the other side of the racks.

Caden reacted first. "Morlum?"

"Not so often as I would like," he said.

Another figure took a much heavier step forwards, and stopped just behind Morlum. It towered over him. It was as tall as Bruiser.

"And this would be...?"

"Prem; Penvos Robotics Exterior Maintenance. You see, I need maintaining."

"I don't know what you're talking about."

"They needed me, but I'm resistant in some ways. They couldn't empty me out. This here" — he gestured at Prem — "this is my... chaperone, I guess you'd call it."

"Chaperone?"

"Yes. I programmed him to try and fight them. I suppose they thought it would be fitting to do the opposite."

"He's nuts," Throam called across to Caden.

"How I wish I were," said Morlum.

Caden stepped closer. "Who brought you here?"

"Oh dear, I knew you would ask me that."

Prem shifted and looked down at Morlum. The man was now sweating, Caden noticed. He cast his eye over the android. It was a common model, designed for prolonged tasks in hostile environments. Its chassis was basically humanoid, with a thick flexible covering. He had no idea where the actuation processors were. If it became hostile, it would not be put down quickly.

He noticed Norskine and Bro were edging silently around the outside of the racks, one on each side. They looked like they were aiming to take up positions behind the android.

"Those people back there." Caden nodded back towards the doorway. "What are they?"

"Vassals. Thralls. Servants. We're called different things, depending on who you ask." He looked Caden right in the eye. "I hear some call us Rasas."

"You heard that *specific* word? Where?"

Morlum's eyes drifted to Prem uncomfortably, as if he were testing a limit. He spoke very deliberately. "We hear things... all over the place."

"So they're everywhere. And you're... like them?"

"Almost. As I said, I'm resistant in some ways. I don't always sing the song, not if there's no choir to join."

Caden glanced at Throam, and saw that he was stood stock still, his rifle aimed unwaveringly at Prem's head. He could not tell if the counterpart was making any sense of Morlum's words, if he recognised their significance. Was he too remembering Aldava right now? There was no way to tell.

"Amarist Naeb, you're the same as her?"

"Not quite. Poor Amarist. Totally swept away by the current. I left her for you, you know."

"Why?"

Morlum's wary eyes again travelled to Prem, then back to Caden. "To start the trail," he whispered.

"The ones back there. Why don't they move?" Caden asked.

"Nobody to tell them to." Morlum made it sound as if the explanation should have been obvious. "There were enough to tell them before, on the surface; you must have killed them."

"The Viskr?"

Morlum actually smiled, as if Caden had made a deliberate joke. "No. No, not the Viskr. The—"

Prem made a very discouraging sound. Caden saw Throam take a half-step forward, and sensed him tensing up. He did not need to look to know that the counterpart's finger had started to tighten against his trigger.

Morlum waved his hand at the racks, and changed the subject. "These are all that are left."

"The others?"

"Taken. Distributed. I don't know where, I don't know why."

"We're going to take them back. Will Prem try to stop us?"

"I don't know."

"Prem," shouted Caden. "What do you think about me taking back these warheads?"

The android gave no reaction.

Throam smiled grimly. "Guess that's your answer."

"He's almost as helpful as you, Morlum."

You're so close to the truth, why don't you just take it?

The words burst into Caden's head like a white hot spear of pain, so blinding that he almost forgot to remain standing.

No, he thought. Prem will kill Morlum if he gives us anything concrete.

What does it matter?

I won't get him killed.

The worlds think him dead anyway.

I won't do it!

One meaningless death could be worth millions of lives. Billions!

We don't know that.

You have killed so many already, do you want the blood of whole worlds on your hands as well?

Stop it.

Murderer, they'll call you.

Stop it!

Murderer, like they called Maber Castigon. Butcher.

STOP IT.

You and he should team up again.

Caden felt a sudden wave of anger burst inside him, from deep inside, from the place he had almost forgotten about. It burned through him and forced its way into his thoughts. His scalp crawled and the back of his head felt empty.

"Morlum, whose song are you singing?"

"I... I can't..."

"Tell me Morlum. Who's in charge?"

Morlum looked at Prem, and took a faltering step away. "I mustn't, no, don't ask me that!"

Prem turned to face Morlum, and took a step of his own, closing the space between them.

"You know I need to know this. TELL ME!"

Throam advanced, side-stepping diagonally to keep Morlum out of his line of fire. Caden was peripherally aware of Norskine and Bro doing the same thing.

"No..."

Morlum was wild-eyed, panicked, stepping back away from Prem as quickly as the android reclaimed the ground.

"Tell me, or I'll shoot you myself!"

Morlum stopped, and turned to look at Caden. A pistol was pointed directly at him.

The wretched man looked at Prem one last time, sniffed, and looked straight into Caden's eyes. Caden felt the meaning: you killed me, you can watch my light go out.

"Shaeld Hratha!" He hissed.

Prem had more than enough time to smash Morlum's throat, before a hail of bullets took the huge android down.

○ ○ ○

"*Disputer* Actual, this is Lieutenant Volkas, acting commander of Bullseye Company. Glad you could join us."

"Bullseye Actual, we have your signal locked in. Hostile contacts fled the system on our arrival, so we will be able to recover your forces immediately."

"Copy that, *Disputer*. Be advised the planet has a formidable quarantine network in place."

"The quarantine network has been disabled, Bullseye. We're sending landers to your position now."

"Any word on the *Hammer*?"

"We've picked up nothing at all from the crash site, but recovery is inbound. Stand by on that."

The channel closed abruptly.

"Captain Thande," Volkas said apologetically. "She always was brusque."

Throam nodded. "They came, that's what counts."

"Oh right, yeah. All *they* had to do was turn up."

"You did good, Volkas. Worked for me, anyway. I wasn't expecting to see even more bodies out here when we came back out of that place."

"What about him?" Volkas nodded towards Caden. "He still going to be giving me a hard time for no reason?"

"I don't know," Throam said. "I honestly don't know."

He stepped away from the lieutenant, and picked his way slowly through fused rubble towards the Shard he had sworn to protect.

Caden was standing at the edge of a mound, looking out across the hillside along the length of the road they had used to reach the chemical works. Far in the distance smoke still rose from the long scar *Hammer* had gouged in the ground. Landers were beginning to descend towards the smoking wreck.

Throam knew that look. Caden was staring *through* the view.

"Hey," he said. "Come back to the world."

The Shard seemed to return from a place far, far away.

"*'Shaeld Hratha'*, that was what Morlum said. What in the darkest worlds is that?"

"Never heard it before today," Throam said.

"Me neither."

"You certainly had a way with words in there," Throam ventured cautiously. "Got him to *talk*, didn't you?"

Caden gave him a look that discouraged following that line of conversation.

For once, Throam thought, I'm going to find out what happens when I ignore that look.

"You knew Prem would kill him, and you made him tell you anyway."

"Lives are at stake."

"We could have separated them."

"Could we?"

"Probably."

"At the time, 'probably' wasn't good enough."

They stared at each other for a few moments.

Caden spoke first. "Throam, something big is happening. I don't know who's behind all this, but you heard what Morlum said: these 'Rasas' are everywhere. They have a head start on us. They probably know us inside out. I really need to know that you're in my corner."

"Like you even need to ask."

"I *am* asking. I'm asking because you've never questioned me like this before, and I have a feeling that Morlum was the tip of the iceberg. This is going to get much worse before it gets better. So are you with me?"

"Always," said Throam.

"Good," said Caden. "Now where the fuck did we leave Eilentes?"

– Epilogue –

Omin ran along the earth that was embanked against the base of the battered wall, ran through the wreckage of Camp Camillion, ran as fast as he could towards the steps that would carry him up, up, up to what remained of the battlement.

Directly above him, the stars were as bright and sharp as diamonds set in a black velvet sky. Not a single wisp of cloud marred the perfection of the firmament on this night, and the band of the Milky Way snaked overhead enticingly.

Breathing heavily he reached the first step, stumbling towards it and scrabbling forwards with both his hands and his feet.

"Come on!" A shout high above him. "You have to see this!"

As he climbed the steps, the sound came again. The greatest sound he had ever known. A sound from the end of the world.

"You're missing it!"

He found his footing and raced up the steps, careful not to fall on those that had been knocked out of place. Vibrations from the ground-shaking sound shook stones and clods of dirt loose, sent them skittering past him into the darkness below.

He reached the top at last, where Junn Delanka crouched behind a block of stone. Omin knelt down next to him, and saw that in the distance a great wall of cloud appeared to stretch across the width of the world, in defiance of the otherwise clear night sky.

"At the horizon," said the private.

Omin looked out into the night, saw what Delanka was pointing towards, and his mouth flopped open.

"What... what in the many worlds are those?"

"I don't know," Delanka said. "But they just keep coming. Watch."

Moments passed in which Omin could do nothing but stare out into the night, mesmerised by the structures that had transformed the distant landscape entirely.

It was *impossible*. They simply could not have just appeared there, and they were far, far too big to have been built since the evening light had faded.

Delanka pointed to the clouds as the sound began to build up again. "Here comes another."

The noise rose to a thunderous crescendo.

It was as though the very heavens were crashing to the ground, in the final apocalyptic moments of the fall of creation itself.

To Be Continued...

The story continues with *"List of the Dead"* and *"The Ravening Deep"*, available now.

The beginning of the end will arrive with *From Shattered Stars*, due 2016!

Also watch out for two companion episodes:
— *I Dream of Damastion* —
— *The Granite Whistle* —

The Armada Wars novels are all available in paperback form, and to buy or borrow for Kindle devices and the Kindle apps.

Reviews on Amazon and Goodreads are greatly appreciated.

ArmadaWars.com

– About the Author –

R. Curtis Venture was born in the United Kingdom in 1978. A graduate of Applied Biology, he has previously worked in entertainment and hospitality, business development, and intelligence analysis. His first great passion was for science fiction, both in books and on the screen, and he spent his childhood years imagining far-off places.

He is currently employed full-time in the legal sector, and somehow also finds time to write.

You can find R. Curtis Venture on both Facebook and Twitter, where he welcomes interaction with readers and encourages feedback. To see what he's reading these days, follow him on Goodreads.

55969856R00192

Made in the USA
Charleston, SC
12 May 2016